OTHER BOOKS BY CRAIG TERLSON

NOVELS

CORRECTION LINE

FALL IN ONE DAY

SAMURAI BLUEGRASS

SHORT STORY COLLECTION

ETHICAL ASPECTS OF ANIMAL HUSBANDRY

NOVELLA

BENT HIGHWAY

LUKE FISCHER

SURF CITY ACID DROP

MANISTIQUE

THREE MINUTE HERO

PRAISE FOR SURF CITY ACID DROP

"Quirky, shadowy, and compelling... the characters are dark and complex, and the trail Luke follows satisfies both the desire for a good story, as well as a glimpse into the dark undertones of human motivation."
- Beth Burton (CAN)

"An absolutely fantastic read that has you rooting for Fischer from the start. The perfect blend of Pacificos, peanuts, and knees to the balls."
- Andrew Giesbrecht (CAN)

"There's plenty of humour, many opinions on coffee, beer and breakfast options, as well as some absolutely kicking fight scenes... This was one road trip that had me absolutely tripping. Great stuff."
- Lagoon (UK)

"An exhilarating read with memorable characters and high action excitement. Buy the book, take the ride."
- S.L.Keenan (UK)

"God I love detective stories set in hot places...There's something about that heady mix of violence, danger, clever quips and tropical sunsets that just spells out perfect escapism for me. Definitely worth reading!"
- Amy Gagnon (CAN)

"A crime novel filled with good food, good drink, and punches to the head. The character Mostly Harold takes over any scene he is in and takes us all on a menacing and often hilarious road trip from border to border.
- Kenneth M. Gray (USA)

PRAISE FOR MANISTIQUE

"Manistique is a MOOD! It's a tense, fast-paced crime novel with an irresistibly atmospheric literary tone and a cast of unforgettable characters."
- Theresa Therrien, author of Saint Joan Blackheart (CAN)

"Luke Fischer is to Travis McGee as Lew Archer is to Phillip Marlowe, his own man and a worthy successor."
- *Mark Atley, author of The Tulsa Underworld Trilogy (USA)*

"Terlson creates an atmosphere I cannot get out of my head. The characters, made me laugh, they made me ponder life mysteries. Great action, great dialogue."
- *Scott M. Frederick (USA)*

"There's plenty of slam-bang action in this story, and a good dose of surprising twists and turns. Highly recommended for fans of noir crime drama with unforgettable characters."
- *Douglas W. Lumsden, author of the Alexander Southerland, P.I. books (USA)*

"What a phenomenal book Manistique is... A masterclass in crime fiction."
- *Steve Griffiths author of Kill Sequence (UK)*

PRAISE FOR SAMURAI BLUEGRASS

"Pitch-perfect and haunting. Five stars."
- *Ed Church, author of the Brook Deelman mysteries (UK)*

"A classic stranger in a strange land tale that Terlson riffs on and makes it wholly his own. Bluegrass is chock full of compelling characters, mysterious happenings, transmigrations and absolutely breathtaking turns of phrase."
- *Anthony Perconti (USA)*

"Wildly inventive and entertaining novel—absolutely recommended!"
- *Thomas Trang (UK)*

"The parallels of mastering the stroke, with a brush or a sword were breathtaking storytelling techniques."
- *Margie Peterson (Reedsy Discover)*

"Loved this book! Drew me in immediately. Do yourself a favour and pick up this and/or any of the other wonderful novels by Craig Terlson. You won't be disappointed."
- *Offer Kuban, Host: The Speakeasy Podcast (CAN)*

THREE MINUTE HERO

CRAIG TERLSON

All characters in this book are fictional, and any resemblance to actual persons, living or dead, is purely coincidental… I mean, coincidences can happen, right? Scanning, printing, uploading, electronic sharing of this material constitutes piracy and theft of the author's intellectual property and is also very uncool, and you'll probably get a curse or something. Don't risk it.

Ethelbert House
Cover art: Phil
Book design: Ethelbert House
Support and beverages: The Lovely

ISBN-13: 978-1-7381036-0-7

THANKS MARTINE
(FOR KICKING MY ASS)

CHAPTER ONE

Everyone needs a benefactor, especially in a place that is not your home. After I ditched my home country and headed out for parts unknown, I needed to find a way to put beans in the cupboard. More importantly, after I arrived in Mexico, I needed to put Pacificos in the fridge. Truth was, I rarely stayed somewhere that had the luxury of a fridge—but there were plenty of places happy to provide a bucket of ice for my beer and a good vantage point to watch the sun slip into the Pacific.

I made it a point to know as little about my benefactor's business as possible. At times it was hard to ignore, but generally I did what Benno asked. In return, he paid me well. Sometimes only my presence was required, playing glorified bouncer at his club when he was entertaining clients or making one of his deals. I didn't know if these deals were legal, and my guess was they weren't. Other times my job consisted of giving dead eyes to anyone who might cause some trouble. Then there were situations when more was required. I'd laid out my share of unruly clients. The first time Benno saw me deck a guy who'd been trying to hustle me, he let out a low whistle.

"Did you grow up in a place where this was taught?" Benno asked. "Like they say, the mean streets."

"My streets were pretty tame—the usual small-town fights. I spent some time as a sparring partner in Montreal."

"Sparring? Like in a ring… the sweet science?"

I laid out the story to my new friend over a row of tequila shots. I told him that one day I started driving east. That I left behind the flat prairie and headed into roads that curved around giant rocks like titans from Greek mythology. That I eventually ended up in Montreal, a place I liked for the corned beef, bagels, and Gitanes—back when I still inhaled the coffin nails. I picked up some work at a boxing gym that trained the next great hopefuls. My forearms developed tight cords of muscle, and my legs could run for miles.

"So this is where you learned to fight?" Benno interrupted.

"I always threw a decent punch. More than decent."

Benno did not push the subject and allowed me my pause before he asked another question.

"Did you become one of the hopefuls?"

I told him that like a boxer who sensed the bell was about to ring, I felt the urge to be somewhere else. It was something that happened to me a lot. I was running out of land in my own country. So instead of going east, I turned right and kept going. My beater died just across the Mexican border, and I took a bus to Puerto Vallarta.

I finished the story and swallowed the last shot of tequila. Benno asked if I could do a piece of work for him.

Since that night in the El Rayo Verde, named for the flash of green that sailors claim they see before sunset, I'd been working for Benno both in his home base of PV, and occasionally on the road. I did end up in Montreal again, but I got pulled back to Mexico like a wayward dog who smells something cooking. People called me a private eye. I've never liked the term. Private eyes dragged up images of Philip Marlowe or that guy Rockford with his cool car. Hell, I'd never had anything that looked like a license. I was just a guy who liked Mexican beers, and more than that, red sunsets over the ocean. I'd never seen the flash of green. But if you wanted somebody found, I'd find them eventually. If anything I was perseverant, or just a pain in the ass. Benno said that when I was working, I was like a dog searching for a lost bone. Always with the dog metaphors.

I'd returned to PV five weeks ago, with the hope that Benno would supply me with the kind of work that paid the hotel bill and my bar tab. But not yet. Right now the farthest I wanted to travel was the length of the Malecón and back.

"Luke, I need you to do a piece of work for me."

"So you said," I said. "Not in Mexico, I'm guessing."

"Why would you say that?" Benno asked.

"When you explain it as a piece of work I usually find myself crossing a border."

"More than one this time, my friend."

"Direction, Benno?"

I pictured driving south, winding through a number of Central American countries, each more dangerous than the first. Things had increasingly grown out of control down there as the dictators took turns trying to out-batshit-crazy each other.

"North," Benno said.

"Two borders?"

"Yes."

I put that one together fairly quick.

"Your little empire stretches all the way to Canada?"

"The first rule of good finance, my friend, is spreading out your assets. You've heard the advice about eggs and baskets?"

Benno sipped his J and C. His club was closed for the night and we were in his office. A block away the ocean waves banged against the shore. Benno had cracked the window and the smell of the Pacific wafted in, woven with the scent of what I guessed was fish being cooked over a fire.

"I doubt you deal much in eggs, Benno."

Benno smiled and poured a couple of fingers of dark Jamaican rum into his glass and offered me the bottle. I waved him off and took another deep pull on my Pacifico.

"You have told me you don't want to know my business," he said.

"Still don't. Just if I'm making the trip that far north, I might need a bit more information than usual."

"It is your, how does the song go, home and native land?" Benno studied my face. "Are you no longer welcome there?"

"I doubt anyone would care if I showed up," I said. "Well, maybe a couple of people, but that's not the point."

There were shouts outside, some late-night turistas likely, carousing the Malecón.

"What is this point that you refer to?" Benno asked.

"Doesn't matter." I finished my beer and walked over to the bar fridge. "Why Canada?"

"That may be the eventual destination. I don't have all the information. For now, I'd like you to go to Colorado."

"Who is in—" I plunked back down across from my fedora-clad friend. "Wait, now I remember. Last week you told me an employee of yours was stirring up shit in Colorado Springs. So you want me to find the guy that wanted to put a bullet in me and push me in a hole?"

"I recall it differently, Luke. He brought you back safely. At my request."

I rubbed the back of my neck, pushing against the muscle tension that suddenly emerged.

"What's Mostly Harold been doing?"

Benno gave a broad smile.

"I had forgotten your name for him." Benno reached into his drawer and brought out an envelope. "Our friend, or as you called him, my employee, has fallen out of communication with me."

"I told you that would happen if you hired Harold."

"So you did, Luke. And yes, this does have to do with Harold, or so I believe. He has been doing some work for me in his home city. But there is something else. To be honest, I am not completely sure he is involved. But it is a place to begin."

The shouts outside increased. Benno peered around me, looking through the dark bar and onto the street.

"Problems?" I asked.

"Perhaps."

I flinched at what sounded like gunshots. Benno eased himself out of his chair, took a 9mm from his desk, and slipped it into the pocket of his jacket. I followed him out of his club.

"Turistas getting outta control?"

Benno didn't reply. Outside he moved quietly but with purpose.

The street was empty except for a group of people in a semicircle next to a stone wall. Against the wall was a skinny kid in ripped jeans. The full moon cast shadows across the cobblestones. One of the shadows held a pistol in the air and fired it into the night air.

As we walked closer, I saw the kid had a cut lip and a shiner the size of a plum.

"Gentlemen, there is no need for this. Especially this time of night." Benno spoke in a cool level tone.

The one with the gun swerved to face us.

"None of your business, asswipes. Get lost."

He was white-skinned like me, not a local, working on a tan that showed up as a burn the color of prairie roses.

"Why are you threatening this young man?" Benno asked.

"This little shit pickpocketed my wallet."

"And he won't give it up," said a taller man with a thick mustache, matching red skin, and a Hawaiian shirt.

"Do you have proof of this?" Benno asked, his voice as flat as a beach.

"The punk banged into us when we were leaving the bar. We didn't notice it at first. But when we did, Perry's wallet was missing." Mustache Guy swept his hand toward Perry, apparently the one with the gun.

"Like I said, Señor Asswipe. Move along. We'll take care of this,"

Perry said.

The kid at the wall spoke in Spanish. Benno spoke back, too fast for me to catch much more than "gracias."

"Hey, none of that shit. You know this kid?" Perry pointed at him with the pistol.

"I know his mother very well. And I have known him since he was a small child. He's a good boy and not involved in crime. Did you find the wallet on him?"

A shorter guy with a beer belly hanging over his checked shorts came out of the shadows to add his two cents. "He doesn't have it. He must have pitched it."

Perry fired again in the air, making his friends and the kid jump.

"Enough of this bullshit. We're gonna lay a beating on you boy. I know you took it."

"I agree that is enough. Put down the pistol before someone is hurt. I'll vouch for the young man. How much was in your wallet?" Benno slid his hand into his pocket.

"Oh, someone will get hurt alright." Perry swung the sight over to Benno.

"I wouldn't do that," I said.

"Who the fuck are you?"

"Just a friend."

"Well, you just take a step back, Mr. Friend." He wiggled his pistol at me.

Benno pulled his 9mm out and put a bullet in each of Perry's kneecaps. He collapsed to the street screaming, the gun falling out of his hand.

"Holy crap. You shot him," Beer Belly said.

Benno again spoke to the boy in Spanish, who gave a nod, and ran off down the street.

"He will phone for an ambulance to come for your friend. I suggest you all wait here."

"Hey, you can't get away with this! You just shot someone!"

Mustache Guy came forward.

I stepped in front of him and held up a single finger.

"I'll give you lugheads some advice. Shut the fuck up, stay here, and wait for the ambulance. Go with your friend to the hospital. Currently, neither of you have any bullet holes."

The other one looked like he was going to say something, but then fell silent, listening to their shot friend moaning on the street.

Benno turned and headed back to the club. I picked up the pistol, a cheap .38, from off the cobblestones. I knew not to ask him about what just happened. There would be no investigation, as most of the local policia were on his payroll. They'd fix the guy up, he'd spend some time in PV hospital— decent doctors down here, I'd come to learn. They'd give him some crutches and send the lot of them back to whatever suburban shithole they'd crawled out of.

Back in his office, Benno poured another Jamaican rum, this time straight up.

"Did you really know that kid?" I asked.

"Yes."

"He as good as you said?"

"Perhaps not. But I know his mother almost as family. That is very important to me." Benno paused. "Is it to you?"

"You're asking me if family is important?"

"Yes."

I didn't saying anything for a bit. I reached for the rum bottle and poured myself a couple inches.

"I see," Benno said.

We sat and drank in the silence. The moon cut a line of light across Benno's table.

"Can you leave tomorrow?"

"Am I flying?" I asked.

"I'd rather you drive. If you don't mind. I can supply a reliable car."

"Another road trip, Benno?"

"I want you to talk with someone. They have a package I need you to deliver."

"Of course you do."

"I'll give you the details in the morning. We no longer need to talk of anything this night."

CHAPTER TWO

In the last couple of hours a thought creeped into his brain and stayed. After driving for days, this whole damn landscape reminded him of pancakes. Long stretches of gray highway were broken up with barely-there towns. The odd cow popped up, but even she didn't know what she was doing out here. At least the sky was all right—there was a helluva lot of it. Like someone had taken a roller and painted it tuna-can blue all the way from the bottom to the top. There were clouds, but today they were as scarce as the cattle. But yeah, pancakes. He needed to get a plate of them.

But first he had to meet someone.

He spat on his thumb and wiped out a mark on his lizard boot before entering the bar. Getting out of the car, he'd kicked a stone across the road and almost tripped on the damn thing.

"Clean your streets, you dumbasses."

There was no one around to hear his mutter. He studied the parking lot, gave his boot a last spit shine, and went in through the heavy wooden door under a sign, THE KING'S HOTEL AND BEVERAGE ROOM. He didn't really expect to find her in here, but it was a place to start.

Brown strips of paneling made the room look more like someone's shitty basement rec room than an actual bar. He wouldn't have been surprised to see a La-Z-Boy and a plaid ottoman shoved in the corner. Instead, worn-out tables were filled with circle fossils as memories of beers gone past. The brightest thing in the room was a faded chrome jukebox that probably stopped working years ago. A ghetto blaster sat on a shelf next to a dented trophy. It played that New Country shit, sung by pretty boys with perms who had never seen either end of a horse. The song ended as he took a seat. It must have been the local yokel station, as someone yammered on about a sale on tractors.

Ever damn person in the bar wore a hat in various stages of decomposition—a combination of heavy equipment dealers, drilling rigs, and hockey team logos. One of the younger ones was wearing a Red Wings number. The Wings were his team when he'd lived in that dumpster of a city, Dee-troit. Given the amount of nothingness that he'd driven through to get here, he figured that most of the group in the bar were farmers. When he first entered, the door jangled against some goofy-ass chimes hanging from the ceiling. The farmers gave his black suit jacket the once-over, but went back to ignoring him as soon as he'd sat down. He knew that being the only one in the joint wearing a suit jacket meant he stood out like a turd on the dance floor. Not that he gave a single shit.

The bartender watched the baseball game being played on the soundless TV. He turned to fill a drink order for the sole beer slinger. She glanced over at his table and flipped him a nod.

"I'll get you in a sec."

The bartender filled her tray, and she roamed the room serving the dozen patrons scattered across the room in pairs and trios before coming to him. She looked barely drinking age, with a freshly scrubbed face and healthy body that came from actually taking care of herself.

He told the girl beer-slinger he was waiting for someone and just wanted ice water.

"Water, that it? Nothing in it?"

"Ice."

She shrugged and walked back to the bar.

Jesus, who would live in a town like this? Hamel, a dumbass

name if he'd ever heard one. He'd driven a thousand miles to find a woman. When he got in the car and drove out of Colorado Springs, he couldn't quite figure out what he was doing. For the first time in too long to remember, he'd gotten close to another person. Then she disappeared like one of those kids on a milk carton.

She was gone a week before he got some information on where she might have went. The woman who saw herself as manager of the place told him they'd had a conversation.

"What'd she tell you?" he'd asked.

"She let it slip that she had unfinished business up in Canada."

"In this place called Hamel?"

"That's what she said."

"What kind of business?"

"Didn't say."

He stewed about that for a few days, while he considered her living a secret life that she never told him about. Maybe she was hitched to some stubble-jumper up here—even if that didn't make any sense. On the fourth day, he got into his car and drove north. He'd been up here once before when he was sent after that Fischer guy who worked for Benno. Talk about a pain in the ass.

Sitting in a bar in a foreign land he knew he didn't have much of a plan. Well… no goddamn plan at all. But he'd learned to put himself in a situation, wait it out, and something or someone would come forward.

He didn't have to wait too long. A man walked in and scanned the room like he had done when he entered. He saw the guy's look land on him. He didn't have a layer of dust like the rest of the hayseeds—and he wasn't wearing a goddamn hat. Now there were two people in the bar with suit jackets. The new guy wore a brown tweed job with a white shirt that outshone the jukebox by three-to-one. He came over and sat down, scraping the chair hard on the floor. Someone muttered *son of a bitch*. The bartender roused his head from the silent game and brought a couple of beers to the table. The labels were green with some goofy red mountains and a picture of a speeding locomotive.

"I never ordered one," the one in the black suit said.

The bartender popped the caps and slid both beers in front of the tweed-jacketed man, who took one, leaned back and poured the entire contents down his throat. He belched, and wiped his face with the back of his hand.

"That your car out there?" Tweed Man said.

"Who are you?"

"Taylor."

"First or last?"

"Sure." Taylor ran a finger over the rim of the second beer. The label read *Pilsner*. "Colorado plates. I guess you look like you're from down there."

"What do you want?"

"I'm looking for someone," Taylor said.

"Well I ain't him."

"Not a him." Taylor barked out a laugh. "She was down there too. In Colorado, or Utah, or one of those states."

Taylor leaned his tweed-covered back into the chair and sucked something through his teeth. The black-suited man adjusted his sleeve collars.

"Vodka?" Taylor pointed at the other's glass.

"Ice water."

"You don't drink? Whattya, Mormon?"

The man in black let out a long exhale.

"Listen, asshat. It's bad enough I had to drive here with nothing on the goddamn radio but whining country music—and now I gotta sit in this dump while the radio plays the greatest hits of Johnny who-gives-a-fuck. So cut to it."

"You don't like country?"

He drained his ice water, crunched down on the last cube, and raised his hand to the server.

"Refill."

She pointed at the sink at the bar.

"Help yerself. We got a whole tap full of it."

The black-suited man stood.

"Holy cow, yer a big fella," Taylor said.

He ignored the comment and went to fill his glass, taking a scoop of ice from behind the bar. Just for the hell of it, he added a lemon slice, and came back to the table.

"Who's the she?" he asked.

"Name is Delilah. And like the one in the storybooks, she's pissed a lot of people off."

"The Bible."

"Huh?"

"She's not in a storybook," the man in black shook his head. "OK, look, you're not the brightest turnip on the prairie. You walk into a place where you're a regular and you beeline for me. Why?"

"How do you figure I'm a regular?"

"No one batted an eye when you came in here. And the bartender knew your order. I came in and they looked me up and down like I had a tail."

"You do fill up a place." Taylor took a slug from his second beer, and took a glance around the room. "So you're not up here because of her? Delilah?"

"I have no idea who you're talking about."

"I'm saying bullshit."

"And I'm saying fuck you and the horse you rode in on."

As Taylor began to stand, the black-suited man shot out his hand and grabbed his wrist hard.

"Ow, let go you—"

The man in black twisted harder. The bartender had turned up the sound on the game.

Gonna be a barnburner this afternoon, Gomez has loaded the bases and the Brewers cleanup man is stepping into the box.

Taylor's hand was turning purple.

"Sit the fuck down before I pop you one." The black-suited man's voice was flat, even.

"I—"

"Down."

Taylor slid into the chair.

The game sound fought against the latest tune about someone's dead dog until the beer slinger went and flipped the ghetto blaster off.

"Now listen numbnuts, I've been in this stupid-ass state for—"

"Province, we don't have states here," Taylor said.

The black-suited man still had a hold of his wrist and he twisted again. Taylor let out a yelp.

"You think I don't know geography? I don't need some maple-syrup-sucking asshat to tell me where I'm at."

He let go of the wrist. Taylor grimaced, rubbing the reddened skin.

"You didn't need to do that," he said. "You haven't even told me your name."

"Why should I tell you anything?"

"You can't expect me to do business with someone if I don't know their name," Taylor said.

"Fine. Call me Harold," the black-suited man said. "And what business?"

"Is that your real name?"

"Oh fer shit's sake. I'm done."

It was Harold's turn to stand up.

"Hey, we could help each other. We're both looking for her," Taylor called over to him.

"I'm not looking for anyone."

Harold kept walking. The goofy-ass wind chimes sounded behind him when he got into the parking lot. A white sedan was parked next to his green Ford with the Colorado plates. His mind flipped through the possibilities. Who the hell was this Taylor guy and why was he looking for Delilah? There was no chance in hell she'd get together with a doofus dressed like that. She had too much style—not like one of those runway models, even if she had the looks for it. Delilah knew exactly what she wanted and how to get it.

In the rearview, Harold saw Taylor exit the bar straightening his tweed jacket, dipping his hand inside, and pulling out something black and gun-like.

"You sneaky bastard."

Harold hit the seat of the Ford and laid out flat as the rear window of the car disappeared. He reached under his body, which was pressed hard against the upholstery, and eased his Glock out of its shoulder holster. Another shot through the shattered back window hit the inside of the windshield and spidered the glass. Harold weighed the options. He could pop up and take out the guy, but Mr. Tweed might nail him first.

An opportunity presented itself as the dumbass decided to walk over and peer in the driver's side window to see what he'd hit. Harold squeezed off a shot that caught him square between the eyes.

Harold banged the car door. It opened halfway, knocking against the very dead Taylor. He let out a sigh, then slid his huge frame across to the passenger side. A few of the bar patrons were now in the parking lot playing a game of whose mouth could be opened wider.

"Get back in there, you stubble-jumping peckerwoods." Harold pointed his Glock at the group.

All but one scampered back in the bar. Harold rifled through the pockets of the dead man. He flipped open a brown leather wallet. There was a business card with the man's ID. Harold took the card and a pair of twenties before shoving the wallet back in the jacket.

"You can't just come into our town and shoot the hell out of things."

Harold lowered his gun, studying the last remaining gawker.

"You know that guy?" He nodded to Taylor, laid out next to his Ford.

"No sir, I do not. But I'm gonna let the Mounties figure it out. They got called as soon as we heard the shots."

"Those goofballs in red underwear on horses?"

"That's not underwear. And they only wear those on special occasions. I'm talking the RCMP. They got an office just up the road in Bennett." The man took a step forward. "I figured you for a Yank. Your accent."

"A Yank? What in the fuck century is this?" Harold raised the Glock again and squeezed off a shot into the side of the bar.

The man jumped. Harold pivoted the gun and pointed it at the gawker's head.

"Well, whattya say? Should we make it easier on those Mounties? Two dead bodies in the same parking lot means less searching for them."

"Go easy now. I can identify you, ya know."

"Not if you've got a bullet in your brain."

The guy looked like he was going to say something, then spun and ran back into the bar. Harold sighed. He popped the trunk on his Ford, and heaved Taylor into it.

He peeled out of the lot, thinking about how long it would take Canadian law enforcement to show up. And would they show up on horseback like in those movies? This place was like old-timey land. Harold never worried too much about cops, no matter what country they were from. But there was another thought that was taking up a lot more space in his head. Who else was looking for Delilah?

Back on the highway in the pancake landscape, his stomach started to burn. It had been doing that for the last few months. He went and saw a doc, who gave him some horse pills, and told him it was stress. Harold told him he didn't get stress. The doc said to take the pills. Harold fished the bottle out of the glove compartment and dry swallowed one. The pill burned his throat on the way down. He imagined it kerplunking into his stomach and telling all those juices to settle the fuck down. Being this far away from home, things were not going to get any calmer.

CHAPTER THREE

I counted the next few days by the breakfasts I had on my way to Colorado. Breakfast one was with Benno. I'd slept in and he sent someone to the Esperanza to roust me. Benno never said anything about me being late. In fact he didn't say anything until we'd finished our breakfast of eggs, chili peppers, and some amazing cinnamon pastries with strong coffee. On the third round of coffee, Benno lit a Romeo y Julieta and passed me one.

I nipped off the cigar's end with Benno's gold cutter as he told me a story about his nephew, or it might have been his cousin's kid. It wasn't exactly clear to me.

"You said he's a bit wayward. How do you mean?" I asked.

"As you said when telling me of your early years, there are times when violence bubbles under the surface like a strong pozole. Is it not so?"

"What do you want me to do?"

"It's a sensitive issue. But at the same time a business one."

Benno went on to to tell me how that side of his family was always in trouble. He had hired the nephew-cousin, Benito, to provide some stability.

"The kid's name was Benito? After you?"

"Perhaps. Many dollars have already went into the policía's pockets to keep him out of jail on various charges. I sent him to Colorado to work at a bar and restaurant of mine."

"You got him waiting tables?"

"Among other things. I have many connections there—helpful in that part of the country."

I didn't want to know about the other things, and Benno probably wouldn't tell me anyway.

"Right. So, Colorado Springs. This is where Mostly Harold comes in."

"When he was here in Mexico I told him of my place there. I asked that he return. It is his home, so he was well-placed to handle a number of business deals for me. I gave our friend a position in the bar, and asked him to keep an eye on Benito."

"He must have loved that. And also, Harold is a cold-blooded killer and not to be trusted. I wouldn't call him a friend."

"Harold, as you call him, did what he was asked."

I saw something in Benno's face.

"Until he didn't," I said.

"He was giving reports to another associate, and then those were forwarded to me. Those reports, including information on Benito, have stopped. I contacted the establishment, but the news was troubling."

"Benito was wayward again?"

An even longer pause as Benno looked at me through the cigar smoke.

"Luke, I am offering you some work. This is a matter of deep importance to me. Why are you like this?"

I considered that Benno was the most dangerous man I'd ever known, and remembered the matter-of-fact manner with which he blew out the kneecaps of the turista. I rethought my mood.

"Sorry, Benno. I was looking forward to eating a lot of camarones and studying sunsets for a while before I jumped into something else. I've been feeling a bit rattled. Don't mean to cause offense."

"Offense is not taken, my friend. I understand. Your journey took something out of you."

Benno gestured to the girl with the coffee and she came over with a refill. She topped each of our mugs with a pour from what I knew was not bar-brand tequila.

"I would consider this a personal favor if you would do this for me. On your return, I will give you both the money and the time to experience our fine Mexican sunsets. Where is it you like to visit… down to the bay?"

"Melaque."

"Yes, that is a restful place."

We sipped our coffees as Puerta Vallarta awoke to the sounds of dogs, roosters, and diesel trucks. A shadow passed over Benno's face, and I worried that my reluctance to take the job had pissed him off more than I thought.

"Benno, I want to"

"Benito was found two nights ago in a shallow grave near the Garden of the Gods. I have learned that he had been dead for some time. He'd been shot in the back of the head."

"Damn. I'm sorry."

Benno focused on something behind me. We sat at a small table in front of his place, open only to his friends this time of day. The morning heat had begun to rise along with the dogs' barking. Benno took a deep drag on his Romeo. I'd barely smoked mine.

"When I was his age I was not all that different. There is something in young people's blood that courses like a river current, and drives them into a wildness. It is not what some call an adventure, but more a restlessness, an unease with one's self. Have you felt this?"

"I have."

"Perhaps, like me, someone stepped into your life and helped you out of the river."

I wanted to tell Benno that I was still fighting that river, but instead I just nodded.

"I hoped being away from Mexico, Benito might find some peace. But he was a troubled young man."

"On his own he got worse," I said.

"It seems this way."

"Sorry, Benno, but why do you want me to go there? Are they sending the body back, or you want me to make those arrangements? Are there problems with the police?"

"Nothing like that. But thank you, Luke."

"Then it's about Harold?"

"You are perceptive as always. That is why I'm asking you." Benno waved off the girl, who was back with the coffee and tequila. "I have been informed that Mr. Stevens is no longer in Colorado Springs."

"Stevens?"

"The one you call Mostly Harold," Benno said.

I'd never heard Harold call himself that. It made him sound more like an accountant than a hired killer.

"Where did he go?" I asked.

"There is a possibility that he went as far as Canada. But I have been unable to find this out."

"You think Harold killed Benito?"

"It is difficult to know what to think. Some of the reports from Colorado were troubling. The numbers were not adding up, and I asked one of my associates to look into it."

"Someone has been skimming," I said.

"Perhaps. It is a complicated matter. It often is when family is involved. I feel that I owe it to his mother to find out what happened to her son. I would like you to find the truth, Luke."

Benno had a softness on his face that I'd seen before when he talked about his family.

"You said you wanted me to drive. If Harold is on the run, shouldn't I be flying?"

"This is not a chase. I want you to do what I know you do best."

"Which is?"

"You have been gifted with a perseverance in matters of discovery. This will take some time, and travel. I think it better you have a car," Benno said. "The man who has provided me with the most current information is in Durango."

"He's the one with the package."

"Yes. Go and talk with him. There is no need to telephone me until you have found some answers."

"What if I don't find any?"

Benno smiled and handed me a set of keys.

The Pontiac LeMans was the color of crushed mint leaves in milk. It was showing its age, rust on some of the wheel wells, but Benno assured me that it was a reliable vehicle. A pair of nephews, or maybe cousins, had added some horsepower to it.

"Where did you get Texas plates?"

"Travel well, my friend."

On the road to Durango I chewed on that perseverance line. Benno was referring to my doggedness—what I called the need to fill in that last square in a crossword. I stopped replaying the morning in my head, as I drove over the Balurate Bridge. Peering at the chasms on either side of me I grasped at something symbolic. I pretended to live a quiet, relaxing life in Mexico, but I was skating above all the corruption, the violence and death. Or maybe the chasms were just another pretty vista in the country in which I longed to stay.

Benno's nephews had done a nice job with the LeMans. It handled well, and when I pulled out to pass a semi, it had more than enough power. I was a bit nervous to floor it and see what it really could do—maybe when I was across the border.

I found a cheap hostel-like place on the outer edge of Durango. After two Pacificos and the best beef stew I've had in my life, supposedly Pancho Villa's favorite, I was out like a light.

***

Breakfast two was at the address Benno had given me, a

restaurant with orange walls, concrete arches, and wrought-iron chairs. Walking in, I saw a familiar face. He looked a few pounds lighter than the last time I'd seen him, but still had the bolo tie with the turquoise stone, and a brand-new straw hat.

"Looking sharp, Arkin. Hitting the gym?"

"Caught some stomach bug a while back and dropped some poundage. Working my way back. You still got that hungry-dog look, Fischer. But with more bags under your eyes."

Arkin pointed at a couple things on the menu and held up two fingers to the waitress, not bothering to see what I wanted.

"Trust me on this one," he said.

"You jet across the Mexican border just to deliver Benno's messages?"

"Still a smart-ass, Fischer. Let's cut to it. Benno's looking for Stevens, so that means now you're looking for Stevens."

"Mostly Harold," I said.

"Mostly what?"

"I can't get used to calling him Stevens, and for sure not Mr. Anything. He told me once that he went by a lot of names, but mostly Harold."

"Cute."

Coffees came. They were laced with cinnamon and dark as a moonless night.

"Damn, they know how to do it here," I said. "So Harold shot Benno's boy and headed out of Dodge, or in this case, Colorado Springs?"

Arkin tipped his hat back. He wiped the band of sweat caused by the Mexican sun that poured through the restaurant's huge windows.

"I told Benno I wasn't sure who killed him. On the surface it looked like it was Stevens. A woman who worked with him said he'd been acting odd, distracted, like something was bothering him."

"Something's always bothering Harold."

"Say what you want, but the guy is a total pro. Benno gave him a job and it was done. Clean, not a loose end in sight."

"So what happened?" I asked.

"A week ago Stevens stopped giving reports. When I phoned the bar he wasn't there."

"What kind of work was Harold doing for Benno?"

"Doesn't matter. Things were collected, other things were paid. He kept a log and three times a week he sent it to me."

"People at the bar know where he went?"

"They said he was talking about taking a trip," Arkin said.

"Hey, hit men need holidays, too."

The food came, chilaquiles with red and green sauce, Christmas style, with a plate of warm tortillas and a bowl of hot salsa.

"Serranos," Arkin said.

Damn, I should plan on taking a food tour with Arkin across Mexico. A few bites in and I knew this was seriously one of the best breakfasts I'd ever had.

"How does Benno's dead nephew fit in here?"

"Stevens reported to me that he thought Benito was taking more than his share. And that he suspected he was working some sort of side deal."

"Skimming from Uncle Benno? Never a good idea." I said. "Who was the side deal with?"

"He didn't say. But he might have discovered it before he left town."

"And took him out," I said.

"Maybe. Or something happened that he didn't want Benno to find out about."

"You figure he left Colorado a week ago?"

"Likely. I heard different stories from the workers at the bar. Some say a week ago, some say more."

"What do you say?"

"Could be another reason he left," Arkin said.

"Hang on. I need a moment." I held up my hand and took a bite of soft egg with fiery chili on a fresh tortilla. "Damn, that is fine."

"There was a woman who Stevens had been seen with," Arkin said.

"Harold?"

"I gathered they'd been spending time together."

"Harold found romance? OK, you think they headed out of town to get hitched? Knowing Harold it would be a shotgun wedding. Or maybe a Glock one."

"Benno told me you didn't really want to do this."

I sopped up the lake of golden egg yolk and chiles, and took some more coffee from the girl.

"Listen. It wasn't my choice to leave PV—for sure not to go after a guy who wanted to put several bullets in me, all at once, or spaced out over time."

"But here you are." Arkin pointed a tan finger at me. "How about you start acting like a professional and stop being such a pain in the ass?"

Arkin was right. I swallowed the *fuck you* I was about to deliver.

"Tell me more about the woman," I said.

"Not much is known, except she'd left the Springs around a month ago. Maybe less."

"But Harold only went after her in the last week? Wait, how long do they figure Benito was dead?"

"He'd been rotting up there in that park for a while. A couple of hikers found him," Arkin said.

I went quiet, thinking on this. The chili burning on my tongue wasn't providing any answers.

"Do you know where she went?" I asked.

"North."

"How north? Montana?"

"Canada."

"Hmm, yeah Benno said that. But where? It's a big fucking

country."

"No idea. No one seems to know."

"People that worked with Harold, do they know it's Benno's place?"

"The manager does. But she's been on a long trip east. Getting back today."

"Harold wasn't the manager?"

"His job was to do what Benno wanted."

The place was starting to fill up. Arkin and I were the only non-locals. The clink of coffee cups sounded amidst the rising tones of Spanish—it was a morning music I enjoyed. I caught the odd word, but since coming to Mexico my Spanish had only got marginally better.

"Why don't *you* go back and talk to the manager," I said.

"Benno wants me in Texas. He wants you in Colorado."

Arkin's mouth was a straight line.

"If I find out where she went, and chase down Harold… then what?"

"That will become clear when you find him," Arkin said.

"You mean if he tries to put another bullet in me?"

"Something like that."

Arkin called the girl over and peeled off some money—too much for the cost of the breakfast.

"If you already told Benno all this, why didn't he tell me himself?"

"Benno said getting you out the door was the problem. Once you were on the road you wouldn't stop until the job was done."

"And you believed that?" I asked.

Arkin ignored the question.

"I'm guessing you'll need a gun. But Benno said it might be hard getting across the border with it. If you want, I can set something up in Colorado."

"I've never thought of the Springs as that tough of town. It might kill you with its beauty."

"So you don't want one?"

"I don't need to be packing if I'm just going to ask questions," I said.

Arkin stood and took his hat off to dab the sweat with the napkin. "Call Benno when you know what's going on."

"What happens if I'm dead in a ditch in Canada?"

"Reverse the charges."

Before Arkin left the café he gave me a thick sealed envelope and a piece of paper with a phone number.

"Give this to the manager. Name is Alex. It's from Benno."

"I know who it's from," I said.

"If you change your mind about the gun, call me at that number."

I fingered the envelope. I never knew what Benno was shipping into the U.S. I didn't really care. Being paid to be an errand boy was fine with me. Being sent after a known hitmen created a bit more resistance.

I took one more refill from the girl. Given the tip Arkin had left, I thought about ordering another plate of eggs. I decided on just the coffee. The rich smell of cinnamon and earthy brew filled my nostrils. One table over a group of four started talking loudly, on the verge of shouting. A tall guy with a massive beard suddenly stood. The woman next to him shouted at him a flurry of words. He reached into his pants and I expected him to pull out one mother of a blade. I'd heard a lot about Durango. Come for the breakfast, stay for the knife fights.

"Para ahora mismo!"

Damn. I didn't know what she meant, something about stopping. Her voice cut through the place like a machete. Beard Guy sat back down, never taking his eyes off the guy across from him that he was about to fillet.

The table settled down, and the muttering turned to what sounded civil to my ear. I finished my coffee and threw a hundred pesos on the table. Arkin wasn't the only big spender around here.

CHAPTER FOUR

Harold flicked off the radio in the middle of another goddamn country song. What was wrong with the people who lived here? The land was flat as hell and even the cows looked lonely— so what, the music's supposed to make you feel even worse about yourself? His stomach had finally stopped burning, but the bad music threatened to make it start again.

He took a gravel road off the highway and drove to some trees he'd seen in the distance. Groups of them were rare around here. He didn't have a shovel, so he dragged the body into the trees and threw a few leaves over it.

"Hunting accident," he said. "One of the deer shot back."

Harold spent the night in a mom-and-pop motel that specialized in lumpy mattresses. He parked his car behind the motel, on account of his whole back window had been shot out. Now back on the highway, he drove with the wind whistling through the car, not sure of his next move. The card he'd taken from Tweed Guy was for a car dealership in some place called Bennett. The map of Canada he picked up back in Colorado didn't list little nowhere places. Where the hell was Bennett? He needed to find a local map that showed these backwater burgs.

It was bad enough driving with no back window and the whole passenger side of the windshield so cracked that it was hard to see through, but what really pissed him off was the no tape player. Then, at least he could have brought some Bacharach along. He had bought the car a couple of weeks ago in the Springs. He never got around to getting a player installed. When he bought the car he was already thinking of coming and looking for her—except he kept giving himself excuses not to leave.

Harold thought back to when Delilah first showed up in the bar. She ordered two shots of gin straight up, telling the bartender that if he put an ice cube in it she was going rap him one. Harold felt a twinge that grew into a wondering. They ended up closing the place together. He showed her his Louis L'Amour collection at his place and she spent the night. Then she spent a lot of nights.

Why didn't she tell him why she lit out? They had something going, something he hadn't had for years. Not since the one who ended up dead on his account. He didn't like thinking about her. Delilah was edgy, tough, and he liked that. She looked great in a pair of Levi's, and she was more than pretty. Harold thought words like gorgeous were dumb, but it fit. It wasn't her looks that had brought him in. One day he landed on a TV show that he'd normally zoom past. He listened to some guy in a pale suit talk about how to connect as a couple. That's what it was. They were connected. The revelation surprised the hell out of him.

But then they weren't.

He asked one of the servers—early twenties, bright eyes—if she knew anything about it.

"The two of you talk," he started. "Did Delilah tell you she was leaving?"

"No. But the other night she got talking."

"About what?"

"She'd went through a steady stream of gin-and-tonics, followed by straight-up gin."

"So?"

"She got talking. Told me I reminded her of someone from back home. A place called Hamel."

"She's from Canada," Harold said.

"Oh, that makes sense. I'd never heard of it before. She said it was in that middle province with the long name."

Harold grunted.

"You two have a fight?" the young server asked.

Harold wanted to tell her that they didn't have an anything. She just disappeared.

"Thanks," he said.

It took a lot to get Harold to leave Colorado Springs. Whenever he did leave, there was a big price tag attached and clear instructions on who he needed to put down. Now that he had only one actual employer, he hardly ever left the city. Benno's work was starting to bore him. He was starting to feel like he was a bag checker at the Piggly Wiggly, working hard to make produce manager. So he bought the Ford, and the crappy map, and headed way the hell north.

He found Hamel, but he didn't find Delilah. The asshat he laid out in a parking lot was looking for her too. And he knew about Colorado. It was the plates on Harold's Ford that tipped him off. But Tweed Guy wasn't going to be giving answers to anyone but the guy digging his hole.

The whole thing made his stomach burn in a way that the doc pills wouldn't help. Again he wished he had some of his Bacharach tapes. Whenever things got shitty, old Burt had a relaxing effect. He might have a hard time hearing them over the wind roaring through the blown-out window. Damn. He needed to either get it fixed or find another car. The next one better have a tape player.

Harold was humming the raindrops song in his head when he spied something up the road. He made out one of those big-ass farmer machines on the shoulder. It covered half of the lane he drove on. He slowed to pass, saw that a car was parked in front of the machine. What the hell did they call those things? A combinator or something? The trunk was open and a couple of thick guys dipped down and came up firing. The first shotgun blast hit the grill. Pellets sprayed the windshield, spider-cracking the rest of it.

Harold cranked the wheel, starting a long slow spin. He grabbed his Glock off the seat and fired out the passenger window, shattering it, and tagging one of the pair in the shoulder. The other fired and Harold ducked low. But the shot was lower, ripping apart his back tire. The spin threatened to turn into a roll. Harold fought it back, the car squealing, smoke and steam shooting into the air. A pellet had tagged his neck and he felt the line of blood sliding down the back of it. The car finished a complete three-sixty. Harold had kept it on the road. Slower and slower it spun. He opened his door and rolled out.

Any second one of the semis he passed was going to barrel down the highway and Harold pictured becoming one of the lines. As he scrambled across the road, he almost tripped on a dead raccoon whose head was flattened on the pavement. *Well, fuck that, I'm not gonna be next.*

He waited for another blast, but nothing came. He edged around his dead Ford, his gun tight against his chest. He spun around and fired. He hit the open trunk hood. The guy he hit was on the ground and his buddy was tending to him. The un-shot guy pointed up to the farm machine.

"I think you want to put that down."

"The fuck you say."

Harold heard the chk-chkk.

"Easy, boy."

The last time someone called him boy, Harold shot him on principle. He kept a bead on the pair on the ground, and slowly turned his head upward. A guy with a fat nose and one of those goofy hats, this one forest-green, pointed a shotgun down on him.

"Who are you supposed to be?" Harold asked.

"I'll be the one scraping your brain goo off the highway if you don't drop your gun."

Harold considered his options. He didn't find any. He lowered the Glock and placed it on the road.

"All right then. Who's running this show? And if you think I'm joining your farmer club you better"

The guy on the farm machine jumped down and interrupted Harold with the butt end of the shotgun. As he fell, Harold had a thought.

Combine. That's what they're called.

CHAPTER FIVE

I'd driven through the state of Chihuahua before. All I remember was the advice I'd gotten from an old-timer at a gas station: *Don't get out of the car until you're north of El Paso—not even to piss.* He handed me a bottle of mezcal with one shot left in it.

I stopped for gas and aqua con gas, one of the few things I could ask for in Spanish. Arkin's verbal poking in the Durango café still ground on me. I knew I was being a pain in the ass, even more than usual. I wanted to help Benno out, but Jesus in a rowboat, did I have to track down Mostly Harold? When I first met Harold, he laid his lizard boots into me in the Hotel Esperanza. On further meetings, it seemed like he was always on the edge of putting me down for good. How he ended up working for Benno was not so much ironic as batshit crazy.

After a full day and most of the evening driving I climbed into a bed made of mostly springs at a small motel in El Paso. I was so exhausted that the bedbugs would have to chomp hard to wake me. I slept late, got up at the crack of noon when someone rapped on my door and told me I needed to check out or pay for another night.

The motel had some decent coffee that surprised me, along with a plate of fresh-baked biscuits and preserves.

"My mother," the tall skinny guy behind the counter said.

"She made these?"

"Yes. And the coffee. She told me if I was going to host visitors I needed to treat them like family."

My next jaunt was shorter, as I wanted to stop in and see Franko in Tesuque. The motel owner's comment got me thinking about family. At this stage in my life, Franko stood in for family… maybe even Benno did. It's hard to tell who is family when you're set adrift and you've long since escaped the ones that shared your blood and hairline.

Sure, I took my time getting to Santa Fe. If Benno wasn't in a helluva hurry, why should I be? Driving through the small town of Hatch, I rolled down my window to smell the chiles being roasted at so many roadside stands. I stopped and grabbed a bag, still warm, and was glad that I'd also picked up a six of sodas to wash down the fiery beasts. I pulled off the road to spend some time at a wildlife refuge, where I watched a group of sandhill cranes dance in a river. I gassed up and ate some fish tacos in Albuquerque. By the time I pulled into Santa Fe, the purple sky was holding up an egg-yolk moon. The last time I'd seen Franko, he was just getting over being shot, and I was on my way to getting shot. I didn't spend a lot of time thinking about how close I came to getting my ticket punched. It could have easily went another way.

In Teseque, Franko's sister Cecily greeted me on the porch of the house they shared.

"I'd say you're looking good, but I'm not sure I'd be telling the truth," she said.

"You look just like you did when I last saw you," I said.

"And why wouldn't I?"

Cecily broke the awkward silence with a warm hug. She smelled of corn flour and the night air.

"I'm sorry, you're probably on your way to bed," I said.

"I was. But I knew someone was coming."

"A premonition?"

"Hah! This time of night I can hear car tires from a long way off. But yes, I had a feeling someone would pay me a visit."

Under the moonlight Cecily had the look of a desert sage, or at least someone that always knew more things than they let on.

"How is your brother? Is he already in bed?"

"I don't know what time it is in Spain right now, but he could be."

"He went back home?" I asked.

"Just for a time. He'll be back sometime next month. You need a place to stay, you're always welcome."

"I can drive on a bit and find a motel on the highway."

"Don't be foolish. I've got a bed already made in the back room."

"You did have a premonition."

Cecily smiled and held open the door for me.

The next morning was the last of my breakfasts before I drove to the Springs. A line of light escaped from the curtains and cut across the bed. I was disappointed to miss Franko, but after one of Cecily's breakfasts with fresh rolls and farm butter, I was very glad I decided to come by this way.

"You headed back north to see that sheriff friend of yours? Where was she again? Indiana?"

I took a sip of coffee, laced with a good dose of cinnamon.

"Michigan. But not this time."

"Something happen between you two?"

"We decided to give each other some space. Easy to do when you live a couple thousand miles apart."

"Space. Is that what they're calling that?" Cecily tied back her hair and poured me a fill-up. "Well, you didn't come all this way to see my brother. I can see that."

"What do you see?"

"Oh, enough of that horsecrap. I'm no soothsayer, but I'm a good judge of character, Luke. You're headed somewhere, with something to do, and something to find."

"I've been asked to look into what happened to a friend of mine's nephew in Colorado."

"And what did happen?"

"He ended up dead."

"Then why bother?"

"There was a guy—might be involved. He's the one I'm looking for."

"You and my brother follow people into the darkest places. Is the one you're looking for still in Colorado?"

"Not any more."

"Where's he at?"

"Might be Canada."

Cecily's skin glowed in the New Mexico morning light. I didn't need to imagine her as younger; her lined face showed a wisdom and a life lived that had its own deep beauty.

"So now you're going all that way to find a man who doesn't want to be found," she said. "As I recall, that's your home. Canada."

"Used to be," I said.

"Home is always home. It looks different at different times."

"Where's home for you, Cecily? Back in Spain where Franko is?"

She sat back in her chair on the porch. The morning sun was climbing and soon the last block of shade where we sat would be gone.

"It was, yes. Those first years I especially longed for it. But when I look over those hills, or I hear the hawks overhead, and how the coyote sings under the moon… well, now this is home." She watched me sip my coffee. "Would you like something stronger?"

"I'm good." I laughed. Besides, it's pretty early."

She leaned toward me.

"Why don't you want to go to Canada?"

"Why do you think that?"

"You have the look of resistance."

"New Mexico is a beautiful place. I could stay here," I said.

Cecily stood. She may have thought I was commenting on the beauty of something more than New Mex. It was hard to make out on her tanned skin, but I saw some red in her cheeks. She dusted her hands off from some nonexistent flour.

"How about you just say what the hell is going on for you?"

"What do you mean?"

"You know what I mean. You're just pissing around. You came here looking for my brother, or an excuse."

"Excuse for what?"

"You don't like to be told what to do—even if someone's paying you to do it. If you and me were together I'd forever be kicking your ass."

I smiled and almost laughed until she leaned forward with a look that said she wasn't putting up with a single ounce of my bullshit. I hadn't spent much time with Franko's sister, but enough to know that when she looked at a person like she was looking at me know, it was time to come clean.

"I don't want to go," I said.

"I gathered that, Luke."

"I'm headed in a direction that's going to take me to the place I escaped from."

"Colorado or Canada?"

"Colorado's fine. But I don't think that will be the end of it."

"You're afraid of something you're going to face up there," she said.

"Or someone."

Cecily leaned back and softened her gaze. The sun cut a hard beam across her face. She didn't even squint.

"You need to go back home, Luke. Make things right. You'll not find peace until you do."

"You mean find the one that killed my friend's nephew?" I asked.

"That's not the only reason for your trip. It ain't even the main one. You know that."

Before I could respond, she strode into the house. The banging of the screen door told me our morning conversation was done.

I gathered my things, made the bed, and made a last trip to the bathroom. Cecily met me at my car with a sack of food and a travel mug of coffee.

"I'm sorry. I didn't mean to be short with you."

"You thought I needed a push," I said.

"If I were twenty years younger we'd do a different kind of pushing."

Cecily raised her eyebrow and it was my time to feel the heat run across my face.

"I—"

"Come back this way next month. You and my brother can share a glass of that whiskey of the angels that he drinks."

"Only if you join us, Cecily."

She laughed and threw her head back. She gave me another warm hug and a kiss on the cheek.

"Now go figure it out, my wayward friend."

I looked back as I drove out of the yard, but she was already out of sight, tending to some chore needing to be done.

CHAPTER SIX

Harold woke tied to a chair in the middle of windowless room. His head hurt, his ass hurt, and his stomach was burning. Meaning he'd been there for a while. His jacket lay in a crumpled pile in the corner. Sons of bitches could have least hung it up. His shirt was ripped at the shoulder, and he had a flip memory of being held down and given something that sent him to the dark side of town. His lips felt mumbly, but they hadn't gagged him, so he thought he'd try a word.

"Fuck."

All right then. Time to get it together. The ropes were tight against his skin, but there was a bit of give as he twisted his body. Not much, but enough to work out some space. Whoever put him in the room would probably be paying him a visit, so he better get to it. There were two doors into the room. The one by his coat was open a crack and a line of light bled out the door. The other looked more sturdy—a metal knob on what looked like a security door, made of steel or something thick.

He twisted his body again just as the security door opened. In waltzed a guy in black jeans and a white collared shirt. The doofus had a pair of suspenders like he was in a movie, or maybe that's how these hayseeds dressed up.

"Tied them ropes myself. Doubt you're gonna make much headway."

"Who the fuck are you?"

"Did you say *fluck*? Mouth still a bit warbly?"

Harold pictured himself punching the guy in the head. It was a good picture.

"Oh, now you're smiling? Never will figure out you 'mericans."

Suspenders pulled over the only other chair and flipped it around to sit on it. Harold hated when people did that—sit on the chair the right damn way. Suspenders ran his tongue over his teeth and cracked his neck.

"That tongue some kind of sex thing? I hear you Canadians go for that weird shit," Harold said.

The guy pointed a finger pistol at him, then opened and closed his hand. Harold waited for the hit, but it never came. He would have liked if it did. Instead, Suspenders rolled his neck again.

"You've got a line of dried blood on your neck. Almost got your number punched by a stray bullet."

"Untie me and I'll punch your fucking number," Harold said.

"Ha! How's about we quit dancing and you just tell me where she is?"

"Glad to." Harold spit a huge loogie on the floor. "Who?"

Suspenders wiped his forehead like he was trying to remember how to spell that big word for the school bee. Damned if he didn't snap those stupid-ass straps. Harold had to stop himself from looking around for a camera.

"We got a call. From the King's."

"From the what?"

"The bar where you killed Taylor."

"Never heard of the guy."

Suspenders pinched a spot between his eyes.

"Taylor said he spotted your plates. Said he was gonna check it out. Then we got a call from our guy."

"Seems like you got it all figured out then."

Suspenders looked like he swallowed a bag of lemons.

"We know you're up from Colorado, and that she was down

there. That ain't no coincidence."

"So?"

"We're looking for her, too."

"Who?"

"Delilah. Don't play dumb with me."

"Oh yeah, that Taylor guy said her name. He was the guy I shot in the head."

"We know you shot him."

"Wanted to make sure you were keeping score."

"Score of what?"

"How many dead people I lay out before I put you in the ground."

Suspenders swallowed in a way that showed Harold he was getting to him.

"Look, we can forget about Taylor."

"I already have."

Suspenders jumped up from the chair and came at Harold. He stopped himself, which was disappointing. He really wanted the guy to hit him. He wanted at least one punch to get his anger going—before he stretched this asshat out.

"Like I said. We can forget things." Suspenders sighed. "Just tell us where Delilah is. We'll check it out. If you're on the level, you can go on your way. Back to those Yoo-nited States of yours."

"You watch a lot of old movies?" Harold asked.

"What?"

"*On the level.* Who says that anymore?"

"I—"

"Well twenty-three-skidoo, Mr. McGoo."

"What?"

"Boogidy-boogidy."

Suspenders scrunched up his face and gave his head a shake. As Harold figured, he was too confused to notice that he'd worked one of his hands free. Now that free hand grabbed the back of Suspender's' head and drove his face into Harold's knee.

The guy's nose spurted and he was out like a light. Harold scooted his leg away to avoid getting blood on his lizard boots. Too late. He'd have to wipe that off later. Harold worked away at the rest of the ties. Turned out that Suspenders never got that Boy Scout badge, and Harold was free in a couple of minutes. If the guy had waited a bit longer before he came into the room, his nose might be unbroken. Maybe.

Harold got his coat and gave it a shake. Suspenders moaned. Harold went over and gave him a nightcap with the tip of his boot. He searched his pants pockets and pulled out a wallet. *Evan Kuz*. What the hell kind of name was that? Kuz… was that some Kraut name? Harold checked the door to make sure one of the farmer boys, like the one on the combine with the shotgun, didn't rush in. Kuz had a Beretta. A douchebag's gun, but it would do in a pinch.

He held the gun up to Kuz's head. Dammit. It pissed Harold off to kill guys he wasn't hired to take out. It went against his personal code. Though, he did break it when he shot Taylor. Probably should have shot the farmer who gawked at him in the parking lot. It was likely the guy that phoned it in.

Lately, Harold's code had been feeling a bit shaky. The hell with it. He brought the gun down hard, sending Suspenders into a long woozy dream.

The non-security door led to a small bathroom with a window. Harold figured that'd be a better way to go than running into the farmer boys who could be all locked and loaded. A couple of shoves and the window popped out without breaking. Harold jogged through the yard. There was a trio of cars, but nobody in them, and nobody outside the house. He decided to boost the last car that nosed in. It was one of those foreign jobs with a quiet engine. He'd rather have a Ford with a rumble to it, but the other two cars would have taken more work, and someone was bound to go check on Suspenders.

Peeling down the gravel road and out of the farmyard, Harold checked his rear view. He kind of hoped he'd see them back there. It would be breaking the code again. But if those asshats came after him, well, when in Rome… or however that saying went.

He'd drive to this Bennett place, find the dealership and see if they knew Tweed Guy, Taylor, that he'd shot in the bar parking lot. It was doubtful they knew where Delilah was either. But it could help him put it together. None of this crew seemed like they could find a zipper on a pair of pants. Harold knew he could do better.

Now, all he had to do was figure out where the hell he was in the province. What a dumbass name for a place. Why don't they just call them states like everybody else?

CHAPTER SEVEN

Colorado Springs was one of those towns where you thought you drove into a postcard. The mountains were perfectly pointed, the skies were powder blue, wrapped with carefully sculpted clouds, and the parks were full of healthy-looking people who all jogged seven days a week and got more Vitamin D than I'd ever see. Dammit if the dogs didn't look better here.

Sitting in a dark bar was a welcome escape after all that beauty. The place I sat in was nice, for sure. I doubted the Springs even had a dive bar—the beers were arctic cold and they had a decent selection of draft. A few Mexican brews had snuck across the border into their fridge, the skunky popular one whose name I'd never say, let alone order it, but they also stocked Dos Equis and Sols. I was on my third Sols while I waited for the manager, who I was told would be there within the hour.

Zapata's. I expected it to be cheese-ball, with a big framed black-and-white photo of the Mexican hero looming over the room, but it wasn't. Something about the place had Benno's stamp on it. It wasn't in Mexico, but the way the tables were set up, the candles, the menus, all felt similar to his place in PV. I ordered a plate of fish tacos with pico de gallo. They were tangy, hot, and as good as I'd had from my favorite taco stand in Melaque.

"You've been waiting long?"

She had long blond hair that curved up at the ends like a surfer's wave. Arkin never told me the gender of the manager, and I didn't really care. She wore one of those little black dresses that get mentioned, and this one fit her form as if it had been poured it from a mold.

"You're Alex? You worked with Harold?"

"Harold worked with me," she said.

The waitress delivered a PBR to her. Well, at least it wasn't a Bud. I waved off the server, nursing my Sols before I made any big decisions.

"Fischer, is it? Arkin told me you'd be coming. I just got back."

"So I heard. Where did Harold go?" I asked.

"No idea."

"Nice place. You taking over from Harold?"

"He wasn't the manager."

"What was he?"

"A pain in my ass."

She cracked open the PBR and drained half of it.

"Never get used to the dryness here," she said.

I handed her the envelope Arkin gave me. She eyed it before sliding it into her big bag that was more luggage than purse. As she bent down to put the bag under her chair, her dress gaped and exposed a intricate butterfly tattoo.

She came back up and must have noticed my gaze.

"This dress gives me an inflated sense of cleavage."

I tried my best to think of baseball and church hymns.

"Benno wants to know what all went on. I'm guessing he signs your checks too—so let's cut to it."

"Arkin told me you were kind of pissy."

I finished the Sol and stood to leave.

"Oh, sit down and relax."

She reached across and took the last remaining taco off my plate, shoving half of it in her mouth. I'd be lying if the sight of a beautiful woman taking down a taco like that didn't spark my interest, or something. I sat back down and watched her finish the taco in two more bites. Damn.

I raised my hand to the server, signaled another round for the both of us.

"Look," she said between her final chews, "I told you Harold was a pain—kind of like I'm guessing you are. I didn't really care when he left, because I knew I could do a better job. This place will be packed tonight. The food's great, the beers cold, and the beautiful people in their beautiful clothes love to come here. Our boss gets a big fat deposit from this place."

"What did Harold do here?"

"What are you doing here?" she asked.

"Didn't Arkin tell you?"

"I want to hear it from you."

She lowered her chin and pointed at me like I was the kid who didn't do his homework.

"Benno wants to know what happened to Benito."

"His cousin?"

"I thought he was a nephew?"

"Who knows. Anyway, yeah, he hung around here. Harold had him running errands, or selling drugs, or shooting cats, whatever they did."

"You didn't like either of them," I said.

"I don't like a lot of people."

She leaned back and crossed her arms. I considered leaving again.

"Who was in charge here, you or Harold?"

She laughed.

"Oh I'm sure Harold thought he was. I did all the work. He'd leave to go do whatever shady shit Benno wanted him to do. I was away visiting my mom in Virginia when he lit out."

"You know why he left?"

"Nope," she said.

"Now that he's gone, what happens?"

"What do you mean, what happens? I run things like I've always done," she said.

"What about Benno?"

"Who gives a fuck about him? We send him his money. That's it."

Something flashed in her eyes before she regained her composure. She sighed.

"I'm waiting for Benno to ask me to do the same shit Harold did."

"But you won't," I said.

"Still thinking on it."

Our beers came and Alex ordered another plate of fish tacos.

"If you're here to ask me if Harold killed the kid, I really don't know. I heard Benito had some sort of side deal going on, but I couldn't say what it was. I doubt Harold's leaving had anything to do with Benito."

"What then?"

"More to do with her."

"Harold's girlfriend." Saying the phrase out loud sounded even stranger than I'd imagined.

"I don't know what they were to each other. But she had her hooks into him in a way I'd never seen before. Big bad Harold didn't let anyone get close. He never chatted with any of the customers. Too many times I explained to someone that, no, he wasn't pissed off at them. He just looked like that."

"She have a name?"

"Delilah."

"You're kidding."

"Good thing Harold didn't have long hair."

"And you think he left because of her?"

"Could be," she said.

The tacos came and Alex held up her hand.

"These are the best damn things here. I swear I've had an orgasm eating them."

I let that line hang in the air, still attempting to look anywhere but below her neck. I waved off her offer to share, as she made her way through the plate. In the corner of the bar someone tinkled on a piano and woman with a Bacall voice started singing. After the tacos and a few jazz standards, I asked Alex to tell me more about Delilah.

"She showed up one night and started ordering tequila shots. Harold was behind the bar. I don't know what she said to him, but he took over from the bartender and started pouring for her."

"What'd she look like?"

"Tall, but curvy, filled out her black t-shirt and jeans that night. Long hair like mine, but she's a brunette. Even longer, it stretched down the middle of her back."

"You ever have a conversation with her?" I asked.

"Not about anything that mattered. She told me she was from Canada."

"Why was she down here?"

"Arkin said you were from there. You tell me why y'all come here."

"The warm hospitality," I said.

She flipped me the bird.

"Delilah say where in Canada? It's kind of a big country," I asked.

"She mentioned it once. I wrote it down just in case."

"In case of what?"

"Whatever," she said.

Alex went back into her bag and brought out a coiled notepad like something a cop would carry. She spun the pad around and pointed at a name that was both distant and right in the room with me.

"Heard of it?" she asked.

"Like I said, it's a big country."

She tore out the page and handed it over.

You gonna write notes on me?" I asked.

She put the pad back in her bag.

"So Harold left to go find this Delilah," I said.

"Beats the hell out of me. Harold's gone and I'm not missing him. Canada can have him."

"You ever been there?"

"Never had the slightest interest. Snow, cold, and big flat areas of fuck-all."

She stretched out the *fuck* and raised an eyebrow. She leaned across the table.

"I have to tend to some things. You can drink and eat on Benno's tab. We've got an account over at the Holiday Inn if you're staying the night."

"That it?"

She leaned back. Her face opened into a wicked smile, she flipped her eyes down and up again, taking stock of what I was trying my best to ignore.

"If you're thinking we're gonna end up making the beast with two backs…" She paused, then gave me one of those finger-off-the-nose flips like we were in an old heist movie. "I'm afraid you're playing for the wrong team."

"I'm just looking for Harold," I said.

"Uh-huh." She reached across and squeezed my hand, and narrowed her eyes. "I could almost be convinced to switch sides. But I've got someone at home that would be pissed."

"Gotta keep the home fires burning," I said.

She let go of my hand.

"Of course, I've been known to play for other teams."

I made a sound that seemed like a word.

"You need anything else? Arkin told me to set you up with whatever you needed," she said.

"I'd take another Sol, maybe with a shot of decent bourbon."

She gave me a final nod and I watched her leave.

I'd hidden my reaction to the name of the town in her notebook.

Of course I knew it. I didn't know the game she was playing, dropping sexual hints and then pulling them back like I was a sucker in a game of three-card monte. I admit she made the chair feel unstable underneath me.

I followed the beer and bourbon with a couple more, waiting for Alex to come back. She never did. I no longer saw her in the bar, so she must have went home to the partner she'd alluded to.

I checked the watch I wasn't wearing. It was late on a bunch of levels. I nursed one final shot of bourbon, thinking on the series of breakfasts that had brought me to this point.

Over cinnamon pastries and cigars, Benno had guessed that I'd end up in Canada. Arkin in his dapper straw hat tried to kick my ass down the road with Christmas-style chilaquiles. Then finally Cecily's warm rolls and warmer smile told me that I'd never find peace until I went home. It was clear that I couldn't delay it any longer.

The thing about moments of clarity is they drive a stake into an alcohol-filled night and steady the sea legs. Well, almost. I only hit two of the chairs as I weaved out of the bar into a starry Colorado night, in search of a hotel room with too many pillows.

CHAPTER EIGHT

The ring of the phone ripped a hole in the soft morning light and broke into one helluva dream about surfing. The wave dropped underneath me as I picked up the phone.

"Mr. Fischer, we have a long-distance call for you. There will be a charge for this. Do you want to accept?"

"What? Yeah."

"I'll patch it through."

I grunted and wiped sleep from my eyes.

"Luke, you are still in Colorado."

"I'm talking to you on the phone, Benno."

"I will admit my friend, I was disappointed to hear that you had checked in, rather than continue your journey."

"You said it wasn't a chase," I said.

"Hmm, so I did. Our friend in Durango said you might need a bit of encouragement."

"Arkin told you I was dragging my ass."

"He said something like this, yes."

"The Springs is a nice place. I can see why Harold stays here."

A few seconds of silence stretched out. Benno was never one to show his anger, but I sensed it in his long pause.

"Benito's mother came to me. She was very upset, which I understand. If this happened to my son, I would share her emotion. I have told her that I will provide answers."

Benno took another long pause.

"I know you have you own ways of doing things, my friend. And you also know that I have given you much assistance these last few years." I heard my benefactor exhale. "But there comes a time when I must insist—"

I cut him off. "I'm going to Canada, Benno."

"Ah, then my phone call was not needed," he said.

"It's always good to talk with you."

Benno laughed.

"There is no need for storytelling, Luke. What have you found out about Mr. Stevens?"

"Only that he left."

"We already knew this," he said.

"But now I know where. Goodbye, Benno."

As I placed the phone on the receiver, I thought back to the moment of clarity from last night. I knew where I had to go. But Benno also knew me, a bit too well, and how like a first-time skydiver, I'd need one more boot out the airplane door. I just hoped my chute would open.

***

Driving the road back to the place where it began, where I began, memories seeped in like river water from a poorly built dam. I'd pushed events from the past into the darkest corners of my mind, quite happy to never have them emerge into the light. Like a lot of people who grow up in a nowhere place, my future split into two options: stay or go. The ones who go might return to bury a parent, but mostly they are gone for good, and sooner forgotten than they might have imagined.

After high school, I considered the option of being gone for good. I thought about getting an education at some place of higher learning, or at least moving somewhere where people were different than the several hundred I'd known my entire life. I packed up the beater my father bought me, briefly considering which direction to point, when she appeared. It wasn't like she walked out of mystical lake with a sword in hand, or more likely, a slough carrying a shovel—but she had an effect on me. I'd even call it transcendental. Or maybe just weird.

For starters, in a town the size of Marvelle, how had we never met before? I guess she'd studied by correspondence, and then went abroad. I've never met anyone who used that phrase and actually meant it. Neither of us felt like we belonged in a small town, but together we made a spot for ourselves.

Our lives intertwined with equal amounts of passion and anger—who knows what we were angry at. We were both Brando, asking, "Whattya got?" The longer I stayed in my hometown, the longer I couldn't leave. I sank into a bog of familiarity. Better the devil you know. So we lived, and drank, and made love, and fought, for months, maybe years. I didn't even own a calendar that could track that kind of time. Somewhere in there my father died.

Then on a cold rainy day in May, I threw a wilted flower into my mother's grave. Most of the people who knew my mom had either left town or were buried in the same graveyard. I stared into that hole and wondered how long before they dug one for me. I didn't really think of it as a premonition, but seven days later I threw the punch that started, or, I guess, finished it all.

I'd only known Benno for a few years, but he knew I was like a dog that won't move until he's kicked—and then one who won't stop running until someone makes him. After his phone call in the Colorado Springs Holiday Inn, I chugged some hotel coffee and a muffin that promised blueberries but only delivered sugar. It was the right kind of fuel I needed to shoot across Wyoming, and then for an even more barren ride, Montana.

As I got closer to the Canadian border, I pictured that hole they dug for my mother. The image of me standing over her grave came out of the dark corner where I'd kept it, and became a retina burn on my brain.

The border crossing took longer than usual as I had to answer a bunch of questions on why I'd been in the US for so long.

"I've actually been mostly in Mexico. Puerto Vallarta."

I produced a resident visa that Benno had set up for me. The square-shaped border guard studied it.

"You said it's been five years. What have you done for income?"

"I haven't been working. An aunt died and I was the last one standing. She left me everything."

"And then you ran out of money?" he asked.

"No. But now my other aunt died. I came back to pay my respects."

"She leave you money, too? You must be some nephew."

After he went through my car, he ran my passport and the visa, then sent me on my way.

"Welcome home, Mr. Fischer. I hope you stay with us a while."

***

I'd couldn't count the number of times I'd been on this highway. Miles of long straight road where the only curves were correction lines—places where the roads needed to adjust or they'd converge. No matter what those nut-bars said, we lived on a ball-shaped earth. Whenever I drove this highway, I heard a guitar strumming. It sounded like wind moving over a field of wheat, fingers plucking out a sad song, and a voice sang an even sadder song.

I'd been away long enough that I struggled to connect the word *home* with this landscape. My body still felt it. My heart did, too, but that organ was buried in so much scar tissue it was hard to get a solid reading from it.

I never really thought of Mexico as a foreign country. When I first drove across the border, and then made my way to a very different highway than the rail-straight I was on. It was the 200, a winding road that hugged the Pacific. Back then, driving that coastal highway felt somehow familiar, though I'd never been there in my life. I couldn't draw a parallel to that twisting road and the vast stretches of flat prairie with skies that went on forever. My connection to Mexico made me reconsider the whole reincarnation thing—or maybe it was the winters. I always hated them in Canada. I never learned how to ice-skate, and the curling rink was just a place to get cheap beer and secondhand smoke.

So once again the person who paid my PV hotel bill had asked me to do a piece of work, or as he called it, *a matter of deep importance*. Benno had suspected all along that Harold was in Canada. Of course he was right. Benno was one of those guys who always guessed right. A couple of years back he'd sent me on a wild chase that led me through Montana, all the way to Montreal, hundreds of miles east of here. It seems like I had only just returned from Upper Michigan—though that was to help my friend, Franko, who I am always indebted to. Being in the U.P. was like knocking on the doorstep of home. Now, this time I had to walk on over.

***

It took several roads, some backtracking, and a sign that the locals had been using for target practice to find what stood in for a main road out here. Harold drove the single-lane highway until he spied a gas station. There was no town in sight, only a big yellow orb that said GAS with most of the S peeled away.

"Fill 'er up. You got maps?"

"Yes sir. Whattya looking for?" The jockey was a tall pimply kid.

"Paris, France."

"Excuse me?"

"What d'ya think I need, numbnuts? For this area."

"Oh, oh, oh, for sure."

Kid sputtered like Curly from the Stooges—no way was he

getting laid anytime soon.

Harold spread the map on the hood and had the kid point out where they were. The kid pulled out a black marker and drew a fat circle around the nearest town.

"I'm gonna buy this map and you mark it up like that?"

"Oh, oh, I'm sorry, I didn't think"

"You ever hear of Bennett?"

"Oh yeah, it's up here." The kid pocketed the marker and pointed at a spot on the map. "Take you a couple of hours. If the traffic is good."

Harold looked out at the empty highway. A car had not drove past since he pulled into the station. He held out his hand, opened and closed it."

"Give it to me."

The kid looked confused, then dug in his pants pocket for the marker. Harold grabbed it from him and drew a circle around Bennett.

"How much for the map?"

"Oh, um, that's on the house. A welcome gift. I hope you enjoy exploring our province."

"Better than Disneyland."

Back on the highway, Harold went through the first convo he'd had with Delilah. Thinking back on it, he should have known she was going to cut out. For the last two decades, he'd made a point of not letting anyone into his life. Being alone suited him. Sure, he'd have the odd night with a woman. But he made sure they knew it wasn't going anywhere. He didn't go in for the cheap motel sex. He liked to have a dinner, go back to his place, and show off his shelf of Louis L'Amours. If things went in the direction of the bedroom, he let them. It was usually a twenty-four-hour thing, sometimes it stretched to seventy-two. But that was it.

"You don't look like you belong here."

That was the first thing she said to him. It wasn't the words as much as they way she said them. The usual bar banter dropped away pretty fast. Before he realized it, he was talking about himself in a way that he never did.

"You don't seem the type to be in a place like this talking to a guy like me," he said.

"What kind of guy are you, Harold?"

"The usual."

"I doubt that very much."

They talked until last call, and then he asked her to hang around while he closed up. The pain-in-the-ass manager was gone on one of her trips again—supposedly to visit her mother. At the bar, Harold put the last of the dishes in the machine and gave the counters a final wipe. He'd told the staff to all go home.

"Well how about you?" he asked her.

"How about me what?"

"Do you belong here?"

"Not usually. It's not long before people start to piss me off."

Harold saw a lot of her over the next three months, showed her the Louis 'Amours a number of times.

Delilah was cagey about what she did for work. Harold knew she had some connections up there in Canuckland. She was involved in some sort of land business. It was the reason she was in Colorado. Whenever he pressed her for more info, she shifted the conversation. He got used to her being around. He wanted her to be around more. It had been twenty years since Harold had considered being with another person.

"It's a nice offer," she said.

"You've seen the place. You could have your own room."

"Let me think on it. I'm working on a deal right now. One that requires some subtlety."

"What kind of deal?"

She smiled at him like she did.

"*Magnificent Seven* is on channel five tonight. How about we grab a pizza and settle in?"

Harold was not one for romance, even less on sentiment. But damn, he really liked that smile.

CHAPTER NINE

There were a few guaranteed spots to go for information in a small town like Hamel. The place where I grew up was ninety miles northeast, but all the towns around here laid out pretty much the same. This time of year there wouldn't be much going on at the rink, though they'd keep the ice on year-round. It was too early in the day to hit the bar, but the nooner crew would be there. Best bet was either Ray's Café—where I remembered having some decent breakfasts and burgers as greasy as young Elvis' hair—or I could try the hardware store or the lumberyard.

The lumberyard was bustling with a parking lot full of half-tons, and folks loading up boards, shingles, and various buckets of paint or fertilizer or who knows what. People would figure on me being an out-of-town snoop if I didn't buy at least a flat of shingles. I decided on the hardware store, as waltzing into a café full of locals would mean all eyes were on me. Doubtful I'd be recognized, it had been more than a decade since I last visited Hamel, and even then I'd never spent more than an afternoon drinking Pilsners here. For sure I'd not been in Robinson's Hardware. I don't think it existed the last time I was in town.

A pair of men saddled up a long wooden counter. One wore overalls with pockets that bulged with small tools, pens, and whatever else he crammed in there. The other wore a pair of slacks with a razor-sharp crease, a collared cream shirt and a tie the color of burnt toast.

"What can I set you up with?"

The guy working behind the counter had a buzz cut and wore a plaid shirt tucked into his faded Wranglers. My upbringing came back to me in strange ways, as I right away could tell those from a pair of Levi's.

"Just poking around, thanks."

"Well poke away, but know that don't pay my mortgage." Buzzcut Guy grinned and the other two threw in some guffaws.

"Speaking of which, you should come by the bank, Darren. We need to get you locked into a good rate."

"Shit, Francis, I thought you came over for the free coffee, not to bug me about my financials."

Francis the banker downed his Styrofoam cup and straightened his toast-tie.

"You sure you don't need something?" asked Darren, the owner of the buzzcut and the store. "Got a sale on a nice set of sockets. The ones with the push buttons so you don't get a hernia trying to change' 'em."

"How much?" I asked.

"For out-of-towners, thirty-nine ninety-nine. A steal at twice the price."

"I'll consider it. How do you know I'm from out of town?"

"You read the population sign when you came in?" The guy in overalls had teeth that were a near shade to the banker's tie.

"Guess you got me there. I'm just rolling through on my way to Alberta."

"Isn't everybody?" Darren asked.

"Could I have a cup of that coffee?" I asked.

"Fifty cent and it's all yours. I'll throw in the creamer."

I put a couple of quarters on the counter.

"You up from the States? I'm not giving you exchange on that," Darren said.

"I've been living down there for a few years," I said.

I dumped in a creamer and settled into a story, being careful how I spun the tale. I didn't want to let these three know that I'd drank and fought my way through many towns around here—including theirs. I told them I had relatives in the province, but that I'd grown up in Ontario. I was quick to point out it was nowhere near Toronto. Growing up here, I knew how people felt about that city.

"I went to the Big Smoke one time. Visited the Hockey Hall of Fame. Shook Bobby Orr's hand," Darren said.

"Oh black Christmas tree, you're gonna tell that one again?" The guy in overalls with the stained chompers was named Jimmy.

"Wasn't telling you Jimmy, I was telling…" Darren pointed at me.

"Fischer."

"First or last?"

"Sure," I said.

That got me a scowl from Jimmy.

"After I met Mr. Orr, and I'd seen the Cup, I hightailed it out of there on the next train."

"Didn't visit the CN tower?" I asked.

"All that shit looks the same from higher up."

The three of them talked about how Hamel was doing, the crops, and how the government screwed up everything. Soon enough, they started peppering me with questions.

"Why d'you head south and live with those 'mericans? They're crazy as shithouse rats down there. Plus, you get hit with a shovel, it's your dime to get stitched at the hospital."

As the talk spiraled down into a useless banter, I knew I'd get nothing of use out of this bunch. I told Darren I'd consider those sockets wrenches and left them to it. Not having another plan, I rethought the café.

As expected, walking into Ray's Café I got the once-over by the locals. They needed to make sure I wasn't a serial killer or worse from Alberta. I sat down to another cup of coffee and a slab of flapper pie that reminded me of my mom. A woman in a corner booth barely looked up when I came in, but I noticed her. There was a crisp snap in her collared shirt, almost a man's style. I doubted she was from around here. She could be visiting a relative, or like me, tracking down a hired killer.

I chuckled at the thought of someone else looking for Harold. For one thing, the guy was so huge he wouldn't be that hard to find. For whatever reason she occupied a booth at Ray's Café, I convinced myself it was pointless to talk with her. The information I needed was from the locals.

She walked over to my booth and slid in like she knew she'd be welcome.

"How's the pie?"

"A bit flabby. They should change the name," I said.

"The sign outside says homegrown cooking, but I saw them slide it out of a plastic box in the pass-through."

"Health inspector?"

Her laugh was like a warm summer rain.

"I was about to ask you the same question," she said. "Except you don't seem—"

"Clean enough?"

The left edge of her mouth curved into one of the best smiles I'd seen in two thousand miles.

She called over to the waitress and asked for tea with real cream on the side, no sugar. She didn't wear much makeup, skin was on the pale side, hair the color of coffee much better than the swill I was drinking—someone got paid a lot for that cut. A soft pink lipstick was all she needed against that backdrop. The clothes, the skin, hair, and smile made me draw my conclusion.

"You do some modeling?" I asked.

"Is that what stands in for a pickup line these days? Besides, did you forget that I joined you?"

"Only wondering," I said.

The waitress brought the tea. My booth partner dropped in a dollop of cream before pouring in the hot water.

"I did a bit. Even had an agent in New York before things went sideways. Shitty business full of shitty people."

We did some of that awkward back and forth chit chat before I called the waitress over and asked if they served beer.

"It's only two o'clock," she said.

"It's five o'clock somewhere. Hell, five thirty in Newfoundland," I said.

"We don't serve beer. At any time. Would you like a Coke?"

"You put some rye in it?"

The waitress turned her back on me and someone gave a hurumph or pfft… could have been a combination of the two.

"Friendly place. You got a name?" I asked.

"Nah, I'm just a dame." She let that one hang for a moment before she finger-pistoled me. "You talk like those books you get at the drugstore. Next thing you'll tell me you're a private eye, like on TV."

"Nope. Wrong on that count."

"What brings you to such a happening metropolis as Hamel?"

"Driving through. Had a hankering for flapper pie."

The waitress came back and slammed a Coke down in front of me.

"Theresa Swain. Can I have a sip of that?"

I slid the icy glass toward her and watched her drink.

"Fischer. Luke."

"Well Fischer Luke, I happen to know the bar down the street starts serving at noon. I'm done with tea and soft drinks, how about you?"

"Sure. There's too much light in here," I said.

"I was thinking the exact same."

***

We left Ray's Café and walked down the main drag. Half of the shops we passed were either closed, for now or for good. Like a lot of these small towns, it was near impossible to make a go of it when people drove to the big city for everything from gas to cans of beans. The hardware store had a better chance, given that something always needed fixing or replacing, and usually in a hurry. But the clothing-store mannequins had a layer of dust on their shoulders and wore a style that was popular a decade or more ago.

"The town is booming," she said.

"I feel bad for them. Every high school student has their last class in June and hits the highway."

"There's no money in the town businesses, expect maybe the lumber store. But there's plenty in the fields and farmhouses. Grain prices are high, crops are lush, and Farmer Joe just bought a hundred-thousand-dollar combine."

"You met Joe?" I asked.

"Not yet. But I plan on it."

Bars in towns like Hamel were in hotels that had a few rooms upstairs that almost no one used. Some arcane law said that if you are going to set up a bar, you had to set up a place to stay as well. The King's Hotel had a dark brick exterior and an even darker interior that sucked up the afternoon sun. The neon signs advertising beer choices seemed low on gas. The place was about half full, chatter levels dropped when we walked in, but came back fast enough that I wondered if I'd imagined the shift in sound.

"You must have been here for a while now."

"How do you figure that?" she asked.

"Seems like a few of these folks know you. They settled in fast, even though you came in with the dangerous stranger."

"You don't look very dangerous."

A young woman in a checked shirt, blond hair tied back, took our orders. Theresa ordered a Pilsner and like Pavlov's beer-dog, I followed suit.

"Were you one of those high schoolers that lit out?" she asked.

"I wish I would have been. I stayed past my welcome."

"How so?"

Some hurting country music whined out of a ghetto blaster from behind the bar. I saw the bartender eyeing us before he returned to pouring rye whiskey into a trio of glasses. The woman with the ponytail sang along as she circled the room with a tray of beers and highballs.

"Look, as much as I love a good banter in a dark bar, let's cut to it. Why did you come up to me in the café?"

"You're kind of touchy," Theresa said.

The woman delivered our beers and I ordered two more. Something told me I was going to need backup.

"You looked like someone interesting to talk to," she said.

"Hmm. Not sure I buy that. How about telling me why you're in town. Start with Farmer Joe."

"Lot of Joes, Harolds and Franks around here. They've all got fat bank accounts, and are looking to spend."

"Why Harold?" I asked.

"Hmm? Just a name from around here. Petes, too."

I studied her face.

"What do they want to spend their money on? More tractors?"

"They're full up on those. I'm here asking them to invest on something that will bring them even more money than their crop. Plus they'll have something to fall back on if the rain stops falling and the hoppers get hungry."

"Like what?"

"Land." She clinked my beer and gave me a wink. "As the saying goes, they aren't making any more of it."

We settled into it, got a basket of peanuts, and kept the tall brown ones coming. Pilsner is one of the beers of choice around here—it was no Pacifico, but it went down my throat like an icy slide in February.

Theresa was a land developer, selling potential she called it. The lots she was selling were not around Hamel—most of the land here was being farmed on, either with grain or pastureland for cattle. She had the inside track on lots that had just opened up outside of Edmonton. Albertans weren't always the most popular around here, but the farmers knew how things were booming there.

"And the urban sprawl will eventually spread into those lots," I said.

"It sure will," she said. "And those lots are going to be prime locations for subdividing. Then comes the lovely little suburban houses with fat lawns, and a mall, and a movie house, all within walking distance."

She told him she'd been in Hamel and the surrounding areas for a month now, making the rounds, doing her pitch.

"Is that what you're doing, pitching me?"

"You got a fat bank account?"

"It's almost see-through," I said.

That elicited another warm laugh.

"I just liked your face," she said.

She took the last swallow of beer and clunked the bottle down.

"People really got that kind of money around here?" I asked.

"Not all of them. But those that do are what you'd call loaded."

"How do you know which ones?"

"To begin with I picked the ones with the most half-tons in the farmyard. They usually have the biggest machines and maybe even a boat in one of the outbuildings. Boys and toys. After I talk with them about the land they tell me about their neighbors—or they don't."

"How so?"

"Some of them see the deal I'm offering and want to tell maybe a brother or a pal who lives down the road. There are a few that try to keep it to themselves."

"But word gets out," I said.

"It surely does. I've got a guy who called my motel room this morning, asking me to drop on by. Like I was just coming over for a cuppa. But no doubt, he smells money."

"How do you know?"

"Something in the urgency in his voice and how he tried to hide it. Hey, why don't you tag along?"

I did a quick gauge of my faculties after the Pilsners. She had matched me with every round.

"You think that's a good idea? A pair of us fresh from the bar showing up and posing as big-time developers?"

"I *am* big-time. And I figure it might be good to go in as a pair. A single hot woman sitting across the table from the husband has not always been the most welcome."

"By the farmer's wife," I said.

"Uh-huh. And I was raised on Pilsners. I'm sober as a judge." Theresa looked up to the clock behind the bar. "Oh shit, we better mosey. Let's go."

She didn't wait for an answer from me. She picked up the tab and I followed her out to the parking lot, thinking on her line about being hot. She wasn't wrong.

CHAPTER TEN

Harold drove into the outskirts of Bennett, the name of the town on the business card he'd fished out of dead Taylor's suit. After the shootout in the parking lot, and then getting shot at by those farmers, knocked out, and tied to a chair, he'd had about enough. He thought about going back to where they held him and cleaning house. Taking them all out would make him feel better, but he wouldn't be any closer to figuring out where Delilah was hiding. She was holed up somewhere. The jokers with the guns and farm machinery didn't know where she was, and neither did old-timey Mr. Suspenders. Damn, he should have stuck around and banged a few heads until someone gave him a fuller story. Why were they looking for her anyway?

So Delilah was hiding out while he traipsed along this flatter-than-fuck landscape sniffing out clues like a coyote looking for the dead bunny. She had surely pissed off somebody. If she was dead, well, he didn't really want to think about that.

There was barely a sliver of sunlight left when he entered the small town. A few dim stars appeared. All the shops on the main drag were dark. He figured on the dealership being closed. Harold got a room at the DewDrop Inn and convinced the guy in the kitchen to make him a cheeseburger, even though they were closed. He thought about staring him down, maybe stomping his foot, but decided to throw a couple of twenties at him instead.

"You want fried onions on that?"

"Burger, cheese, ketchup. Hot sauce if you got it. It's a simple damn recipe."

Harold ate in his room and watched Bruce Dern shoot John Wayne. He always liked that part and wished that big galoot got shot in more movies.

He slept in the next morning, got woken up by someone banging on his door and telling him that checkout time was noon. He was surprised at how tired he felt. He drank some rotgut coffee and ate a year-old muffin from the motel office before going to find the car dealership. He followed the sign that said City Centre—they didn't even know how to spell things up here. His stomach was more settled than usual, which was surprising after last night's burger. He thought, not for the first time, that the doctor had no idea what he was talking about.

The car he'd boosted turned out to be a real smooth ride, as he'd guessed. He still felt out of place driving it, too chic-chic for him. At least it was a dirty beige color so it didn't draw attention. He turned a chrome knob and pushed a couple of buttons on the radio. The sounds of "What the World Needs Now" filled the car.

"I'll be damned."

Harold sang along with Burt, something he only did when he was alone, as he drove onto what they called Main Street. Pretty original. It was the usual small-town shit, a couple of clothing shops with corny names, a small bank next to place selling insurance, and a grocery store with handwritten signs in red showing the latest deals on corn. The cars were all parked on the diagonal, which was about the stupidest use of space he'd ever seen.

The address on the card said Main Street, but there was no dealership that he could see. Harold followed the road through a four-way stop and across a set of tracks. The radio jockey came on to tell him they were playing all oldies today on account of his mother's birthday. Harold didn't think of Bacharach's music as old. It was always around, like air, and it always would be.

He rolled his neck to get the cracks out. Buildings on the road were spaced further apart now. Yards were full of big machines, like the combine where the guy with the shotgun had stood. Up ahead he spied a large circle sign with the name Prairie Motors in red block letters.

Harold drove onto the lot, glancing at the price cards propped up on the car windshields.

"No damn way I'd pay that for a Chevy."

Inside the showroom, next to a pair of brand-new sedans, was a guy in a beige suit carrying a clipboard.

"Hey there. What can I get you driving today?"

The guy flashed him a wide-gapped smile. Harold fought the urge to pound him in the crotch. It was turning into that kind of morning.

"You do trade-ins?"

"Surely do. That your vehicle outside? That's a nice one. I'm sure I could put something together for you. You looking for another sedan or something sportier?"

"I'm actually looking for a guy who works here." Harold pulled out the card. "Dwayne Stiltson. He in today?"

"You bet. Dwayne's the manager here. But I can help you find anything you need."

"I need Dwayne," Harold said.

"Are you sure I can't—"

"Get your manager or I'm walking."

The toothy smile wavered and fell. The salesman gave a nervous laugh.

"Well OK. A man who knows what he wants. I'll go see if Dwayne's free."

While the salesman in beige disappeared down a short hallway, Harold went over to the coffee pot he'd noticed when he came in. He filled a cup with a smiley-face design, annoyed that they didn't have paper cups, and that he had to drink out of some salesman's mug. The coffee was bitter as hell, fitting Harold's mood perfectly.

"I've heard you're looking for me. Straight to the top 'eh? Don't believe I've had the pleasure."

Harold turned to see a man in a blue suit and red tie, his gut straining at the buttons.

"The pleasure of what?"

"Dwayne Stiltson."

"Right."

Harold looked at the man's outstretched thick hand.

"Well, what can I do ya for?" He pulled back his hand, seeing that Harold had no intention of shaking it. "Were you looking for new or used?"

"I'm here to ask about Taylor," Harold said.

The name produced an eyebrow move from Stiltson.

"Don't believe I know any Taylors. Barry, have you helped a Mr. Taylor?"

Harold sighed. The bullshit in the room was getting thick—time to cut to it.

"He's the one that got laid out in the bar parking lot. Someone shot him in the head. Does that help?"

"Bar? Parking lot?"

"Hamel. Some stupid name like the Royal," Harold said.

This time the man's eyebrow move was accompanied by a lip curl. The fat guy was a regular silent-movie actor.

"Barry, can you take that Fairlane for a spin? Someone said it had a funny noise. Check it out, will ya?"

"I had someone take that out yesterday. Ran like a watch," the salesman said.

"Then try out that Charger in the backlot."

"What's wrong with the Charger?"

"Just check it out, Barry."

The other guy looked like he wanted to say something and then left the showroom. Harold considered rapping them both in the head just to get things moving. He had zero patience for this dancing-around shit.

"Let's have a chat in my office, Mr…?"

Harold walked past him down the hallway. Stiltson followed.

The office was a wood-paneled affair, photos of chubby kids and an ugly wife next to a framed shot of Stiltson dressed in hunting gear and holding a dead goose. He plopped down in his leather chair, noticing Harold study the photos.

"Do you hunt?" he asked.

"Dumbass thing to do. Wading through fields to kill things that can't kill you back," Harold said.

"Well, I like the sport. And cooked wild goose is one of the pleasures in this world. Now, I get the sense you're a man in a hurry. How about you tell me who you are and why you're here."

"I'm looking for someone."

"Yes. You said the name Taylor. 'fraid I don't know where this fellow is at."

"I know where he is. I'm the one who put a bullet in his forehead."

Stiltson coughed and sputtered like an outboard that wouldn't start.

"See here you son of a bitch! If you're gonna come into my place and threaten me…" He didn't seem to know how to finish.

"Taylor knew a friend of mine—he didn't say so, but I'm putting that together. Her name's Delilah. She's the one I'm looking for."

Stiltson's eyes flashed.

"What does all that have to do with me?"

Harold let out a sigh. The bad coffee was gnawing a hole in his stomach. Dammit, his pills were in the other car.

"Tell me what you know or I'll blow your fat ass into the wall."

Harold took out Kuz's Beretta and pointed it at the manager's head. Stiltson grabbed the phone on his desk and pounded numbers on the pad. With his free hand, Harold reached over and tore the cord out of the wall.

"Talk."

"I didn't know Taylor. Never even met him. He got hired because we got a tip that someone might come looking for her—up from the States. I guess you're the someone. That's all I know." Stiltson spit out the words.

"Who's we?"

Stiltson pushed himself back and opened a drawer.

"Easy," Harold said.

"I'm just getting my medicine."

He fumbled with the vial, twisting it with his chubby fingers and spilling out a capsule. He pointed at a water cooler in the corner of the office. Harold thought he'd let Stiltson choke back the pill dry, but this whole damn thing was taking too long. He brought the manager a cone of water and waited as he took the pill.

Stiltson held up his hand, his eyes clenched and then his face relaxed.

"You're gonna end up dead, face-down in your desk."

A look of panic slid across the manager's face.

"Not from me, numbnuts. You should drop some pounds, do a push-up or two."

Stiltson pocketed the vial.

"Acid reflux. It just happens. My ticker's fine," he said.

"Uh-huh. Who sent Taylor looking for me? You said *we got a tip*, so you must be one of them."

The manager looked at the clock on the back wall like it had an answer.

"I don't know why I said *we*. Shit, you gave me the heebie-jeebies. You know what it's like to get a pistol pointed at your head?"

"I'm usually the one pointing," Harold said.

Stiltson swallowed like the pill was stuck in his throat.

"They're meeting right now. I can take you to them."

"Right now, huh?"

Stiltson nodded. There was flop sweat across his forehead.

"All right. Lead the way," Harold said.

He followed the manager down the dark hallway to the back door.

"You forget to pay a bill?"

"Oh, ha. The light down here never seems to work. We've all gotten used to it. My Buick is parked out back. You good riding with me or you wanna follow in your car?"

"Let's just get going," Harold said.

Stiltson opened the door and bright sunlight filled the hallway making Harold squint. He took a step back. It took half a second before he saw beige-suit Barry charge him. Harold had already holstered his gun, so he clocked the guy one. Barry said *oof* and slid to the floor like a dress falling from a hanger. Two other guys in bad suits pushed through the door. Stiltson squeezed his fat gut past them and ran into the asphalt lot. One of them threw a punch that connected just above Harold's left eye. The other one grabbed Harold's arms and tried to pin them back. Harold brought his lizard boot up, hard, into the first guy's crotch.

Stiltson yelled something from the parking lot. There was a squealing of tires and Harold watched a maroon Buick spin out as it raced by. The puncher who Harold nailed in the nuts was bent over, sucking air. He threw up a puddle.

Harold jerked one of his arms and the guy behind struggled to hang on. He let one of Harold's arms go and was met with a elbow smash into his face. Harold spun around. Somehow the guy still had a hold of one of his arms, but like he didn't know what to do with it. Harold head-butted him, opening up the cut above his eye where he took the punch. Nut-cruncher Guy had started to get it together so Harold drove an upper cut into his chin.

Barry was still out like a light. Listening to the other two moan, Harold thought about putting bullets in all three of them.

"Fuck this," he said.

Stiltson's Buick was long gone. Harold went back into the

showroom, poured himself another coffee, dabbed at his cut, and then threw the pot at one of the brand-new sedans. Son of a bitch didn't even break.

"Stupid-ass Corelle Ware."

CHAPTER ELEVEN

We left the LeMans at the bar and drove out of town in her vintage half-ton Ford. That's what she called it, *vintage*, and then laughed that laugh of hers.

"Driving an old half-ton makes a better impression than pulling into the yard with a Buick and wearing a power suit," she said.

Theresa didn't have the suit, but she dressed like someone who was used to being in charge. I could see how her presence with the locals might push a few buttons, but at the same time they'd be intrigued by her. Just like I was.

We passed a pair of car dealerships and the farm machinery lot on the edge of town. The road rose into what passed for a hill around here, and then dipped down into a long curve around the town cemetery. The greenery behind the black iron fence was lush, and from the road I caught glimpses of fresh flowers and wreathes. A man and a young boy stood over a grave, the afternoon sun illuminating them in a way that made the scene less somber.

"Not a bad final resting place," she said. "I saw a sign saying they were selling lots at a discount."

"Different kind of land development," I said.

I didn't tell her that it reminded me of a very similar place, almost an exact replica, an hour and a half away in Marvelle. I hadn't visited my parent's matching pair of headstones in years, and had less than zero interest in going there.

When we'd walked from Ray's Café to the bar the sky was clear and bright, but now the sun had started to dip and long clouds slipped in like someone was drawing a set of heavy curtains. The crops we passed looked lush, with golden waves of wheat that undulated in the soft breeze, a sound that must have whispered dollar signs to the ones who farmed it. Though, none of the farmers I grew up around spoke of money being made. More often the talk was about the rain, or lack of it, or hail, or infestations that threatened to wipe out that year's crop. Sure money was being made, but the risk of losing a boatload of it always loomed in the minds of the ones watching the sky.

We pulled off the highway onto a grid road that arrowed to a farmyard in the distance. A ring of trees surrounded a modest house, and off to the west a few cattle lumbered and munched the day away. She was right about the number of vehicles in the yard being a sign of prosperity. I counted three shiny half-tons, a four-wheel-drive and a maroon Oldsmobile that looked like it just came off the lot.

"See what I mean," she said, reading my mind.

"A lot of car payments."

"Pfft. Most likely paid in cash in some sort of back-of-the-showroom deal."

She marched up to the porch in her crisp white shirt, ignored the lit doorbell, and gave three quick raps. There were some scuffling sounds before the door opened and a large figure filled the frame.

"Mr. Johannsen? I'm Theresa Swain. We spoke on the phone."

"Call me Ollie. The Mr. makes me sound like my father and he's been six feet under for years. C'mon in, the wife just made a pot."

Johannsen was a solid five inches over six feet with shoulders as wide as a Mack truck. He was muscular in the way a guy got after working a farm for a few decades. I put him in his late fifties, or a very fit sixty-year-old. His jug ears poked out under his International Harvester hat, which he took off to reveal a salt-and-pepper brush cut.

"This is my associate Mr. Fischer. He's new to the company. Head office wanted him to tag along for my trip to the province."

Johannsen grunted and looked me over.

"You got a first name? I don't like all this Mr. and Mrs. crap."

"Call me Luke. Good to meet you, Ollie."

"You didn't mention an associate. Neither did Jerry."

"Jerry Saunders, your neighbor up the way?" she asked.

"Uh-huh. He said you worked alone. It don't matter. Lay it out. I need to go check on my cows in about an hour."

"Cut to the chase. A man after my own heart," she said.

Ollie gave another grunt. Theresa brought out a folder from her bag, opened it, and began to lay out the deal. She was articulate and smart without being aggressive. She pulled out sheets, pointing to aerial photos and diagrams, tugging responses from Johannsen. He had a quick mind and his questions drilled down into the details of the deal. It was no surprise that Ollie ran a very successful farm.

Theresa finished up her pitch and leaned back.

"So why come here?" he asked.

"To give people around here an opportunity. People like you, Ollie, who know the value of land."

"Yeah, but this is land in Alberta—why not sell it to those folk?"

"Our company has a mandate to spread ownership across the prairie provinces. It's an economic decision, diversifying the owners, bringing different players to the game."

"You make it sound like poker."

I heard the suspicion in his voice, and I'm sure she did too.

"This is no gamble, Mr. Johannsen."

"Ollie."

Theresa smiled and launched into some complicated financial talk that gave answers of a sort. Ollie seemed to follow it, and the way he picked up a sheet and studied the sketched-out property lines made me think she had a buyer. As she talked, I realized that I'd heard another pitch like this in the backroom of Benno's place in

PV. I wondered if her deal was as shady as my Mexican benefactor.

"It's an amazing opportunity, Ollie."

"Gonna need to think about this. That's a lot of money for land I can't see in person."

"You could make the trip," she said. "But the value is not in what it looks like, but what it will become. Edmonton is bursting at the seams, and people are going to gobble up these plots at three, four times the price."

"And if I get in on the ground floor, I get it at this price?" He pointed at a number with his thick weathered index.

"You sure do," she said.

"All right. But I need a day or so to think on it. And I gotta go check on my cows."

"Of course." Theresa scooped up all the folders but left him one. "You can reach me at the motel. I wrote the number on the back. Hang onto these sheets, you can review them with your wife, or whoever else you need to show."

"That's the motel over by the bar? I heard they fixed it up. Used to be quite the dump."

"Not a lot of choices in Hamel. But it's nice and clean," she said.

"Helluva thing that happened over there. I think they're still looking for that guy," Ollie said.

"Yes, I heard about that. Someone was killed right in the parking lot," she said. "Not the sort of thing that happens much around here, I imagine."

"There's all sorts of shit, pardon my French, that goes on around here that never gets reported. Not usually in broad daylight, though."

"Sorry to interrupt. Could I ask what you two are talking about?"

"New guy in town. No one tells you nothing 'eh?" Ollie grinned and put his Harvester hat back on. "There was a shootout, like in some damn Western movie. One dead, shot right in the noggin. No description of the killer. Or nobody's saying."

Theresa quickly packed up her bag and we followed Ollie outside. She went over a couple more broad specs as they walked, but Ollie's mind was already elsewhere, likely thinking of the work he still had to do that day.

"I'll talk some to the wife, and give you a shout over at the motel. I'm guessing I can just write a check on this deal, or are you going to want a bank draft?"

Theresa smiled.

"A check and a handshake is just fine with me, Mr. Johannsen."

"Ollie."

She shook his hand and we watched him climb into one of the half-tons.

"He's already talking about how he wants to pay," I said.

"He's a sharp one. No wonder he's doing well."

"The land deal, is it really that good?"

"I wouldn't be selling lots if it wasn't. Listen, I need to head back to the motel to do some paperwork. I can drop you back at your car."

As we drove the grid back to the highway, I sensed a shift of mood between us. I wasn't sure, but my asking about the deal had triggered something that she wasn't telling me.

"You know anything more about the shooting at the bar that Ollie mentioned?" I asked.

"Shit like that goes down around here more than you'd think. We like to bitch about all the guns the Americans have, but we've got them, too. Especially out here."

"For hunting, though," I said.

"Uh-huh."

CHAPTER TWELVE

Theresa dropped me back at the King's bar and headed over to the motel. She told me the place was clean and the beds only had a few dips. I still didn't have a place to stay for the night so I figured on heading over and getting a room later. First I wanted to grab something to eat, and more importantly find out what happened with the shooting that Ollie mentioned. Theresa knew something about it too but wasn't saying anything. I had more than half a hunch that a guy named Mostly was involved.

The bar was half full, nearly all men. I counted three women. Like before, everyone was wearing either plaid or denim or both, like they'd phoned each other ahead of leaving home. A group at the longest table shared a couple of those bar pizzas that had more grease in them than an Indy pit stop. My entrance raised a couple of heads but, seeing that I was no one to take note of, everyone returned to their Pilsner and peanuts. I took one of the two stools pushed against the bar. The female server must have finished her shift, as the bartender worked the room himself.

"You're welcome to a table."

"On my own. I'm good here," I said.

"Your gal-pal not coming back?"

The bartender had a square chin and hair slicked back with enough grease to compete with the pizzas. I noted his look when we were in here before, chinos and a solid black shirt with a couple of buttons open to show a thatch of hair. He must have missed the plaid memo.

"She's turning in for the night to do some work. I'll take a Pilsner and one of those bowls of peanuts."

He grabbed a beer from the cooler behind him, filled a wooden bowl with peanuts, and gave me another empty one.

"Put the shells in here. I don't want to sweep your mess."

The pizza table yelled for another round.

"Hold your horses, you bunch of jackasses."

"Keeping you busy," I said.

"Uh-huh."

The bartender went over to the table and took orders while I drained half the icy Pilsner. It was the beer that reminded me of my former home. Pacificos reminded me of my new home in Mexico. A lot of people picture landscapes, buildings, or their old Aunt Sally knitting on the porch as a way of remembering home. Trust me to think of beer. But it's hydrated me on hot days in both countries, and it's been the fuel that drove me into more than a few skirmishes. Besides the work for Benno, I tried to stay away from fights now. But some were unavoidable. If someone took a swing at my head, I'm not going to go all Gandhi and hand them a daisy. Some people just need a rap. There are those guys who lose their balance and reflexes when they drink—after a few cold ones, mine get sharper. Right. And that's why I've ended up on the floor of a bar like this one with cartoon birds swimming over my head.

The bartender came back and I signaled for another.

"You have anything to eat here beside peanuts and pizza?" I asked.

"Chips and bars." He pointed to a metal rack. "And no one's complained otherwise."

I held back my smart-assery, and decided to dig for some information.

"I heard some bad stuff went down here last week."

"Went down? You sound like one of those crap shows on Detroit

TV. Nothing goes down around here," he said.

"Two murders, right in the parking lot. Were you working?"

"You a cop? You look more like a hobo," he said.

"Nope. Just interested."

"Then I don't know anything about it."

He gave me another beer and went off to take more orders, or maybe to get away from me. I cracked a few more peanuts when I heard a voice behind me.

"You won't get much from these peckerwoods."

I turned around to see a guy with a shaggy haircut wearing a black cable-knit sweater. I guess he didn't get the plaid memo either. He looked like the guy in the cartoons with the dog. I half-expected him to say *zoinks*. He looked to be in his early thirties.

"And you are?"

"Different than them. Can I grab a seat?"

I swung my open hand to the stool next to me and offered him my bowl.

"Mi casa es su casa."

"That's talking about houses, not bar peanuts," he said.

"Still working on my Spanish. I didn't see you come in."

"Being as though your back is to the bar, and you flinched when I came up behind you, suggests you aren't paying that much attention. Except you're anxious about something. Most likely about the guy that got killed last week."

"Are you Hamel's version of Sherlock Holmes?"

"Some things don't need elementary to figure out. Why do you want to know about the shooting?"

Along with the stylish sweater he had on a crisp pair of gray chinos—damned if the guy didn't own an iron. He looked fit, moved like he knew his way around a gym or a hockey rink.

"Luke Fischer. And I'm not anxious about anything. Just surprised."

"Could have fooled me. Damien Price."

He set down the glass he'd carried over with him.

"Get you another, what, vodka-Seven?"

"Just the Seven. I don't imbibe."

"Then why are you in a bar?" I asked.

"Met a customer here. Was going to take off until I saw you talking to Charles."

"That's the bartender? Doesn't seem much like a Charles."

"Call him Charlie and you'll never get another beer. He's kind of an asshole."

Charles the bartender was still talking to the pizza table. Music had started up from somewhere—that New Country shit sung by people who were cowboys just like I was an international spy.

"So you're gonna tell me things the bartender won't? Why talk to me?" I asked.

Damien called across the room.

"Hey, Charles, all right if I help myself to the pop?"

The bartender raised an arm without looking at us, and kept on with his conversation. I knew I was back home when he called it pop instead of soda. Damien went around the counter, got a fresh glass with ice, and filled it to the brim.

"I like when new people come to town. Freshens things up. But I'm not gonna talk about what happened in the parking lot. Not in here anyway." He took a long sip, squinting like he was drinking rotgut.

"Go easy with that stuff. It'll go right to your head."

"Rather have a sugar rush than the hole that alcohol is chewing in your stomach." Damien took another longer drink and belched. "You know they used to put lithium in this. That would have really been the pause that refreshes."

"Why don't you want to talk in here? You seem friendly enough with Charles the butler."

"Where you staying? We can go there. If you buy me a pizza, I'll tell you what I know. But not one of those." He pointed over to the table. "They're called Tombstones for a reason."

"Haven't checked in anywhere yet. Looks like I have two choices, the one down the street, or the other in the outskirts. You got a recommendation?"

"Three if you count sleeping in your car." He pulled something out of his pocket, unwrapped it and took a bite. "Granola bar."

"For serious?"

"Hungry as hell. And I don't do chocolate."

"You don't seem to fit into a place like Hamel."

"You think everyone's a conservative redneck up here? Well, there's a fair share. But I grew up here, and my folks and plenty like them are open-minded and believe it or not, even well read."

"I know," I said.

Damien gauged my look.

"Didn't figure you being from around here," he said.

"Ancient times, when Pharaohs ruled the land. Your folks still live in Hamel?"

"Moved to Florida seven winters ago. Mom was originally from the US, so they're not really snowbirds. They come back every other year."

"Well, Damien, I think I'd like to buy you that pizza. Do they deliver to motels?"

"I gotta better idea. You come over to my place, we'll pick it up on the way."

Damien finished his 7-Up and I drained the last drop of the Pilsner. Out in the lot he told me his car broke down and he was still waiting on parts. We took the LeMans and stopped for a large vegetarian pizza before going to his place, which was a few miles out of town.

"Long walk," I said as we drove.

"Good for the lungs and the mind."

Damien had a fairly modern-looking bungalow, a half-mile off the highway, surrounded by a ring of trees. I guessed they were poplars, the foliage blocking out most of the moonlight. Coming out of the trees, I saw that the yard was neat. A small garden with tall tomato plants bordered a post and wire fence that drew out the edges of the property. A dark sedan was parked by the house.

"That your car?"

"Yeah. Distributor fried. The garage in Hamel told me they'd give me a shout when the parts came in."

"Tomatoes are looking good," I said.

"Inherited my mom's green thumb. I'll give you a tour later. Let's go in, I'm starved."

We sat in Damien's bright kitchen and chomped down on some of the best pizza I'd ever had.

"Right?"

"Have to admit, yeah. I was suspect when you didn't want any bacon on it," I said.

"I don't do meat," Damien said.

"Yeah, but bacon. C'mon. Even vegetarians lie about that."

Like the yard, his place was simple and neat. A pale green couch and two matching chairs, both with clean lines, were next to a low table made out of something expensive. I guessed teak.

"I don't think you buy your furniture from around here either," I said.

"I had to get those shipped in special. I like Danish design. In my blood, I guess."

"As much as I'd like to discuss Scandinavian furniture with you, I'd rather hear about what happened at the bar."

"All right. You wanna beer?"

"Thought you didn't drink?"

"I keep some on hand for my customers."

"Just what is it that you do, Damien?"

"I'd tell you but I'd have to kill you."

His voice was level, and he flashed a decent set of dead eyes before his face broke into a grin.

"Ha! You are a gullible sort. Hang on."

He went over to the stainless-steel fridge opened the French doors and pulled out a large bottle of 7-Up and a six of beer with the sunny labels I knew so well.

"Now where in the hell did you get those?" I asked.

"Went to the States last month, needed to pick up some supplies. One of my customers likes Mexican beer, but you can't hardly get it around here. I picked up a couple of cases for when he drops over. I've also got Sol or Dos Equis, if you'd rather."

"Pacifico is fine," I said.

He pulled up a stylish tall chair next to a kitchen table made out of the same wood from the one in the living room.

"I'm a kitchen guy, if you're good with that."

He handed me a Pacifico and I took the last slice of that damn fine pizza. Hamel was full of surprises.

"The bar," I said.

"Right. Why were you in there? Supposed to meet someone?"

"Just passing through on my way to Alberta," I said.

"So who told you about the shooting?"

"How about you go first? I'm here because you told me you could fill me in."

"All right. I go to the King's a few times a week to meet customers. Last week, Tuesday night, I watched this guy come in. He was a big one in a dark suit. Hell, the whole bar watched him come in. He was joined by another guy in a suit. Him I'd seen before."

"Did the big guy wear cowboy boots?"

"Yeah, now that you mention it, he did. The other guy was wearing tweed and brogues."

"You studied their footwear?" I asked.

"I notice things."

"Sure. So the guy in tweed, you'd seen before?"

"Like I said, he looked familiar, from a nearby town. Could be Loren. Doesn't matter where he was from. He was the one that got laid out in the parking lot. The bar emptied when they heard the shot. A guy named Robertson, a real dumbass, challenged the guy in the cowboy boots. He might have ended up just as dead, but I guess the big guy drove off.

"Interesting."

"Anyway yeah, the big guy's boots were made out of some kind of reptile. Could be lizard?"

"That's what he thinks, too," I said.

"Come again? You know this guy?"

"We've met. Repeatedly."

"Ah. He's the reason you're in town. Here, I thought you came for the beer and pizza."

"Speaking of which."

I held up the empty Pacifico, which Damien took and replaced with a full one. Putting the bottle in a tub under the sink.

"Kinda doubt you'll get any money back for foreign beers," I said.

"Yeah, but I know a place that'll recycle them. We only have one earth, gotta take care of it. What'd you say your name was?"

"Fischer. Call me Luke."

My host went over to a cabinet and opened a pair of doors to a significant record collection. As he flipped through the albums I tried to figure this guy out. OK, maybe he had a pair of hippie parents that leaned left and would vote Communist if they could. Maybe the whole free love and granola bars was a ruse. There was something he wasn't saying. The laid-back hippie thing didn't seem to fit. Still, if he offered me an organic Popsicle, I was leaving.

"You like ska, Luke?"

"I know a bit of it, I like the beat. But I prefer Dick Dale."

"Surfer guy, eh? I think I might have something." He flipped through the rows of records before plucking one out. "Yep. Haven't spun this one in a long time."

The stereo was a wood-and-chrome job, I recognized the

turntable as high-end, made by the Swedes. The guy liked his Scandinavian things. Strains of "Pipeline" filled the bungalow. Damien did a small groove step as he walked back to the kitchen. I took a swig of the Pacifico and imagined how good a bowl of salty peanuts with hot sauce would taste.

"Great sound. Nice setup," I said.

"You ever ride a board?"

"Always thought I might, surf that is. But nah. I'm only an admirer. Hey, can we get back to the shooting?"

"Sure, what else did you want to know?"

Dick Dale let out a loud twang, which matched my thoughts about this guy. Was I getting played?

"You haven't said much. No reason you couldn't have told me any of this in the bar."

Damien rotated his glass of 7-Up, drawing a finger through the condensation ring on the table.

"How about you say why you were in the bar? On your way to Alberta, you said? How do you know this big lizard-boot-wearing fellow?"

"Someone told me Harold might show up around here."

"That his name? And who shows up in Hamel? You some sort of cop, Luke?"

"Not any sort of cop."

Damien's lips narrowed and the dead eyes showed up again as he studied me. Before I could launch into a made-up story, his expression shifted into a wide smile. Then the bugger winked at me.

"Forget about it. You asked about my business. You wanna see it?" Damien flipped finger pistols at me.

"Thought you'd have to kill me?"

"Man. Loosen up. It's Friday."

"It's Wednesday."

"Whatever. Follow me."

He walked through the living room into a bathroom that seemed too large for his house. I finally started to put it together, on why he invited me over to his place.

"No offense, Damien, I don't swing that way. Fine with me if you do." I stepped back outside the bathroom. "I'll leave you to it."

"You don't what?" He looked over his shoulder at me. "Oh fer shit's sake, no. Here look. This is what I wanted to show you."

Damien slid a bath mat out of the way, uncovering a small golden disk embedded in the floor. He pressed down on the disk, it clicked in place, and a door rose up on some sort of hydraulic. After a push, the door glided to the side and exposed a set of stairs, a glowing light.

"Nifty hey? If you didn't know a hatch was there, you'd never guess," he said.

"Hold on. I've seen this movie. I'll show myself out."

"Oh relax. I just need to check the Ph levels."

Damien disappeared down the stairs as the familiar smell drifted up.

Oh… so that was his deal.

CHAPTER THIRTEEN

Harold was driving because he didn't know what else to do. After the run-in at the dealership, he'd walked around Bennett for a long time. He wasn't even sure what he was looking for.

He ate a long slow meal in a diner with frou-frou curtains in the windows. His digestive track was burbling, but behaved itself—good thing, as his pills were long gone, stuck in a glove box. Maybe them farmer boys who got the drop on him will try them out.

The car lot was a bust. But he figured that fatass Stiltson had to be connected to the whole deal. Harold didn't know what the deal was—the guy he shot in the bar parking lot must have been hired by Stiltson. Harold considered that it was time to pitch it in. It'd be tricky getting across the border with his boosted foreign vehicle. He could always ditch it and fly back. There had to be an airport up here somewhere.

It wasn't like him to give up on a job, even though no one had hired him for this one. He came up to find her, to ask her some questions. He liked talking to her, a lot. And wanted to do it some more. He sure as hell didn't figure on having to play hide-and-seek in pancake-land—or that there'd be a bunch of square-headed asshats looking for her, too.

When he met Delilah, Harold saw something burbling underneath her. The two of them weren't all that different. She didn't put bullets in people like he did, but she was working the dark places. She never said anything about that, but Harold sensed it. He never told her what he did, or what he'd done, but he knew she sensed it in him, too. It didn't seem to bother her. They'd talk late into the night at his place. She stayed over about half the time, but even when she didn't being with her made for a good night.

Harold felt the streak of anger that she kept under wraps. He had a streak like that, but he didn't keep his under anything.

Now up here in flat-fuck-central, the hidden stuff about Delilah was coming out. If she was working with guys like Stiltson or that tweed-jacket joker, then there was a lot she didn't tell him. Harold wasn't big on pulling mysteries apart like some Sherlock Holmes type, checking mud on shoes or some damn perfume on a postcard. He preferred Louis L'Amour over that fancy-pants elementary-my-dear jackass shit. Right now, all he could guess was that Delilah got involved in a deal with these farmers and stubble-jumpers and did something to piss them off. Most likely it was about money. It was always about money.

The next town rose up as he hit a big curve in the highway. The last bit of light had been sucked out of the horizon, and small yellow lights winked on in the metropolis that was Loren, another dumbass name for a town. POPULATION 1399, so said the sign.

"Let's make it a round number."

It was as if someone took a chunk of time out of his day like it was a slab of pie. *How did it get so late* and *Why the fuck am I still here* were the two questions that burned inside him.

Loren looked about the same as Bennett, maybe a bit smaller, the same insurance agency, bank, grocery store strip, all dark inside. A group of cars, parked on the diagonal again, lined up against a brick building with those small windows you can't see through. Harold figured no one wanted to let people know they were drinking away the afternoon. *What would the preacher say?* Hell, the collar-wearer was probably in there.

He took a table in the back, gathering the usual stares when he walked in.

"What can I do you fer, big fella?"

"You speak English?" Harold asked.

"Come again?"

The server was a skinny fencepole in a striped shirt with rolled-up sleeves. One arm showed the start of an anchor tattoo. Harold fought the urge to rap Popeye in the head.

"Do you fer... Jesus. Is that how you talk around here?"

"Now, listen fella, this is a friendly place"

"Bourbon. Jack Daniel's is fine, Jim Beam will do."

"Afraid you're on the wrong side of the border for that, my friend. Tell you what, you head out how you came in, take a hard left or right, whatever direction south is. If you drive about an hour you'll hit Montana."

Popeye started to walk away.

"Just give me whatever whiskey you pour here. A double with no ice. You got anything to eat?"

"Like I said, this is a friendly place."

"Use that word one more time, Popeye, and I'm gonna see how far I can put my boot up your ass."

"Popeye?"

Harold sighed. A tiredness crawled into him again. All he wanted was a drink and something big and full of meat—stomach be damned. He'd had enough. Maybe she was just meant to stay hidden. Maybe Stiltson and the crew would find her. Maybe he'd sleep in the car and go back to civilization in the morning.

"Sorry."

A part of Harold died whenever he was forced to use that word.

"Hey, we all have those days. I get it."

Popeye reached out to touch Harold's shoulder and he flinched—instinctively reaching inside his jacket for his holster.

"You make cheeseburgers here?"

"Sure do. Piled high and full of onions. Comes with fries."

"No onions. Hot sauce instead of ketchup."

"HP sauce OK with you?"

What kind of fucked-up backwards land was he trapped in? Harold nodded at Popeye and rolled his neck listening to it crackle like a campfire. He looked around mentally comparing this bar to the one he'd left in Colorado. In the Springs, the walls were freshly painted, the tables black and smooth, and light was low and pleasing. He didn't normally give a shit about things like that, but sitting in a badly lit, wood-paneled, one-step-away-from-a-bingo-hall broken-table dump like this made him take stock. As tired as he was, he might eat and hit the road anyway—drive south and escape every last one of these stubble-jumping asshats.

"Buy me a drink?"

Harold saw her coming at him, dark jean jacket, faded jeans and nice eyes and nice hair that went along with the rest of the niceness. She reminded him of Delilah. They could be related.

"What do you want?" he asked.

"Well, that's a helluva line. You come up with that yourself?"

"A woman like you comes over like that, if you're not a pro, then you're after something."

"I'll ignore the comment about being a hooker and I'll buy you a drink. How about that?"

She dragged a chair out and plunked down across from him.

"Listen lady, I don't want to be rude"

"Lady? Ha! And sure you do. I bet you're like this all the time."

They were interrupted by the server with his whiskey and a drink for the woman.

"Smirnoff and ice? I saw you sitting over here."

"Thanks, Carl."

"Watch him, I think he bites," Popeye the server said.

Harold eyed the woman.

"So if you're not a working woman, what do you want?"

"Working woman?" She laughed. "What TV show from the

fifties did you walk out from?"

Harold drank his whiskey.

"Listen, I came over here because you looked interesting. I know you're not from around here, because this place is so small that a stray dog is going to get noticed."

"You calling me a dog?"

"Biggest hound I've ever seen." She laughed again and rattled the ice in her vodka.

Harold wasn't used to women coming up to him and starting conversations. This one had some scam going on, he was sure of that.

"Where are you on your way to?" she asked.

"Why do I need to be on my way?"

"Because no one comes to Loren on purpose."

Her eyes flitted over to Popeye Carl the server and back again.

"Someone sent you," Harold said.

"And how do you figure that? Was that a spy movie you walked out of?"

"I don't know why you're talking movies, but I do know you're working something." He downed the rest of his whiskey in a fast gulp. "And I'm not in the mood for any of it."

Harold stood to leave.

"She told me about you," the woman said.

"Who?"

"Said you met in a bar in Colorado. You were pretending to be some sort of manager."

It took Harold another moment before it fell in on him.

"You know Delilah."

He sat back down.

"I met her a couple times, we talked."

"So where is she?"

"Was hoping you knew that. Isn't that why you came up here?"

Harold put something together.

"How did you find me?"

"Well, I figured you'd either be here or Grassdale, another twenty miles up the road. Someone told me what happened at the King's over in Hamel, and then I heard about the thing at Stiltson's dealership this morning."

"What does that have to do with me?"

The woman chewed on her bottom lip.

"News travels fast—even in backwater burgs like this," she said.

"It was Stiltson. He hired you to find me."

"Nuh-uh. Somebody else. But it doesn't matter."

She was around the same age as Delilah, a softer face, and fuller lips.

"You gotta name?" Harold asked.

"Most people do. You're Hank, if I remember what Delilah said."

"Harold."

"I'm Reyna. Like it's gonna."

"Weird name."

"So what do you actually do, Harold?"

It bugged him that she knew his name. Her back was to the rest of the bar. Harold scanned the other tables. No one seemed to be paying attention to him, even if they knew he wasn't from around here. The last time he was in a bar like this someone got stretched across the parking lot.

"I find people that don't want to be found," he said.

"What do you do when you find them?"

"Why were you talking with Delilah? Come across." Harold clenched his fist.

"Sounds like a threat, Harold."

Heat crawled up the back of his neck. Reyna rattled a cube into her mouth.

"You punch a lady in a public place?" She crunched down on the ice cube.

"I've done worse."

"Ha. I bet. OK, I met Delilah when she first got back from Colorado. The guy I work for had a deal set up with her. We hung out for a couple of days as they went over the details. I got to know her."

"Who do you work for?"

"His name is Michaelson. He has a place north of here."

"Does he know where Delilah is?"

"She disappeared like candle smoke. Made a lot of people unhappy."

"How much money's involved and who has it?"

"You're sharp, Harold. I bet you find a lot of those people you go looking for."

Harold studied her mouth. It was a nice mouth, but it could be a lying one.

"So this Michaelson guy told you to come find me?"

"He also heard about what happened at the King's. Then after recent events, well, we both put it together. Just like you're trying to do right now. He asked me to drive up from Hamel, and see if I could track you down. Ha. I guess we're in the same business."

Popeye Carl arrived with another vodka and set down a whiskey for Harold.

"I didn't order this," he said.

"I assumed the two of you were getting into it. Don't try matching her though, many have tried and gotten dragged out of here."

Harold pulled in the whiskey, and waved his hand at the server like he was swatting a fly.

"If you live in Hamel, why do they know you here?" he asked.

"I like to mix up the places I drink. This is a frequent one."

"Rain your real name? Sounds made-up."

"Rey-na. And you'd think I could make up a better one. Harold your real name?"

"Real enough."

She laughed.

"Well, this is fun. Now we can keep up the verbal ping pong or you can get off your ass and go find Delilah. With your experience it should be easy."

"Then when I find her this Michaelson will want to talk with her," Harold said.

"We can do it as a team. Like those buddy-cop shows."

"Again with the TV."

Harold thought he saw someone at the back of the room looking over at them. Reyna was chewing on her lip again.

"Fuck it. You're lying and I'm leaving."

"When I last saw Delilah, she said she'd call me and tell me where she was."

"Bullshit."

"She always planned on screwing over Michaelson. That's why we got talking. She was gonna cut me in on the deal."

Harold eyed the guy at the back of the room, who looked away when he saw Harold studying him.

"Why all this back-room-dealing shit? Doesn't make sense."

"You were right. There's a lot of money involved, and Delilah is in control of it. She has both Michaelson and Stiltson on the line. I was supposed to get here before someone else came looking for you."

"And how is this someone else going to find me?"

"I did, Harold."

"They better come in with more than their plaid shirts and goofy-ass haircuts."

"Whattya got against plaid?"

"Reminds me of that show with the donkey and the cornfield."

"*Hee Haw*? Ha! You don't strike me as a *Hee Haw* fan."

Three men entered the bar, two in suits and one wearing a blue plaid shirt. The one who'd been eyeing Harold jumped up and went to them.

Reyna turned back to see what Harold was seeing.

"My car's in the back. Red poncho, big boat," she said.

"Poncho? A what?"

She sprang up and darted past the bar, through a pair of doors with circular inset windows. Harold hesitated, then took off after her. The three men at the door bolted. Carl the server yelled something. Harold burst through the doors into a kitchen where a guy flipped burgers on a grill. He dipped into his jacket for the Beretta.

"Who the hell are you?" the cook asked.

The guy in plaid was first through the kitchen doors. Harold spun around. Plaid- Guy fired into the wall next to Harold. He put one in the guy's leg, tumbling him like a kid's Lego tower.

Harold banged the back door open with his ass. A car engine revved to life and he sprinted toward the headlights. She had the passenger door already open and Harold dived in just as the two suits came through the bar door. Reyna cranked it hard spraying gravel at them. Harold expected the gunshots to start, but either Plaid Guy was the only one packing, or they couldn't get their guns out of their pants.

"Circle around. I'm gonna take those assholes out."

"Nuh-uh. We're getting out of here."

She floored it. Harold tried to get a shot off as they spun into the alley. The car fishtailed as he fired in the dark, unsure if he hit the suits, the building, or some raccoon searching for garbage. He hoped it wasn't a raccoon, they were cute little buggers.

CHAPTER FOURTEEN

I didn't know what I was getting into with this guy Damien. When he opened the hidden trap door, I thought about bolting. But when the smell wafted up I understood what the prairie hippie's business was.

"That's pretty strong. How do you not smell that upstairs?" I asked.

"This portal is vacuum-sealed—and no vents go to the upstairs. I've got a five-thousand-dollar air filtration system that cleans and humidifies. The plants love it, and people going by don't catch a whiff of my girls."

"Girls?"

I followed Damien down the metal stairs into a room lit by warm lights, casting luminous patterns on the leaves of what must have been a hundred plants.

"They better all be girls," Damien said.

"Didn't realize that pot plants had sex."

"Just like in real life all the males are useless. If a plant turns out to be male, I pull it out and shred it as fast as possible. Cross-contamination happens in a helluva hurry."

"Contamination as in what? Girls become boys?"

"I don't have anything against that with people. Had a cousin that went that way, surgery and everything. But yeah, with cannabis, that can happen." Damien studied a line of plants, inspecting the leaves. "Don't say pot. This isn't some high-school-kid thing. This is science."

The plants actually looked quite beautiful under the light. I'd seen them before, but never this many. They were differing heights, the tallest four feet, brushing the ceiling.

"Just starting to bud out," I said.

"Ah, you do have some knowledge. Yes, these calyxes will soon thicken into colas."

Damien picked up something that looked like a wand and placed it in the dirt. Red lights appeared on small screen.

"You gotta keep the acid-base balance just right." Damien placed the wand in several other pots.

"How do you know when you have a male?" I asked.

"Little clusters of balls appear."

"For real?"

"Yep. Mother Nature just keeps repeating herself."

I followed as he checked the dirt in several other pots. Besides the whir of the filtration system, it was dead quiet.

"I can barely hear the music from upstairs," I said.

"Extra insulation in the walls, sound dampening tiles in the ceiling."

"For what? These girls might start singing or something?"

"Ha. Only to me. I don't know—I like to be safe and secure. Away from prying eyes and ears." Damien walked over to a small box on the wall. He removed a panel and a beam of thin moonlight shone in.

"For spying on the neighbors?" I asked.

"Or whoever."

He closed up the peep hole, went back and tested a few more plants.

"Things are looking good. Let's go back upstairs. You want another beer?"

"I'm not one to turn down an offer like that. But I should go check into the motel."

"Why don't you just hang here? I've got an extra bedroom."

"Wouldn't want to put you out. You've got a whole room full of women to take care of."

Damien smiled.

"I like you, Fischer. And these girls take care of me. Best thing ever for my mental health."

I ran my finger along one of the leaves. Leaned in and took a deep smell. It was earthy, sweet, almost citrusy.

"Nice."

"It's a strain I've developed. Customers like it, smokes well, good balance of THC and CBD. I call it Lemon Squares. C'mon, I'll give you a taste."

I followed Damien back up the stairs to the portal door, which had closed behind us. He pushed it open, I heard a click, and then it moved out of place.

"High-tech operation. You must be doing all right."

"I sell at a fair price. I've got a good stable of clients who know how to keep their mouth shut. I stay away from the organized-crime shit."

We stepped back into the bathroom. The door slid into place and Damien covered it with the mat.

"Didn't think there was much of that around here. You saying Hamel has a mafia?"

"You're smarter than that, Fischer. It's everywhere. And mafia? You watch too much late-night TV." Damien took a sealer jar out of a cupboard above his fridge. "I'm not talking Cosa Nostra and old Italian guys in suits. But, there's groups of people making sure they get their fair share."

"An odd way to put it."

"Grab another beer. I'll change the music and you can tell me your life story."

My host put on something with a reggae beat, but sped up. I'd heard stuff like it before, but this was faster.

"You said you knew ska?" Damien asked.

"Feels a bit slow for that."

"First wave. Good ole Desmond Dekker. You probably know his tune"

"The Israelites."

"Ha! I knew I liked you." He held up a well-rolled joint that he'd taken out of his sealer jar. "Do you imbibe?"

"I gave up smoking, wasn't doing my lungs any favors," I said.

"Agreed. It's why I only do this occasionally. Wouldn't be right if I didn't do some quality control."

"Any dealers I've known were massive potheads."

"Please. Dealers? Potheads? Where'd you grow up, Fischer? Language like that went out with the gramophone."

"Not that many miles from where we're sitting."

I laid out as much of the story as I felt like telling. How I left here, went east and ended up in Montreal before going south. Damien passed the joint and I decided to take a hit. The smoke was smooth as silk and damned if it didn't taste a bit like a lemon square. I popped the cap on a Pacifico and settled back into the couch. The reggae had sped up, and I recognized some of those early ska beats.

"How far south?" Damien asked.

"Ended up in Mexico. PV, sorry Puerto Vallarta. But there's another smaller town where I like to hang out, Melaque. Full of pelicans, great tacos, and cold beer in a bucket."

"Ah. That explains the love for the Mexican brews. But you kinda slid over why you left here in the first place."

I felt relaxed listening to Desmond and his boys. But I wasn't ready to spill my story to a guy I'd just met.

"Long story."

"Fair enough," Damien started. "How does the big guy from the King's fit in?"

"I'm doing a favor for a friend."

"A friend from Mexico? Lots of organized crime down there. If that's who you work for I better watch my back."

"You're looking right at me."

"So I am."

Damien passed me the last of the joint, gestured toward the jar.

"This will do me. But you go ahead," I said.

"Nope. I'm a guy who believe in moderation. You staying?"

"Yeah. I think I will."

"Solid. The other bedroom's got clean sheets. I'm gonna head to bed now. I've got a small TV in there, and I believe there's a late night showing of *Magnificent Seven*."

"Appreciate the hospitality."

Damien nodded, went to the stereo to shut off the record.

"Leave it on," I said.

He nodded again and disappeared into the bedroom. I heard him flick on a TV and the theme song I knew well drifted out and mingled with Desmond. The last of the reggae/ska beats faded and the turntable shut itself off with a click. I padded down to the other bedroom. It was more of the simple Scandinavian furniture, a gray comforter on the bed, on the wall a circle mirror hung over a dresser. Above the bed hung an aerial shot of a farm with a bright red barn and matching silos.

Damien still hadn't told me anything about the shooting in the bar, or why he didn't want to talk at the King's. I believed he saw Harold talking to the other guy. He might have even seen the shootout. Though with Harold, it'd be over quick. And how about the RCMP, what did they know?

Damien knew more than he was saying. He wanted something from me. He trusted me enough to show me his grow-op—though maybe he was just too proud to keep it hidden. I'd see how far that trust went in the morning when I pressed him for more information.

Strains of Bernstein's Western theme came from Damien's room. The bed was soft and the sheets high-quality—a lot better than I would have got in the motel. I wouldn't have minded a night cap with my new land-developer friend. I drifted off into dreams of riding the countryside with Steve McQueen and Desmond Dekker. Turned out Desmond was a helluva horseman.

CHAPTER FIFTEEN

Like she said, Reyna's car was a boat—a big old Pontiac Laurentian, circa back in the time of free love and too many hippies.

"What's a Poncho?" he asked.

"I guess being an American, you've never heard the term."

"It's what Eastwood wore in those westerns."

"Ha. Up here it's what they call Canadian Pontiacs."

She eased the car around a long curve. Harold didn't see that they were going around anything. The headlights shone two long beams illuminating the yellow lines on the black road.

"So what, the highway makers get bored and need to put in a bend?"

"Correction Line," Reyna said.

"Correction what? Like a prison?"

"Roads are built on a grid system out here. If you don't put in a s-curve like this every twenty-four miles, they'd come together."

"Uh-huh."

"On account of us living on a ball," she continued. "Or do you not believe that? You seem like you could be one of those flat-earthers."

Harold didn't bother following her explanation. It burned him that he didn't take out the guys back at the bar. He should have put one in Plaid Guy's head instead of his leg.

It was a clear night, with dots of light in the distance that were people's homes. Out here a person could believe the world was flat. One neighbor could wave over at the other forty miles away, and let them know they needed a cup of sugar.

"Where are we going?"

"A friend of mine has a place out here."

"So what? Those jokers at the bar are going to be following us."

Reyna checked the rear view.

"Nobody coming up yet," she said.

"Your friend is that Michaelson guy?"

"No. His place is a couple hours north of here. We're going to Frank's. He's down in Florida. Asked me to look in on his property once in while," she said.

"Probably glad to get the fuck out of here."

"You don't like our fine province?"

Harold grunted.

"So we peeled out of town just to go pay a buddy of yours a visit?"

"I told you. He's not home."

Reyna slowed the car and turned onto a gravel road. A small copse of trees stood next to a metal building lit by a tall lone light. Piles of corrugated metal, and large wooden spools were spread across the yard.

"That your friend's place?"

"Nope. But he owns the business. Shut it down when he went on holiday. His house is three miles up. So are you going keep looking for Delilah or what?"

"What? You said she was going to phone you. Cut you in on some deal."

Harold's head felt foggy. It was either lack of sleep or the fact that he didn't know what the fuck was going on. Not knowing things always fogged his head and pissed him off.

"She'll call when I'm back in Hamel—and we're not there, are we?"

"I'm done here," he said.

"You forget that your car's back in Loren?"

"Then I'll rap you in the head and take yours. The size of this thing I could throw you in the back and still have room for a Little League team."

Reyna laughed. She pointed at a yard light that lit a twin row of trees and a road going through them.

"What did Delilah ever see in you?"

"You get to know me, I'm charming as fuck."

"Yeah, I can see that."

They pulled onto a road bordered by tall cypress trees that stretched up like sentinels on watch. The moon was a fat yellow egg shining down on the yard, the cypress caught the light and made it seem brighter than it was. The house was a split-level job, big bay window, a half-ton and sedan parked up against it. The yard light cast long shadows on them as they exited the car.

"Not sure if they followed us. Didn't see anyone out on the road. But you should be ready just in case," she said.

"Your buddy leave any food in there?" Harold asked. "Popeye never did make me a burger."

"Who's Popeye?"

"The guy in the striped shirt and anchor tattoo at the bar. You two knew each other."

"Ah, Carl. I'm sure there's something to eat in the freezer. You can look in the fridge, but I think Frank cleaned it out before he left."

Inside the house, Harold went to the kitchen as Reyna opened a door to a set of stairs to the basement. The fridge had a few jars of pickles, some ketchup, and a bunch of almost empty jam jars. Harold hated when people did that—finish the damn stuff and throw away the jar. There was a row of beer on the fridge door's shelf. Harold took one and tried to twist off the cap.

"Son of a bitch, this is a backward country."

He poked around a drawer until he found an opener. He was at the kitchen table when Reyna came back carrying a couple of bags.

"Found some sausage and pierogies. How's that sound?"

"What the hell is a pie-rogee? I don't eat no weird animals."

"You don't travel much, do you, Harold?"

"I go where I have to."

"A pierogie is like a dumpling." She read from the bag. "These have potatoes and onions in them. And this is some of Frank's sausage, which I happen to know is excellent."

"Why's the guy living in Florida?"

"Not living, vacationing. He's not a snowbird."

Harold considered asking what that meant but decided he didn't care.

"Keep an eye out to see if anyone enters the yard. I'll make us some food. I'm hungry as hell," she said.

Reyna grabbed a couple of pots, filled one with water, and threw the sausage in the microwave to thaw. Harold scanned outside, checking for hidden holes he might need to use if this all came down to a firefight with the jokers from the bar. He hated getting pinned down in a house, so he wanted to think ahead to his movements outside. The yard light cast a large yellow circle, but there were still spaces hidden in darkness. One of the outbuildings—a barn, he guessed—was bordered by two smaller sheds. If he heard a car come up the road, he'd slip into the space between one of the sheds and the barn. The minute they exited the car, he'd pop them and be done with it. None of this facing them down like the OK Corral shit.

He turned back to her, watching her take the sausage out of the microwave and into a hot pan. He couldn't quite figure this one out. She was fiery in a way that reminded him of Delilah. Maybe that's how they grew them out here. He kind of liked it.

"You going to tell me what her deal was?" he asked.

"Delilah?"

"No. The queen of England. I heard you stubble-jumpers still pay attention to her."

Reyna laughed.

"I can see that charm, Harold." She gave a queenly wave and went back to stirring the sizzling sausage, then dumped in some cut onions. "One night after Michaelson went out we finished a bottle of gin and got into it. Delilah said she wanted to go somewhere warm and stay there. Tired of Canadian winters. She'd be a snowbird, but for good."

Harold sighed.

"OK, what's a snowbird?"

"People who escape Canadian winter and fly down somewhere warm like Florida."

"Anyway," he said.

"That's when Delilah told me she was going to take it all."

"This Michaelson guy have a lot of money?"

"He was connected to some sort of group."

"Like a syndicate?" Harold asked.

"Could be. She never used that word. I knew it wasn't strictly legal, probably not legal at all."

Harold sensed something at the edges of what she said. He wasn't getting the whole story.

"What do you do?"

"Mostly I work in an insurance and real estate place in Hamel."

"Sounds boring."

"It has its perks. Because of some clients, I came across information and made some money on the market. Nothing big."

"What kind of market?"

"Stock market, Harold. You know with the suits, ties and commodities."

"Thought that was all those Wall Street assholes."

"Don't need to be on Wall Street to make money," she said.

"Michaelson one of those clients?"

"Yeah. Sometimes."

Harold heard the skip in her voice. Reyna drained the pot and spooned the pierogies onto a couple of plates. She put the sausage and onions on top.

"You like sour cream?"

"In my coffee?"

"Jesus, Harold, you seem like a smart guy. You got a lot to learn."

She pulled a white plastic container from the fridge. Brought the food to the table, took a spoon and put a huge dollop of cream right on top of each plate.

"Trust me," she said.

Harold studied the food. It looked like something he'd eaten before, sausage and potatoes, but the sausage was the wrong color and the dumpling things sure weren't potatoes. He dug in. A few bites in, he was surprised. There was just enough grease and salt to soothe the pit in his stomach. And damned if that cream stuff wasn't pretty good, too.

"Right?"

Harold chewed and grunted.

"So Delilah and Michaelson were doing deals on the stock market. She was going to screw him on that, and cut you in. Why?"

"It wasn't just stocks. There was other money. A lot of land development deals around here. Farmers love to buy more land. The rich ones anyway."

"To grow crops?"

"No. Urban land. And not even from around here. Cities in Alberta like Calgary, Edmonton, even Lethbridge is spreading out. Lots in the outlying areas, sometime miles away, are picked up for a good price. They get developed, thinking that people are either gonna move out of the city, or get sold to those coming from other provinces. There's always a migration to Alberta. When oil prices are good, anyway."

"You know a lot about this. But you still haven't said why she was going to cut you in," he said.

"Delilah liked me."

"Right."

She speared a chunk of sausage off Harold's plate. He watched her chew it.

"She needed me to get some account numbers of Michaelson's. I knew where he kept his books."

"What was she going to do with that?"

"I didn't totally follow it. But money was going to get moved around until she had it all."

"And Michaelson had none."

She nodded.

"Uh-huh. Any more of this?" He forked the last pierogi.

"Make you a Canadian yet, Harold."

As Reyna went to the stove, Harold took another scan outside. Far out on the horizon, a pair of headlights grew in the distance.

"Hold off with that plate. I'm gonna go outside."

CHAPTER SIXTEEN

Morning light poured in Damien's kitchen window, the fields glowed with warm shades of green and yellow. The sky reminded me of a book of paintings I'd taken out of the library when I was a kid. Something about those pictures always stuck with me. It was the light, but also the people. They looked like they were alone even when they were with someone else. I remember the painter was Hopper, and I always meant to go see his canvases in a museum someday. This morning I was far away from any city that would have a museum like that. The light-painting outside would have to do.

I thought I'd missed my host, until he appeared from the bedroom, already dressed and looking like he'd been up for a while.

"Coffee should be done," Damien said.

"It was the smell that brought me out here."

"Cups are above the sink."

"You going out? Kinda early."

"I've got a customer that likes to meet for breakfast. There's bread for toast, jam in the fridge. Hang here as long as you want."

I stumbled over to the sink to get a cup and inject some caffeine into my body—I still wasn't firing on all cylinders.

"Oh one more thing," he started. "Can I borrow your car? My customer was supposed to come out. But now you're here."

He said it like the in-laws had arrived.

"You never said why you didn't want to talk in the bar about the shooting," I said.

"Oh that." Damien grabbed a thin jacket from a hook. "So I can take your car?"

"You're not going to tell me?"

"When I get back."

"How about now?"

I could tell he was sizing me up, not quite comfortable.

"All right. I've got time for one coffee."

The coffee was more than decent, along with the warm sunshine it was doing a good job clearing the morning cobwebs. Last night's dream of driving a long lonely stretch of highway popped into my mind. Where was I headed anyway?

"Good stuff. You must have fresh beans." I lifted the cup toward him.

"It's Charles," Damien started. "He's involved somehow. Pretty sure he knew the guy that got shot in the parking lot. The one in the tweed jacket."

"Charles is?"

"The bartender. I told you that. Things were tense in the King's after the killing. RCMP asked everyone a lot of questions, especially Charles."

"They ask you questions?"

"I got grilled for a bit. I gave them a description of the big guy. Said that I saw them talking but didn't hear much."

"Was that the truth?"

"True enough. I heard the tension between the two of them, but neither were giving the other details."

"So the RCMP are out there looking for him?"

"Probably. Not every day is there a gangster-style murder in Hamel. The next day I was in the King's again, and Charles was talking to a couple of guys. They weren't from Hamel. Two were in suits, another was in a checked shirt. He was another big bugger."

"So Charles talked to some guys. What does that mean?" I asked.

"I went over and got a 7-Up, caught a bit of their convo before they knew I was close. They were talking about hunting down the guy in the cowboy boots."

"Lizard boots," I added.

"They didn't know what they were made of. And then they said something about finding the bitch."

"Who did they mean?"

"Couldn't say. Charles saw me approach and nodded at the men. He's known me for a few years, but something in his face, I don't know."

"Like he didn't trust you," I said.

"The feeling was mutual. But hey, you seem to know this boot-wearing guy. What did you call him, Harry?"

"He goes by a lot of names. But mostly Harold," I said.

"You think this Harold knew the woman they were talking about?"

"Couldn't say."

Damien lowered his head and gave me a pretend smile. He finished the last of his coffee and went to the sink.

"Listen, I really gotta go. This guy is one of my best customers. What about your car?"

"Take it. I have no plans today."

"Thanks, I'll take care of it."

"I have no doubt."

Damien picked up a gym bag by the front door.

"Make yourself comfortable. Me casa eh suh casa." He laughed. "That's how you actually use it. No peanuts."

After he left, I made a few slices of toast and slathered them with a rhubarb spread that looked like it came from a farmer's market. I did some stretches and listened to my joints crack. Sitting by the door was a neat shoe rack, those clean Danish lines again. A pair of sneakers looked to be about my size. I hadn't had a run since I left Mexico and my body knew it. I strapped on Damien's shoes, maybe half a size too big. I rustled through a drawer in his room and found a t-shirt. I didn't find any shorts, so the pants I was wearing would have to do.

Running was the best way to clear my head. Right away, the gravel road felt good under my feet, a lot different than the cobblestones in PV, where I had to watch my step or I'd go down and do a proper face-plant. The morning breeze was light, cooling my face as the sweat started to run. I jogged along the grid we'd drove in on, and then turned down a softer road that ran alongside a muddy slough. A pair of ducks glided on the dinner plate surface. They gave me a couple of quacks, either encouraging me or wondering who the hell I was running from, or toward.

Like the ducks, I didn't know either. I knew that Harold was here causing shit. I also knew that Harold was damn good at his job. If he killed those guys at the bar and then disappeared, he'd stay gone. I doubted the RCMP would find him.

All right, so Alex the manager with attitude told me Harold came up here looking for a woman. Harold had been hanging out with her in the Springs, and it sounded like they were a thing. Thinking of Harold in a romantic relationship was like picturing a cow doing math. Was she the one Charles the bartender and the goons wanted to find? Damien wasn't giving me the whole story, but the suits and guy in plaid were likely goons hired by someone. Hamel had them just as much as any other place.

Muscles started to protest and my lungs reminded me that I'd been sitting in a car eating gas station food for way too many hours. I turned onto another road, this one next to long section of fence. On the other side, some of my bovine mathematicians happily munched away the morning. A flock of black birds, starlings maybe, rose up behind a line of trees, their calls echoing in the blue blue sky that Neil Young sang about.

I didn't want to push my body too much, and then spend the rest of the day dealing with muscle pain. Scanning ahead, I considered where I was, appreciating the geometry of it all. I turned down another road, knowing it would take me back to Damien's place. Back on the gravel, my knees absorbed the pounding of the harder surface. My shirt was soaked now, as the miles of road food exuded out my pores. The starlings swirled above, still following the lone jogger, likely having similar questions as the ducks. They veered off to go do their bird business as Damien's place came into view. Out here there were no mountains, or hell, even hills to obscure the view. A person could see as far as their eyesight let them, the only obstacle being the curvature of the earth. I remembered my dad telling me about correction lines and the reason for them. He drew on an orange with a ballpoint.

"You see Luke, no matter what those jackasses that stuck Galileo in a tower said, we live on a ball."

"Uh-huh."

I was twelve. I already knew this.

"These grid roads are all separated, a mile apart."

"I know, Dad. You told me this when we went hunting."

"Yeah, but these roads, if we kept them all the same distance apart… what happens when we get closer to the top of the orange?"

"They come together."

"Righto. So they need to put in those s-curves. Like over at the Klatt place. That curve in their road doesn't look like it's going around anything—but it's preventing a twelve-car pile-up by making those roads stay separate."

"Kinda doubt you'd find twelve cars on the same road out here, Dad."

I was a smartass at twelve—not sure I ever grew out of it.

As Damien's place grew in the distance a slow burn started in my stomach and spread into the rest of my body. This wasn't a sensation I got from running, it was something else. It was bullshit to call it sixth sense, but I'd always had a physical reaction to danger. I didn't try to analyze it. But when I got that feeling, things were about to go bad— mom's-potato-salad-on-the-counter-too-long kind of bad.

I spied the black Ford parked next to Damien's broken-down sedan. Could be it was one of his customers looking for the month's hot deals. But the guy patrolling the perimeter of the yard didn't look like a bargain hunter.

I turned hard and ran toward the border of trees at the back of the yard. Keeping low, I don't think the guy heard me.

The poplars shook in the wind, helping my steps blend in with the rustling leaves. The guy was about my size, six-foot-nothing, thicker through the shoulders, filling out his blue plaid shirt. His hair was cut short, narrow eyes sat under a forehead as broad as a semi's grill.

I figured on at least one or two more in the house. Another thought popped into my head. This group must have found out about Damien's basement operation, and came to clean out all his product. OK… so why the guy roaming the perimeter? Was he supposed to be watching for the law? The guy turned back and walked toward the front of the house. I stepped out of the poplars, moving onto the grassier parts of the lawn. When I stepped on an unseen branch, the snap echoed like I'd fired a pistol. Blue Plaid Guy spun around. Seeing me, he charged.

"Hey."

It didn't look like he carried a gun. He came at me, his shoulders arched and fists at the ready like a cartoon gorilla. I ducked under his first punch. Another fast jab clipped my shoulder. The guy had fists like rocks. I jumped back as he attempted a kick. He must have caught a late-night Bruce Lee flick and thought he'd give it a go. When his leg breezed past me, I kicked at his knee. I didn't break it, but I knew it hurt like hell. He went down, then rolled over and popped back up—pretty fast for a big guy. I was impressed by the move, until he threw a punch a cotton thread away from my chin. All right. Enough dancing. I hit him hard in the chest and followed up with a slam in his breadbox. No fat on this guy. It was like punching a brick wall. He was either a hard worker or a gym rat. I slammed another one into his gut, and this one made him pay attention. He bent over, trying to grab whatever air he could into his lungs. While he studied the grass patterns, I wound up and gave him a haymaker that would have made my sparring coach in Montreal say "Oof." The crack was a helluva lot louder than the stick I'd stepped on.

Blue Plaid Guy timbered down. Fade to black.

There was no time to wave my hands in the air, as two more goons churned around the corner. I called myself a bad name for not taking Arkin's offer of the pistol. I bolted around the other side of the house. My morning luck held as Damien's garden tools leaned up against the house. I considered the rake, nice and pointy, but I went for the shovel, more heft. I timed it well as I caught the first guy square in the noggin. He bounced off the house and lay on the ground like a nice sleeping goon. The other guy didn't know whether to shit or go blind—my father's saying for catching someone flatfooted.

I wielded the shovel with the long handle like an Arthurian knight. Damned if the guy didn't grab the rake. This should be interesting. We started a strange dance, swinging tools, our implements clacked against each other. I questioned my garden-weapon of choice as the tines of the metal rake slashed through the air and tried to make me into a Fischer-bob.

"Come here, you fucker."

This goon was thicker than the guy I'd put down in the back yard and the one taking a snooze on the ground. He thrust at me, and I knocked the rake out of his hands. The head of the rake broke off from the handle and the goon's face fell like he'd lost the end of his ice cream cone. He let out a yell and came at me fast and hard. I swung for the fence at Fenway and he joined his partner on the ground. I was pretty proud of my gardening victory until I turned and saw a tall guy in a suit. He pointed a fat shotgun at me.

"Drop the shovel."

I made it a habit to listen to guys with shotguns. I put down my new favorite weapon.

"Hands in the air, and walk toward me."

I complied.

"You guys here for the big weed sale?" I asked.

"What?"

I was putting together my next clever quip when something hit me hard from behind. I joined the sleeping goons on the ground.

CHAPTER SEVENTEEN

Harold moved fast, out the door, down the stairs, and sprinted to the shed. His shadow disappeared under the yard light, then reappeared and ran ahead of him into the dark night. Tires spat gravel as the car raced toward the farmhouse. Headlights arrowed into the yard. Harold pulled out Kuz's Beretta, slowed his breathing, racked it.

"OK, Farmer Joe, let's dance."

He followed the car, a long LeBaron with a white roof, as it slid to a stop under the yard light. The doors flew open.

"Just like at the circus. Here come the clowns."

He took the guy coming out of the passenger side first. Spun him right around with a high shoulder shot. The driver and the rear passenger skidded—feet on gravel stopped. Things got library-quiet. Harold looked for their heads above the car, wanting to pick them off like dolls in a carnival game.

"We just want to talk," the driver barked.

Harold considered a shot through the windows, but they were both too low for that, using the car as a shield. If he left his hidey-hole between the shed and the barn, he'd be an easy target under the yard light.

"Nah. Let's shoot instead," Harold said and fired a round into the LeBaron.

The rear passenger popped up and fired off a couple, one hitting the shed a few inches from Harold's head. He jerked back, and a splinter of wood brushed his forehead. The jumpy bugger dropped back down again. The guy he'd tagged in the shoulder lay on the ground and moaned something. Damned if Harold was going to play Whac-A-Mole with these peckerwoods.

"We don't want to have to kill you," the driver again.

"Oh good. You had me worried."

Harold fired another one into the car and took off like a sprinter from the blocks. He moved fast for a guy his size, doing a dipping turn, and another, before reaching the house. They fired at him as he ran, but hit nothing. Harold lay flat against the side of the house. His chest burned. He spied the driver's bent leg poking out from the side of the car. A second before he fired, the guy pulled it in.

"Shit."

There was a bang, the screen door rattled, and Reyna stood on the stoop, yelling.

"Stop it, you assholes! She's not here."

Harold did a fast glance to the car and back to her, gauging the distance.

"Damn. I was getting to like her," he whispered to no one.

He waited for the gunshots, pictured her crumpling on the stairs, bleeding out. But nothing. A lot of nothing. Harold looked up at the moon like it would give him an answer. It was high and bright as a dinner plate.

"Hold on, we're coming out. Don't shoot."

Harold took a bead on the driver as he moved away from the car.

"Well, well. We have a winner in the Dumbass Olympics," Harold said to himself.

A thought zipped past. If he took out the driver, then the rear passenger would likely take out Reyna. Harold didn't know why she was still breathing, but he kinda preferred it. He lowered his gun and stayed in the shadows. The driver held open his arms, including the one holding the gun. The passenger did the same. These guys either had balls the size of watermelons or they were just dumbfucks.

"I told you she isn't here," Reyna repeated.

The driver was about six feet tall in a baggy suit. His partner had a similar suit, but with a baseball cap.

"Farmer Joe got dressed up for the shooting," Harold muttered, and then stepped out of the shadows.

They walked over to the house and up the stairs where Reyna stood.

"How about we just have a look?" the driver asked Reyna before raising his gun to her chest.

Harold took a bead on the driver's head, and pivoted his aim between him and the other passenger.

"Drop the piece before I spread you out on the ground."

"Hey, you're a big one. You must be the one we heard about took out our buddy Taylor."

"Asshole in a tweed suit?" Harold asked.

"Ha, yes, he liked his tweed. So that was you?"

"Never heard of the guy. Now how about you just throw those pistols down on the ground."

The passenger, who had said nothing to that point, raised his gun at Harold. It looked like a .38, useless for trying to hit anything unless you were standing next to it.

"How about you drop yours before we drop you?" he asked.

Reyna batted away the gun pointed at her.

"For fuck's sake. Everyone put away their dicks," she said. "Come inside and see for yourself. She's not here."

The driver looked surprised, then grinned. He followed her into the open door. The passenger stood on the step, his gun still on Harold.

"Well, get in there, you dumbass," Harold said.

The guy in the goofy hat shoved his gun in his pocket and followed the driver and Reyna into the house. Harold went up the steps behind them. He stood at the front door, listening to them rummaging in the bedrooms. He glanced outside to the guy he shot, who was still on the ground. He thought he'd just hit him in the shoulder, but maybe it was lower. He wasn't moving. Harold stepped back outside to listen. There were no moans either. He went back in the house.

The driver reappeared with Reyna beside him, his gun pressed into her side.

"She's coming with us."

"Like fuck she is," Harold said.

"You can't take us both out," the driver said.

"Wanna bet?"

The driver seemed to consider this. He said something low to his partner, then turned back to Harold.

"Hell with this. Let's get Lenny to the hospital," he said.

"Lenny might need an undertaker," Harold said.

"Oh, he's like that. He's been shot before. Lays on the ground for a long time, like a little kid," the passenger said.

Harold glanced over. The guy on the ground was gone. Two he could take, three might be a bit harder.

"Let them go, Harold," Reyna said.

Damn, she reminded him of Delilah—right down to the edge in her voice. Harold backed out the door, letting the two of them pass. He read JOHN DEERE on the rear passenger's ballcap.

"Nice hat," he said.

He watched them go under the yard light. The car interior lit up, and he made out another figure, his hand on his shoulder, sitting in the front seat. They drove in a wide arc and spun out of the yard.

Reyna stood beside him on the step. She smelled good, like flowers or something.

"You know those guys?"

"I've seen one of them before," she said.

"With Michaelson?"

"Yeah. The driver. Maybe the guy in the John Deere hat, too."

Harold walked back into the house. She followed.

"All right. Let's have a drink and you can tell me what the fuck is going on. My stomach is burning like hell."

"You should get that looked at," she said.

"I did."

CHAPTER EIGHTEEN

It was like someone trying to adjust the horizontal on an old TV set. I tried to make the shaky pictures hold still, bring them back in alignment. My head was ringing like a boxer's bell and my stomach gurgled. The world outside came into focus, and the face in front of me was a lot prettier than the guy who recently pointed a shotgun at my face.

"You look like shit, Luke."

"You should have seen the other guy. Or maybe guys, I can't remember." I rubbed the back of my head, finding a good-sized goose-egg.

"Might have a concussion. I can take you to the Hamel clinic. There's no hospital, but I've heard they have some nurses on staff," she said.

"Why are you here?"

"Damien called me. He wanted me to check in on you. He thought someone might come by his place."

Theresa helped me to my feet. The goons I'd sent to dreamy-land where gone, as was Mr. Shotgun.

"*He called you*? How do you know him? I thought you'd only been here for a month, talking to farmers."

"C'mon, I'll drive you," she said.

Her half-ton was parked next to Damien's car.

"Hold on. I'll be fine. Let's go inside for a bit," I said.

"Not sure that's a great idea."

"Because you want to take me to get my head checked, or you're worried someone is going to come back?"

"Doubtful. They left you still breathing. So they didn't find what they were looking for. They don't care about you."

"Ouch."

"Your head?"

"No, the fact they didn't care about me. I thought I was worthy of at least being tied to a chair and questioned."

"You're a strange one, Fischer."

In the house, I swapped Damien's sneakers for my shoes. Then I stripped off the t-shirt I'd ran in, now covered in sweat, dirt, and grass. Theresa watched me dress myself without a word.

I grabbed a Sol out of the fridge, as I'd drank all the Pacificos last night. I held one up for her, but she reached in and grabbed the 7-Up.

"Damien swears by it," she said. "Say the bubbles bring clarity."

I put the Sol back and got us a couple of glasses. Sitting at the kitchen table, the soda and sugar was helping to clear my head. Theresa looked as good as ever, except for the frown lines that I'd caused. The sun had climbed a bit higher than where it was before the gardening implements duel. I couldn't have been out for long. Damien's place had not been trashed. I thought about checking out the hidden door to his basement farm, but wasn't sure if Theresa knew about that.

"Why do you know Damien? He doesn't seem like the land-buying sort."

"I've known him for a while," she said.

"A while like a month or a while like some years?"

"Really not sure we should be sticking around here," she said.

She drained the glass, set it down, and burped.

"Bubbles of clarity," I said. "What were the goons looking for? If you know Damien, then you know how he makes money."

Her eyes narrowed.

"He showed me the basement. A lot of money down there," I said.

"Hmm." She paused. "Doubt they were interested in that. They were looking for someone."

"Like Damien?"

"Damien told me the two of you were seen leaving the bar together. He guessed someone would be paying him a visit. He didn't say why," she said.

"If he already guessed that, why didn't he stick around to greet them?"

"He told me he had to drive north to meet a customer. Be gone most of the day. Must have borrowed a car."

"He has mine."

"Anyway, he wanted me to check on you. Good thing I did."

"And you just came on over—not knowing what you might be facing?"

Theresa lowered her head and fiddled with one of her shirt buttons. She looked past Luke out the kitchen window.

"We should go."

"Where in Hamel can I buy a gun?"

"They have a stock of them at Robinson's. You just have to talk with the owner."

"The hardware store? And how do you know that?"

She wouldn't make eye contact with me. She poured herself another glass of soda, then walked over to a tall cabinet in the corner of the kitchen. She moved liquor bottles, mostly full, out of the way and reached to the back of the cupboard. She came out with gun— reaching in again she took out a box of shells and a shoulder holster. She put them all on the kitchen table.

"Sig Sauer. Looks shiny enough to be brand new." I picked it up.

"Damien takes care of his things."

"Nine millimeter."

"I have no idea. It's a gun. Why do you know so much about

them? What is it you do, Fischer?"

"I find people. Sometimes I run into people who carry guns."

"You find people? What are you, some sort of detective?"

"Nope. I just help out a friend whenever he needs me to."

Theresa's lips drew a straight line. She was putting a bead on me, trying to figure things out, but at the same time hiding information from me.

"You must be pretty good friends with Damien to know where he keeps his guns."

"He told me in case I was out here by myself and needed protection."

"From who?"

"Let's go. I'll drive," she said.

"Good thing, as our mutual friend has my car."

I checked to see that the 9mm was loaded, fit the holster under my jacket, and pocketed the extra cartridges. I followed Theresa outside and climbed into her truck. She peeled out of the yard.

"Tell me about this friend of yours. Why'd he send you here?" she asked.

I flicked on the truck radio and string music filled the cab.

"Longhair music?"

"I'm cultured as fuck," she said.

I spun through a few stations, the requisite country twang and some barking DJs, until I landed on a folky-guitar thing. We turned the opposite direction that Damien had driven in on.

"Town is that way," I said.

"Gonna take the long way. More scenic."

"You stop worrying about my concussion?"

"You seem fine. You look like shit. But you're fine."

We passed another farmyard, this one more on the ragged side. The barn was in bad need of a paint job and it was leaning more than that tower in Pisa. A dog raced in the ditch next to us, then gave up the ghost. I watched him in the side mirror, his head thrown back, letting a flurry of barks out into the sky.

"You going to tell me about your friend? Or who you're looking for?" she asked.

"Well, if we're spilling our stories. I think you've got some 'splaining to do, Lucy."

"You're a strange one, Fischer."

"So you keep telling me."

Roy Orbison came on the radio, his haunting voice drifted through the cab. The sun had climbed high above us in a cloudless sky. A lone bird swooped and spun in the distance. It was too far away to know if it was an eagle, or just a crow with a helluva wingspan. My old man would have known. He tried to show me when I was a kid, but I never had much interest.

"Damien and I were together, but that was some time ago."

"When you lived around here?" I asked.

"Back about a hundred years ago, yes. We've kept in touch. It was his idea for me to come here and talk to some people about the plots. He said a lot of money was floating around. But I already knew that."

"How long have you actually been here?"

"Only a month, like I told you. Damien said I could stay with him, but I said that wouldn't be a good idea."

"Worried something would be rekindled?"

"Yeah. Or I'd kill him."

The Orbison song ended and a loud voice came on talking about a farm equipment sale. I flicked off the radio.

"Why did Damien want you to check in on me? And I guess the other question is, will I be seeing my car again?"

She laughed, and the warmth of it eased some of the tension building up in my shoulders. There was still something she wasn't telling me.

"For a drug dealer, he's a helluva honest guy," she said.

"I don't think he'd call himself a dealer. He's particular about his terms."

"No, you're right. He sees himself as just another farmer. With a helluva cash crop."

"His customers like his product?"

"Don't know much about it. But I've heard he grows some of the best."

"Is that why you left him? Didn't want to get involved with the illegal operation?"

"Operation? Ha. You say you're not a detective, Fischer, but you must watch a lot of *Hawaii Five-O.*" She shook her head. "There's a lot of reasons I left Hamel. Damien was only one of them."

She rolled down the window, and the breeze carried in an earthy smell mixed with the unmistakable fragrance of cows in a field.

"Look at them happy bastards. A day like this, perfect temperature, blue sky, pasture full of fresh clover to munch on, and lots of places to lay their cow pies. There's worse lives," she said.

"Until you get made into cheeseburgers."

"We all gotta go sometime, Fischer. Now c'mon. Tell me why you know so much about Sig Sauers and why did your friend send you here?"

Something in the way she talked was giving me a tap-tap-tap on the back of my neck.

"I did grow up around here," I said.

"Already figured that one."

We passed another group of cows, this one with a few calves, one taking breakfast from his mom. A pasture stretched out behind them, bordered on by a wheat field and another field the color of the Mediterranean.

"Love the color of flax this time of year," I said.

"Farmer-boy Luke? Seems unlikely."

I spilled out some of my story. How I grew up here, but needed to leave for brighter pastures, or at least different ones. I didn't tell her what gave me the final push, only that I'd moved east to Montreal.

"I spent my days working at a gym as a sparring partner, and drinking beers with my friend, Rick."

"You were a boxer?"

"Of a sort," I said.

"So you came out west from Montreal?"

"No. I left there, too. Went south."

"How south?"

"Mexico. That's where my sometimes employer is."

"The one you're calling your friend."

"He's both," I said.

"Helluva long drive from Mexico. Who does your friend the employer know way up here?"

Theresa had driven past a number of roads that I knew led back to Hamel. She continued driving north.

"I'm thinking this ain't the scenic route."

"Changed my mind," she said. "Who you looking for, Fischer?"

"You ever hear of a Mexican standoff?"

"Is that when everyone's pointing a gun at each other?"

"Ha. I see you watch the same movies as I do." I felt the edge of the Sig Sauer under my jacket. "Way I see it, you need to tell me where we're going and why. Then I'll tell you who I'm looking for."

"A standoff. Huh."

That was all she said for the next hour. I was fine with it. I wasn't worried that she was taking me out to some farmer's field where I'd get jumped by a bunch of goons—that had already happened. I had the goose egg to show for it. Besides, I was the one with Damien's gun.

Racks of clouds had slid in, dotting the sky and giving the swooping black birds something to contrast with. I cracked the window. My old man said you could smell when the barometric pressure started to shift. I think he was bullshitting me, but there were a lot of farmers that knew when rain was coming, even when the radio said it wasn't. Olfactory memory. The smells from the fields kept taking me back to my childhood, which were a hell of a lot better than the early adult years I spent here. I filled my days with mostly drinking and fighting.

At least I'd won a lot of the fights. I didn't tell the owners of the Montreal gym that's what made me qualified to be a sparring partner. I had a natural affinity for punching guys in the head. It fit my personality well at the time. Maybe it still did.

"Damien," she said.

When someone doesn't say anything for a long time in a closed space like the truck, the sound does a funny thing, like an echo.

"What about him?"

"That's where we're headed. He told me after I checked on you that I should drive up to where he was."

"I thought Damien was with a customer."

"He met him at his other place. That's where we're going."

"Why?"

"He said it was time to get out of Dodge."

"Hamel?"

"Whatever."

The road ended in a T, and she swung the truck east onto another grid road. Ahead was a stop sign and the intersection to a single lane highway. The asphalt ripped a black swath with freshly painted yellow lines. We headed down the highway. More clouds had moved in. The rain would be here soon.

"How far is it?" I asked.

"Settle in. It will be a few hours."

A couple of drops hit the windshield.

"Let me tell you about a guy named Mostly Harold."

CHAPTER NINETEEN

Harold found a half-bottle of rye and grabbed a couple of tumblers from the cupboard above the sink.

"Thought you said your stomach hurt? Shouldn't you drink some milk or something?"

Harold grunted and poured a few inches in each glass.

"Not much for whiskey," Reyna said.

"Shut up and drink."

He sunk his large frame into a kitchen chair, the smell of sausage and those crazy dumpling things was still in the air.

"So what, we're going to wait for them to come back with reinforcements?" she asked.

"Doubtful. And if they do, I won't be so nice. Now, let's hear it."

Harold took a drink, then leaned toward her.

"Not sure what I can tell you that I haven't already said."

"Bullshit."

She eyed him. Harold already figured she was tougher than she looked.

"I asked you before, but now I'm thinking you *are* the kind of guy that would hit a woman?"

"Only when I need to."

Harold glanced outside. The yard was still illuminated by the tall light, and the moon which had climbed out of view from the window.

"You see something?" she asked.

"Spill it. You said you knew one of those jackasses."

"He's part of the group that Michaelson is dealing with. Name is Simon."

"Like the kid's game?"

"These guys aren't playing games. They're with Stiltson and the others."

She held her drink up and smelled it, wrinkling her nose. Reyna took a sip, shrugged, and drained the glass. She gave Harold a steel-eyed look.

"Look." Harold jabbed a finger at her. "I'm tired and pissed off. Getting shot at by asshats will do that. So quit fucking around or I'm going to get serious."

A flash slid across her face. Harold knew she knew he'd do it. He didn't like hitting women as a rule, but he never was the biggest rule-follower.

"I told you there's a lot of money around here, and it was being moved around. I thought it was land-development cash, because that's what Delilah told me. But Michaelson let on that it was more than that."

"What did you do for him?"

"I found him some clients at the insurance agency."

"Clients for what?"

"The group Michaelson was in with were into all sorts of shit: drugs, prostitution. Hell, Delilah said they dealt in guns."

Her shoulders softened. She was going to spill it now.

"Dealt how?"

"Sold to someone. Overseas, I guess. Doesn't matter. The point is there was a lot of money floating around," she said.

"Not legal money."

"Illegal as fuck."

"Hard time believing all this crime-syndicate shit is happening in these tinydick towns."

"You'd be surprised."

"So Stiltson and Michaelson hired Delilah? For what?"

"Stiltson is the head of the group. Until recently him and Michaelson weren't on the same side."

"And now?"

"They're not buddy-buddy. But yeah, they're together. And Delilah was scamming them both."

Harold pinched a spot between his eyes. This kind of shell game gave him a headache. He realized that all the stuff he'd sensed about Delilah was not only true, but that there was a whole lot more of it.

"Something bothering you?" she asked.

"Only all of it."

Outside a large truck rumbled by. The noise rattled Harold's head.

"Don't people ever sleep around here?" he asked.

"Delilah knew what she was getting into. She knew what would happen if she took the money."

"Wait. What money?"

"That's why they both hired her. I don't know the full amount, but I got the idea it was a lot. They gave her all the cash and she made some transactions. She'd invest it, build some interest, or maybe the market would bump it up. Then she performed some transfers, move it around—I didn't quite follow it."

"She was laundering money."

"I guess that's what they call it."

"So she kept the money and now they want it back and her at the bottom of a lake. There any lakes around here? Seems like it's just fields and cows and shit."

Reyna took the bottle and poured herself another couple inches. Harold studied her body. She was starting to tense up again. She looked outside the window, like she was searching for someone in the dark. Harold didn't bother looking.

"I work in insurance. I don't know much about all this back-room stuff."

"You know enough."

Reyna took another long pull of whiskey.

"I'm kinda surprised you actually came up here. Sounds like the two of you had something going down in Colorado," Reyna said.

"That was before she took off. She didn't tell me why she left—or about any of this organized-crime shit."

Reyna didn't say anything for a while. Harold saw the wheels churning in her, thinking how to deliver the next lie. She had a full deck of them, he knew that.

"You knew Delilah before," Harold said.

She stiffened, then gave a forced shoulder roll.

"I met her at Michaelson's."

Harold dipped his hand into his jacket, fingered the Beretta.

"The kind of work I do has taught me how to tell when someone's lying," he said.

He took out the gun and placed it on the table.

"You'd just shoot me and leave me dead in the kitchen?"

"No. I'd drag your body outside."

A quaver in her voice. Some fast blinks.

"In Hamel. We'd talked," she said.

"I already figured that out. Why?"

"Both of us had been with Michaelson."

"Been with?"

"We were sleeping with him."

"At the same time?"

"Jesus, no. I don't know."

Harold picked up the gun.

"You know where she is," he said.

"No I don't. That's the whole fucking point. And neither does he." She spit out the words like she was a kid in front of a teacher.

Harold ran through everything she'd been telling him. The spot between his eyes throbbed.

"So she was screwing you, too," he said.

Reyna averted her eyes. Harold racked and pointed the gun at her forehead.

"Delilah had tickets to Europe, Spain I think. She said she'd get ahold of me when she landed. Then I could decide if I wanted to fly over. Plans were made. And yeah, I was in on them. But it all changed," she said.

"Changed how?"

"She cut me out. Stopped talking to me."

"Hmm. She's off eating tacos or whatever the fuck they eat over there. Why come looking for me?"

"Michaelson doesn't think she'd left yet," Reyna said.

"What do you say?"

"I don't know."

She was tough, no doubt. The quaver was gone. People who had a gun shoved in their face for the first time usually broke down. Maybe it wasn't her first time. Harold let out a sigh. He lowered the gun, unchambered the round, and put the Beretta back in his shoulder holster.

"Are you awake enough to drive?" he asked.

"I couldn't sleep if I tried. Where are we going?"

"Let's go see this boss of yours. You drive. I'll sleep. But I'll tell you, I'm a light sleeper."

"I bet," she said.

"Delilah tell you that, too?"

"No. But she said you were dangerous."

Harold gestured to her and they walked outside together. He ignored the deep ache in his body and the fire in his stomach. They got into the Pontiac. Harold sunk his head back on the headrest.

"You get too tired, pull over and wake me up," he said.

"All right if I put on the radio?"

"As long as it isn't that country shit."

Harold closed his eyes. He should really get the hell out of here. He'd been shot at before, gotten clipped a couple times. A slug in his back sent him to the hospital for a couple of weeks. Music drifted in from the car radio, one of those English bands. He didn't mind it.

Harold could force her to drive him back to his car, he'd find an airport, and then head back to Colorado. There could be a couple of peckerwoods waiting for him at the bar where his car was parked. Maybe he should just take her boat and leave her on the side of the road. Shit. Why the hell was he chasing this woman? He liked his life just fine in the Springs. Benno paid well for the work he did. It was getting a bit boring, true. But what else was he going to do?

When Delilah came into the bar the first time, there was something in her that lit him up. That never happened anymore—except for the one he'd planned to marry. She taken a bullet meant for him. That was ten years now. Harold didn't like thinking about her.

Delilah didn't remind him of the dead woman. It was too long ago, and she looked and acted different than that one. Something about Delilah seemed familiar. She kept things close to her chest. She told him she was born up here in Mountie-Land, but hadn't been back for years. That was obvious bullshit. Harold questioned how much of her story was real and how much was what she wanted him to know. She'd obviously pissed people off, jackasses like that bunch at the car dealership—or the one who tied him to the chair: Kuz. Who has a name like that? He should have shot him. He was kind of getting used to his Beretta, though.

All right then. He wasn't too far off thinking they were similar. Delilah was doing some backroom dealing. Maybe she had her own Benno. But if Delilah had all the money, why wasn't she flying over the Atlantic right now? Could be she was watching a bullfight right now. They did weird shit like that over there.

Or else she was still here because someone fucked up. Someone almost always did.

"How far is it?"

"About an hour and a half," she said.

"I'm going to sleep now. If I feel you slow down you better have a good reason."

A mountain of tiredness crashed through his body. The ache in his stomach told him he was going to need find some pharmacist up here who he could shake some pills out of. He watched Reyna at the wheel, his eyes half-closed. He needed to get some shut-eye or he wouldn't be worth shit. It was a clear night, that plate of a moon surrounded by razor-sharp stars. He hadn't seen a building or any sign of life for the last twenty minutes.

"This is a lonely damn place. Everything is flatter than fuck."

"Out here you can feel the curve of the earth."

"The hell you can."

Harold murmured the phrase again as sleep overtook him. He drifted into a dream where he was on his back stoop in Colorado eating peaches and reading a Louis L'Amour paperback.

CHAPTER TWENTY

As we drove the long stretch of highway, the darkening sky made it seem later than it was. There'd only been a few drops, but a deep rain was coming. I told Theresa the story of Mostly Harold. It was like I was telling a tale of old, except Harold wasn't a wandering minstrel, he was a professional killer, and damn good at his job. My first encounter with him was when he laid his prized boots into me in a cheap hotel in PV. After that he followed me as I traipsed across the Southwest searching for some art thieves and a brother who was supposedly lost. A lot of people ended up dead, and I was almost one of them. I think Harold would have killed me, but for whatever reason he didn't. I never could figure out if he kind of liked me, or just couldn't be bothered. Benno, against my advice, hired Harold. I never asked about the darker side of Benno's business. Not that he would tell me if I did.

Harold was a helluva tracker. If someone needed finding, he'd do it. Truth was, he was better at it than me. And if someone needed killing, the same. That wasn't so much in my wheelhouse, though I'd done it before, and I'd do it again if pushed into a corner. I didn't tell Theresa that, but I thought it.

"Is this Harold guy tracking someone?"

"I'm not sure. Someone told me he came up here looking for a woman."

"Any woman?"

"No. One in particular that he was with in Colorado. It's weird to think of him with anyone. Harold marches to his own drummer, usually set to a Burt Bacharach beat."

"Bacharach? Like the cheesy raindrops guy?" Theresa asked.

"It's his favorite music."

"Doesn't seem to fit."

"I've learned there's a lot about Harold I don't know. I used to think he wasn't that deep of a thinker. But lately I've wondered if he keeps everything under his hood. And it's a big hood."

"Big?"

"You see a guy like that coming at you and you know things are going to go bad. He's built like a lineman."

"Wichita?"

"No, football."

"Oh, I thought we were still talking music," she said.

I laughed at that one. I told her about Benno.

"So it's more than helping a friend, you work for him."

"He sent me to check in on his nephew in Colorado. Actually, his dead nephew," I said.

"This Harold killed the nephew?"

"I really doubt it. Mostly Harold has this code where he only kills the people he's hired to kill. Not sure how strict he adheres to that, but it's one of the reasons I'm still alive."

"Why do you call him Mostly?"

"When I met him he told me he went under different names. But mostly Harold."

"Funny name for a guy who doesn't seem too funny."

"I've never heard him laugh. I'm not sure it's a sound his body can produce. Anyway, by the time I got to Colorado, Harold had left. I followed his trail. That's what Benno wanted me to do."

"A trail that ended in Canada?"

"Seems that way. Like I said, he's following a woman."

"Does she have a name?"

"Delilah."

Theresa coughed.

"You know her?"

"Just a funny name. Biblical, you know," she said.

We drifted into a quiet as the rain started, the drops beat a Cuban rhythm on the truck's windshield. The color in the field were desaturated as the thick blanket of cloud smothered them. Knowing what I did about farmers around here, the rain could be a blessing or a curse. Always too little or not enough. They didn't all bitch like that, and some seemed to ride through whatever the season brought and produced bumper after fat bumper crop. Those clouds raining down on the fields might completely miss another field just a few miles over, and then drench another one. Mother Nature was a bitch and she didn't care who you were related to. During the high-price, high-yield years, a whole whack of money was made by some while others barely made it through.

"Shit."

Theresa's voice shook me out of my agricultural pondering. I was barely aware of the music coming over the car radio.

"What is it?"

"Those headlights behind us. They've been closing the space for the last while, but not passing."

"Some people just drive that way."

"Yeah, but I think I recognize—"

She stopped mid-sentence as the headlights grew into giant suns, blazing through the now-driving rain. There was a blast that hadn't come from thunder. Theresa jerked the truck hard. I leaned over to flick off the radio.

"Turn it up," she said. "ELO. I like this one."

Light filled the cab. The truck groaned as she hammered down on the gas.

"Hang on."

The tires slipped on the rain-slick road. They were almost on us now. It was a wide Ford sedan, its grill like angry teeth with a hole punched in the middle. Headlights refracted in the rain, the sky darkened like it was twilight, though it was only mid-afternoon. They rammed the back of the truck. I jerked back. One of the figures leaned out the window. He pointed the shotgun that I'd heard earlier.

"Gun," I shouted.

"Yeah, I know."

Theresa swerved the truck again. We went into a fishtail, she fought to keep us on the road. We skated to the shoulder, and then back on the highway. The blast, louder than the first one, clipped the tailgate.

"Son of a bitch," she muttered.

"Who are they?"

"Damned if I know."

They gained on us, ran alongside, and pulled ahead. The guy with the shotgun was a thick goon in a puffy jacket. He was still hanging out the passenger window, rain bouncing off his head. He pointed the gun at the truck tires. Theresa cranked the wheel, sliding into and smashing the Ford's back bumper. The guy with the gun looked like he was gonna come right out the window.

"Easy," I said.

The truck shook like it could fall apart any second and leave us suspended in air. We went into another skid like we were in the Ice Capades, except we were skating with goons. The sedan swung over and rammed into the side of the truck. Theresa pulled back and fought the slide. We hit loose gravel on the shoulder, going into a long spin. I felt the truck lift. I was sure we'd roll. But she brought us back, pumping the brakes, gaining control. Still sliding, the truck dipped into the ditch. We rode the wet ground like it was a washboard. The half-ton slammed to a stop. Theresa jumped out of the cab and sprinted into the field. I ran after her, expecting another blast would cut us down at any moment.

I took a fast look behind. The sedan was up on the shoulder. I saw the two figures, one pointing out toward us. The guy in the puffy jacket no longer had the shotgun. The other goon was in a dark suit, made darker by the rain. We both ran through the field, wheat stalks bending and cracking under us. It was a helluva lot harder than a jog down a gravel road. The rain pelted our bodies, soaking us after a few minutes. A farmyard with a large barn was off to the left. To the right, a small stand of trees. Farther right, fifty yards away, a lone cow stood not giving a shit about the rain, but probably wondering about the two crazy folk running though her field.

I considered spinning around and taking a bead on the figures in the gray light. I brought out Damien's 9mm from the shoulder holster. I was only a few yards from the trees. Theresa pointed toward the barn.

"Trees," I said, gulping air into my burning lungs.

She nodded at me, then veered hard left. She took off like she was at a track meet.

"Wait," I called after her.

The figures came at us hard through the field. I ducked into the trees. They were too spindly to hide behind, but I gave it a shot anyway. The cow let out a long low, bitching at us, telling us to get out of her field. I realized the one hanging out the window never pointed the shotgun directly at us. He'd tried to blow out the tires. Still, that didn't mean they wouldn't take us out now. The two men stopped and stood in the field, the wheat above their knees. I watched them talk to each other before the one in the puffy jacket took off after Theresa. In the gray light I saw him pull out something gun-like. The other goon in the suit did the same and came toward the trees. I took a bead on him.

Dammit. I didn't like shooting someone I don't know—especially when it's not clear why they're coming after me. A shot rang out and hit one of the spindly trees, only a few feet from where I stood. The joker in the suit didn't share my hesitation. Rain suddenly let up like someone had turned off a tap. My body heat contrasted against the mix of sweat and rainwater that soaked my back and chilled my skin.

"Hold up or I'll take you out," I shouted.

He took a fast step, moving right, and fired again. Shards of tree bark sprayed, and a piece hit my face. It stung like hell. A few drops of rain hit me, mixing with what I was sure was a trickle of blood. Far off, I heard another shot. Why did she go that way? I looked over to where she ran, and then back again. Now where the fuck did that guy go? There's no place to hide out here. I scanned the copse—no way he came in here without me knowing. I was about to yell again when he sprung up from the field, covered in mud and wheat stalks. We fired at the same time. I don't know where his shot went, but I spun him around like a kid's toy.

I edged out from the trees, my gun pointed at the spot he went down. The rain had stopped. The crunch of the wheat stalks under my feet and my own breath was all I heard. It was a hair lighter, the sky giving a reprieve, but the sun was still too scared to come out. The body lay still. Then I saw the rise and fall. I circled around him, taking a fast look to where Theresa ran, and back to the suit on the ground. He groaned, swore, and rolled over.

"You got a gun in your hand, you better drop it."

He held up his hands. I scanned the area around him—hard to see in the dim light where his pistol had dropped.

His face was contorted in pain.

"Call an ambulance," he said.

"For some reason they didn't put a pay phone in this field."

"Hurts like hell."

"Let's have a talk. Then I'll drive you to a place that sells Band-Aids."

He moved his hand to the blossom of blood on his shoulder.

"Easy now," I said. "You'll be fine. Best place to get shot."

"Fuck you."

He started to bring his knees up.

"I like you better on the ground." I tapped his leg with my foot.

The clouds had spread out, already heading for another vista. My buddy Mr. Sun glowed to life. The dark-suited goon had a square head with a haircut to match. His collar was open, exposing a thick neck. I imagined the muscles pushing under his wet and grimy clothes. The guy was an ape.

"What do you want?"

"Nuh-uh. That's my question," I said. "Why did you come after us?"

"Not you. Her."

"Ok. Then why her?"

He moaned again.

"Not telling you shit," he said.

"A boot in the head will make you forget about your shoulder."

I stepped toward him. We both saw the gun at the same time. He lunged for it and I connected my shoe to the back of his head. He yelled. I stepped onto his hand, inches away from the gun. I picked it up and pocketed it. I knelt down and pointed the Sig at his face.

"This is a shitty place to die. No one will find you for quite a while. You'll probably get chewed up by a combine."

"Combines don't chew."

I rapped him in the head, producing another yell and a fuck.

"Why her?"

"We were told to go find her. Bring her in," he said.

"Bring her in or kill her?"

"They didn't want her dead."

"Who is they?"

We listened to each other breath for a while. I strained to hear her voice or another shot in the distance, or something. A murder of crows flew overhead.

"Stiltson."

"See, that wasn't hard. Now where can I find this asshat?"

"Bennett. He has a dealership there."

"See. It feels good to tell the truth. Now tell me what the fuck is going on and I'll go get you some help."

"I don't know," he said.

"Oh, I think you do."

I placed the gun against his forehead. I had no plan to fire it, but I'd seen some bad asses do this in the movies.

"Me and Larry work for the group that Stiltson runs. They said she was on the run. We were supposed to track her down and bring her in."

"Your buddy Larry the one in the puffy jacket that went after her?"

"Yeah. He loves that stupid jacket."

"So why go after me?"

"We were told to take out anyone traveling with Delilah."

"Who?"

CHAPTER TWENTY-ONE

Rainstorms show up out of nowhere on the prairie, and then the clouds pack up like a traveling circus, leaving so fast you wondered if they were here at all. The air had gone from cool and refreshing, drying my soaked clothes, to arrows of heat that cooked the back of my neck as I walked with Dark Suit through the field.

I was pretty sure he saw the flash of confusion on my face when he said the name Delilah. I tried to cover it saying, *Yeah, well let's go see how her and Larry are doing*. I got him to his feet. He grumbled and moaned, but I nudged him forward. He now walked a few steps ahead of me.

My head felt like I'd climbed in a washing machine during the spin cycle. *Delilah*? That was who Harold had come looking for—according to Alex the Springs manager, anyway. So the goons were after Delilah and mistook Theresa for her? Running through the field—even with the dark sky and the rain they should have seen that Theresa wasn't her. Unless they didn't know what this Delilah looked like. Could be they were sent to retrieve a woman driving a truck going East on Highway 37—I think that's what the sign said. Some guy named Stiltson had sent them.

Wait. Unless Theresa *was* Delilah. Shit. She'd acted funny when I said the name.

"Hey, what's your name?"

"Johnson," Dark Suit said.

"I'm sure it is. Well, Mr. Johnson, how did you know we'd be driving out here?"

He didn't say anything. He stumbled on the ground, yelped, and regained his balance.

"I have no problems shooting someone in the back," I said.

"Stiltson described the truck. He said you'd be driving north and east away from Hamel."

"This guy sent you after a truck? That's not much to go on."

"He told us what she looked like."

"Delilah."

"Yeah, her."

We reached the edge of the yard. A cousin of the cow out in the field mooed from the barn. A pair of chickens skittered across the ground. They were in a helluva hurry to get somewhere, or running from Old MacDonald with an axe. I walked a circle in the yard, telling Johnson to stay put. Except for the animals, there was no one around. I expected someone to come from the house and ask me what the hell we were doing, but it was quiet as a church. The only vehicle was a small yellow tractor parked next to the barn.

I rapped on the door of the house. It was an old story-and-a-half job, with a row of square windows on the main level, a wider window sat under the peaked dormer, and a clapboard porch. No one came. I twisted the doorknob, locked, then looked back at Johnson who was standing in the yard like the last kid picked for the baseball game. The porch wrapped around the house. I followed it, peering in a couple of windows. Another road snaked out to the highway. It was more dirt than gravel, with a set of tracks that looked fresh in the rain. Someone was digging in, as if they got stuck or had to leave in a hurry like those running chickens. I went back to Johnson.

"You came with someone else," I said.

"It was just me and Larry. Go in the house and call an ambulance."

"Door's locked."

"C'mon, asshole. You shot me."

"I'm sure if the shoe was on the other foot, you'd be calling a team of surgeons to take care of me."

Johnson grunted and winced.

"Kick the door in," he said.

"Did Stiltson send another couple of goons as backup?"

"How should I know?"

"Your buddy Larry a part-time magician?"

"Huh?"

"They disappeared. No tracks against the house, only the ones around the front on that dirt road. Looks like they picked up Larry and Delilah and tore the hell out of here."

Johnson stared at his shoes, then looked up toward the highway.

"Stiltson said there'd be another group."

"Dammit, Johnson, getting information from you is like talking to a grumpy teenager."

I went back to the house and kicked in the door. A cat bolted out of the doorway and scared the shit out of me. Johnson laughed.

"Yeah, yeah." I walked back and pointed the gun at him. "Here's what's gonna happen. You can go in there and call an ambulance, or Stiltson, or whoever the fuck you want. I'm gonna walk back to our truck. If I see you following me I'll shoot you like I almost did that cat."

"You'd shoot a cat?"

I rapped him in the head. Johnson yelped.

"No. I like cats. I don't like you and your dumbass suit. Who wears a suit out here?"

I left Johnson to think about that one. Walking back through the wheat field, the sun hammered down on me, and the dampness now was from my sweat. Theresa had left the keys in the ignition. I looked in the goon's sedan. No keys. Either Johnson still had them or they were gone with Larry. If he had them, then Larry wasn't too concerned about leaving Johnson behind.

I pulled back onto the highway and drove in the same direction we first headed. Theresa said we were driving to Damien's other place. She said it would be a few hours. That could be anywhere. I scanned my brain for a mental map of the province. There were a few possibilities, but nothing said he was in a town, or that the goon-mobile that picked up Larry went in this direction.

I eased the speed of the half-ton as fast as it could go without shaking. I thought about Theresa, who I barely knew. How had she known Damien? A thought popped in that suggested she also knew this Stiltson. Hell, maybe her and Larry were old drinking buddies.

There were times I did things to follow an instinct, an urging that felt somewhere between chili-pepper heartburn and stomach butterflies. More often, I followed something because I didn't know what else to do. This was definitely the latter.

CHAPTER TWENTY-TWO

I'd driven an hour, thinking of nothing but putting miles under my tires. I was slicing hope as thin as it gets, trying to see something that would offer a clue as to where they'd taken her. I was no Sam Spade, Philip Marlowe or even Jim Rockford—I was a guy in a beat-up truck who kept on something like a dog on a bone. I was more stubborn than smart. Maybe those other tough guys were like that too, but I never called myself a detective. Why would I?

I passed a green sign with a mile marker and an arrow that pointed to a small town. I was certain I'd been there as I traipsed the province with my father back when I was a kid. He worked for a fruit company, which was odd for this part of the country with a growing season barely long enough for apples and raspberries, and melons if you played your cards right. The old man was an exporter, talked to grocery stores, and gave them the best deals on oranges and bananas so the whole damn population didn't succumb to scurvy.

No matter which one of these roads I drove on, they seemed like they pointed toward home. I no longer knew what that word meant. Years gone felt like decades. My past here was covered in scar tissue and empty Pilsner bottles. I planned on leaving right after the last bell rung in my high school. Maybe I was born with a restless heart—I knew how stupid that sounded. In truth, it was more anger than restlessness that burned in me.

When I met someone who saw the anger, but still wanted to stick around, my leaving Marvelle got pushed to the back burner… of another stove.

Her name was Marguerite, and she'd grown up in a small French town, one of the only ones in the province. Her family came from France, not Quebec. It wasn't her looks that attracted me, though she'd have given that girl in the giant clamshell a run. It was more how she talked to me, and how she listened like she was peering into my soul.

She was four years older than me, and came to Marvelle right around the time I was thinking of leaving. Against her father's wishes, she had left the wheat fields and went to university in Paris to study psychology. She came back when her father grew ill. He died a month after her return.

I was downing Pilsners in the Royal Hotel, a place as far from royalty as you can get, when she plunked down next to me. She said she needed a summer project, and I was going to be it.

"What kind of project?" I asked her.

"Undetermined. Let's start with you buying me a beer, and we'll see where it goes."

Marvelle was small enough that I usually knew everyone, or at least their faces.

"How come I've never seen you in here?" I asked.

"Is that the best you got… what's your name?"

"Fischer."

"First or last?" she asked.

"Your pick."

We verbally sparred like that, a precursor to the bob-and-weave I'd later perform in the Montreal boxing gym. It was also a harbinger of the next few years we spent together. She had an old-fashioned name for someone who most definitely was not. In the first year her intensity matched my temper. Marguerite caught the eye of other guys. She wasn't beautiful in a runway-model way, but there was something in how she carried herself, how she moved across a room. People, especially men people, noticed her. Sometimes they noticed too much. Shortly after, they ended up on the receiving end of one of my right hooks, along with a boot in the guts while they were on the ground looking for a tooth.

"We're not living in medieval times, you don't need to come to my rescue like some knight."

She was right. Marguerite could take care of herself. She'd wither an onlooker with one dead-eyed gaze and a well-placed *fuck you*. What she didn't understand was that the fights weren't about her, or some kind of misplaced chivalry. There was a fire in me that burned a hole in my guts. In the last year, the blaze had started to spread throughout my body. I couldn't say where the anger came from—but smashing someone repeatedly in the face helped douse the flames.

Neither of us had planned to stay in Marvelle. We were the rabbit glue that prevented the other from leaving town. I was doing any sort of job that gave me money to put gas in the car and beer in my belly. Marvelle seemed to always need ditch-diggers. Roughing in the pipework for houses by hand plowing the ditches for a couple of plumbers built up my back muscles and biceps. The extra muscle came in handy when I was driving my fist into someone's head.

"What were you trying to accomplish?"

The question came one night as she placed a Steri-Strip on the cut over my eye, and cleaned up the dirt and blood on my face.

"Nothing."

"That's what you achieved," she said.

I couldn't even remember why the guy pissed me off—or why we went to the parking lot to square off. My anger burned away every rational thought and replaced it with how to best lay a punch, or a kick, or a knee into the body of my opposer.

We were living in a small basement apartment. She filled out university applications for places in France but never sent them in the mail. I transitioned from ditch-digging to throwing bales of hay and building fences for a trio of farmers.

"Why are we here, Luke?"

"Where should we go?"

"Me back to Paris—return to university. And you… somewhere. Anywhere."

Marguerite knew my restlessness and anger danced together. But it was like I was driving through two feet of mud and my tires were spinning. At that point, I'd stopped the spinning and given myself over to being mired.

The night it all ended we were at the bar. The usual crowd was yakking over too-loud music. Some guy came and sat down next to Marguerite. He was taller than me, but thinner, like a scarecrow in Levi's, with a wispy beard. I'd seen him around, his name was Norman something. No doubt he'd seen Marguerite and me together before, so when he started hitting on her, I asked him straight-up.

"What the fuck are you doing?"

He gave a scarecrow laugh. A half-beer later we were out in the parking lot. Marguerite was pissed. Before she took the car home, she told me I needed to stop doing this. I told her I'd catch a ride and see her at home. It would take less than five minutes to take care of this asshole.

Norman was about as tough as he looked. He flailed and threw a couple of punches at me, and one clipped my ear. The ringing and burning lit something up that had absolutely nothing to do with the skinny guy in front of me. I hit him once hard in the guts. He tried to wheeze out an apology, but I wasn't hearing any of it. I clocked him hard in the head. As he fell, I drove a knee into his face. Right then I pictured my wheels stuck in that mud. Son of a bitch. I needed to get out of that mud before it killed me. I got out all right. When I laid the boots to Norman, it almost killed him.

Someone from the bar had called the cops. Two cars showed

up and were joined by the local RCMP. I got charged with assault and they dragged my ass to a holding cell. Norman got a free ambulance ride.

He spent three weeks in a hospital eating from a tube. I missed doing time in an actual jail because enough people said that Norman had started it. I was protecting myself. The story held weight, as unknown to me, old Scarecrow Norm was packing. A friend of mine knew one of the Mounties who filed the report. Norman was carrying a Black Widow Luger, unlicensed—who knows where the hell he got it. I've spent some brain matter wondering what would have happened if he would have squared down on me and left me to bleed out in a bar parking lot. Never figured out why he held back, but it turned out that fighting a scarecrow was the push I needed to get out of the mud.

Marguerite came to the trial. She didn't say much to me when she visited the holding cell. On my release, she drove me back home and told me to pack my stuff. I didn't even argue. We both knew we were done. The rabbit glue was gone. The mud had dried up. Walking to the car, she grabbed me and gave me a long hug. She whispered in my ear.

"Get it figured out, Luke."

She kissed me. I felt the wetness on her cheeks. I watched her go into the house. I got in the car and drove.

After I got tired of going west, I turned left, and ended up in northern Ontario. I met a guy named Sal in a small bar in Dryden. He had a faraway look in his eye—someone also escaping from something. I never did learn from what. I moved in with him on his small farm near a place called Red Lake. I helped him with his straggly cows and collected eggs from a row of fat chickens. Sal made a bit of money with the eggs, sold a cow once in a while. But most of his income came from the mineral rights on his land. They'd found both gold and silver there, producing a steady stream of cash in his bank account whether his girls were laying or not.

Sal spent his time drinking with me and shooting things. I learned more than I ever thought there was to know about guns from my host. He had a number of legal rifles and shotguns, and then a bunch of handguns that were not. We shot at cans, bottles, makeshift targets made from dinner plates, and the odd gopher. Sal liked shooting but he didn't like killing things. I fired Glocks, Sig Sauers, Colts, and even an old Luger from the war.

The one that felt best in my hand was the Browning Hi-Power. I could nail any target Sal put up with that 9mm. Turned out I was as good with guns as I was with my fists. This wasn't really something I needed to find out. A guy with my kind of inner rage can do a lot of damage with his fists. Teach me how to use a gun, and some folks are going to end up dead.

Sal's moods got darker, in spite of the shooting sessions, which seemed to lighten them. He did like his chickens. I'd go out to the barn and hear him having conversations with them. I decided to move on, even though I had nowhere to go. Sal thanked me for staying with him. He made me a couple of bologna sandwiches, which he packed in with a sleeve of Oreos and a six of Pilsner. He gave me the Browning as a parting present.

"Not sure I should take this," I told him.

"You end up in Quebec, you'll be glad you have it."

"Why Quebec?"

"Cause everyone's pissed off and they're French to boot."

I had no intention of going to Quebec, but after living a month in Toronto, the city grated on me. There was too much traffic and every corner had a guy with a jackhammer.

I left, drove east for about six hours, and ended up in Montreal. Despite what Sal said about La Belle Province, there was a mood to the place that fit my mindset. I found work as a dishwasher, a furniture mover, and flipped eggs at a greasy spoon. I rented a one-room basement apartment, went to work, and then to the bar after. That's where I met Rick, my bio-chemist buddy. Together, we closed a place on St. Denis one night. He told me about giving up his marathon race to tenure at McGill so he could become a high-school science teacher.

"The kids are bright, they ask good questions. There's a whole lot less fuckery."

Rick and I became friends, and we closed more than a few bars together. I talked to him about my restless heart and legs, and my desire to pummel people in the face if they got on my wrong side.

Rick was a good listener, and maybe the smartest guy I'd ever met. He told me about a boxing club in the neighborhood where I rented my apartment.

"Go skip some rope, hit a bag, or someone. It might be what you need," he told me.

I wandered into the club one afternoon, Hank's Gym, and was told to strap on a pair of gloves. Growing up in Marvelle, I knew a couple of brothers who liked to punch and jab at each other with boxing gloves. The brothers had invited me to join them in their sessions. I preferred the feel of my knuckle against someone's face, but I liked the feeling of power the gloves gave me. That feeling came back when I strapped on a pair of gloves in the Montreal gym. They put me in the ring with a guy who didn't have an ounce of fat on him. I had absolutely no footwork or any clue on how to move in the ring. I took a dozen blows to the head and gut before I nailed him. My old man would have said he came out of his shoes. He hit the mat and was out like a light.

The trainer working with me let out a low whistle and called over the gym owner. I faced another young boxer, who was cut like a chunk of granite. I didn't put him out, but one of my punches had him doing a drunk man's turn into the ropes.

I started going to the gym after my dishwasher shift. The trainers worked with me, showed me how to move, had me work the bag, skip rope, and spar with their guys. They had a handful of boxers, most of them seemed like kids to me, who they put in bouts arranged by the gym or clubs in the city. They wanted me to fight in these, but I had no interest. I was lazy about the training, too. But I liked the sparring, and I liked going to the bouts to watch the kids go at it.

"Get in there. Time to be a three-minute hero."

That's what the gym owner Hank told the kids in the corner between rounds. All they needed to do was summon a bit of courage, or strength, or a piece of luck, and whether they were down or up in points, a three-minute round could change everything.

The miles rolled by as I thought about those days spent sparring in Montreal. Living there, I was in the best shape of my life, even with the long beer sessions with Rick. Nowadays, I still tried to do things to stretch out my muscles, ran along the beach in PV, and up and down the cobblestone streets. The sparring I did now wasn't any timed or refereed affair. It was more knocking heads of anyone who gave Benno trouble—or decking someone who was giving me trouble. The burning insides that haunted me while in Marvelle had softened some. I didn't take any great joy in fighting. I recognized the skill for what it was and used it like a guy who knew how engines worked fixed cars.

My body ached from being too long in a car. That ache was matched by the one in my gut that rumbled, thinking about where Theresa and the goon went. Theresa, who might be Delilah. So who grabbed them from the farmhouse, and how did they know to go there? During my time in the field with Johnson, did Larry in the puffy jacket go into the house and call someone? It seemed unlikely.

A town grew on the horizon. I'd never been to Grassdale. Johnson in the suit said something about Stiltson and a dealership in Bennett. That town was an hour west. Something in my aching gut said the goon-mobile didn't go that way. I was starting to think my gut was as dumb as the rest of me. It made more sense to try and find this Stiltson. He'd hired the pair of goons to search for

Delilah.

I decided to get gas, road coffee, a pocket full of meat sticks, and head over to Bennett.

My plans changed when I saw a guy in a puffy jacket pumping gas into a gold Pontiac.

"I'll be damned."

CHAPTER TWENTY-THREE

Harold dreamt of riding a horse over a long hill under the bluest sky. The horse was a mottled color, a pinto, he knew that name from the L'Amour books. It was like Harold was in one of those stories. He looked across the vista, a patchwork quilt of earth tones, dotted with thick brown cows. He'd dreamed this dream before, and whenever he woke up from it he felt sad that it was over, wishing he would have lived back then. Her voice took him away from the peaceful scene.

"Up ahead."

"What?"

"That's Michaelson's," she said.

Harold blinked himself awake. They were driving on gravel, but it was smooth like someone had just grated it. The sun had started its climb on the horizon, blazing like a blood orange against the pale morning sky. Out in the distance, one of those oil pumps from Texas churned like those funny birds that dipped into your glass.

"How long have we been driving?"

"A couple of hours. Was going to stop for gas in Stillwater, but nothing was open. It was too late. I figured we could make it."

"Backward country."

They turned onto another gravel road, eventually reaching a narrow drive that was bordered by scrub brush.

"Doesn't look like much," Harold said.

It was a stretched-out bungalow with a couple of outbuildings, shacks, and the sheds everyone seemed to have around here. Through a garage door, the end of a light green car poked out, another Pontiac. Reyna pulled in behind the other car and shut off the engine.

A guy dressed in jeans and a dark sweater came out the front door and stood on the steps drinking from a mug.

"You didn't call," he yelled over.

"Didn't get a chance."

"You found him?"

"In Loren, yeah. Good guess," she said.

The guy in the sweater pointed to some spot above them, down the lane and out to the grid.

"Anyone behind you?" he asked.

"Not yet," she said. "But they might come soon."

Reyna went to the house. Harold stayed by the car, straightened his jacket and ran his fingers through his hair.

"So what's your deal, big guy?"

"What's yours, asshole?" Harold asked.

The guy on the steps took a long drink from his mug. He eyed him in a way that pissed Harold off. He took out the Beretta and pointed it at the sweater.

"Oh, you're one of those."

Sweater Guy laughed and went back in the house.

"Well, get in here," Reyna called. "Don't forget your gun."

Harold knew this would never happen in a fucking L'Amour book. He holstered the gun and followed them inside. The two of them sat at a kitchen table. The place looked a lot nicer on the inside. It was all light-colored wood, white counters, and a lot of stainless steel. It wasn't the sort of stuff Harold usually noticed, but the contrast to the outside's dumpiness made him think.

"You decorate this place?" Harold asked.

"Nice, right?" Reyna drank out of the same white mug as the guy's.

"Cup of coffee? Brewed fresh, and a lot better than you'll get around here."

Harold joined them at the table, running his hand along the smooth surface, then giving it a knock.

"Where is she?"

"We're also in the dark. Didn't Reyna explain that?"

"She didn't explain shit."

Michaelson eyed him.

"Well, I'll tell you Mr…"

"Stevens."

"OK Mr. Stevens. We'd all like to know where she is. You came up from where, New Mexico?"

"You worked with her? Do the same shit?" Harold asked.

"Depends. What kind of shit are you implying?"

Sweater Guy had a shaggy haircut that made Harold want to smack him in the forehead.

"You look familiar," Harold said.

"I look like a lot of people." He tugged on the neckline of his sweater.

Harold sighed and took a sip of coffee.

"Damn," he said.

"It's good to like good things, Stevens. Now if you're pals with Delilah—"

"How do you know that?"

"—then you must have met her when she was traveling down in New Mexico."

"Colorado. Bunch of hippies in New Mex," Harold said.

Michaelson laughed.

"And yes, Delilah and me were working on some things. I more deal with buildings, and she with land they sit on. No offense, Stevens, but you don't look like a real estate agent, or a farmer. Whattya say you come clean about who you are and why you're here?"

"I'm not coming clean about shit."

"Sorry. But I am spent." Reyna yawned. "Driving through the night after tussling with those bozos, I need to sleep."

"You stay right here," Harold said.

"Oh, settle down. If you need to shoot her she'll just be down the hall."

Michaelson pointed past a fancy-ass looking couch to a pale green wall with framed black-and-white photos. The photos were people dressed in suits and nice dresses. Harold couldn't tell if they were old-timey shots, or just pretended to be.

"Those your relatives?"

Michaelson smiled. He waved Reyna down the hall, where she disappeared into a bedroom.

"People that lived here long before I came. I don't know any of them," he said.

"So why have pictures of them?"

"What do you want, Stevens?"

Harold took another gulp of the coffee. Damn, the son of a bitch was right it *was* good coffee, and exactly what he needed. He still felt a bit fuzzy around the edges, wondering how long he'd slept before she woke him up.

"So you're Michaelson. That's the name she used for you."

"OK."

"And I think you do know where Delilah is." Harold took his gun out again.

"Can't stop fingering that, eh? Someone's liable to get hurt."

"How about *you* come clean? Or I'm ending this."

Harold thought he heard something outside.

"This is a helluva stalemate, Stevens. Neither of us can find the person we're looking for. And it's the same person."

"Well, one of us is lying."

"I don't think you're seeing the picture here. I heard about what happened in Bennett. And in Hamel. That's why I sent Reyna to see if she could find you."

"What happened?" Harold asked.

Far off there were scraping sounds—tires crunching gravel. Harold stood, went to the window, keeping his gun on Michaelson. A dark sedan barreled toward the house. It slid into the yard.

Harold watched as men bolted out of the car—two ran to the shed, and he lost sight of another who rounded the house. Harold moved fast, got behind Michaelson and grabbed one of his arms, twisting, jammed the Beretta into his back.

"Who's coming?"

"Some associates."

"Why?"

"We like to do brunch."

Harold twisted Michaelson's arm again, who let out a grunt of pain. A figure ran past the window. Harold swung the gun up and fired through the glass. A yelp came from the back bedroom, and Reyna ran down the hallway.

"What the fuck D—"

"Get back in the back, Reyna." Michaelson cut her off.

Harold pivoted with Michaelson's body, moving backward, scanning the living room quickly—another doorway, dark, in the corner of the room.

"Where does that lead?"

"Stairs to the basement. Then another door outside."

"What's down there?"

Car doors slammed outside, more scrapes on the ground.

"Usual basement stuff. My preserves."

"What?"

Harold's follow-up question stopped in his mouth as a whole lot of things happened at once. A guy in a plaid shirt and goofy hat appeared in the doorway that led to the basement. He pointed a long rifle barrel at Harold. Harold swung Michaelson over as a shield. At the same time, the front door was kicked in, making

Michaelson yell, "*Hey!*" Reyna, who never made it back to the bedroom, bolted toward the open door, and was stopped by one of the suited goons who had burst in. Harold pulled Michaelson back with him against the wall.

"Everyone put their dicks back in their pants or I'm blowing a see-through hole in your boss." Harold kept his voice cool and flat.

"How do you figure me being the boss?" Michaelson asked.

"You called them right before we got here," Harold said.

Reyna kicked one of the goons in the leg.

"Let me go, you son of a bitch."

"Let her go, Buddy," Michelson said.

The taller goon in the navy-blue suit released his hold on Reyna. He reached down and rubbed his calf.

"Gladly."

Reyna ran outside. Harold heard a car engine rev and spin out of the yard.

"We saw Reyna's car out there. Does this guy own the LeMans in the garage?" asked a shorter goon with a brush cut, wearing a black suit with a plaid shirt underneath.

"No. I borrowed it from a friend," Michaelson said.

"Always liked those cars. Nice color, too," Buddy said.

"You want us to go after her?" Short Goon asked.

"Maybe later."

"Hey, lucky pals, let's all talk shop later. I want each of you take a few steps back before I aerate this guy," Harold said.

"Air what?"

"It's a gardening thing," Michaelson said. "Stevens here must be an avid planter."

"Whattya want us to do?" Short Goon said.

"Not too sure," Michaelson said. "Stevens, you got any ideas?"

"Does he know her? As in, where the hell she is?" Buddy asked.

"Again, not sure."

The goons at the door took a few steps. Harold surveyed the two handguns, one a Glock and the other a revolver, probably a .38. The jerk-off farmer in the basement doorway with a rifle was less a concern. Harold had a feeling he couldn't hit the broad side of a barn. Still, even if he killed Michaelson, his exit was blocked both ways.

"All right, I'm stepping back," Harold said. "Everyone take a breath."

"You got a lot of steel in your pants, Stevens. You got three different guns pointed at you, yet you still sound like you're in charge."

"How about you put that pistol down before we do some air-raising?" Short Goon asked.

Harold laughed.

"Top-notch business partners. Any of them pass grade school?"

"Put it down or we're putting you down," Buddy said.

Harold did a quick run through of the possible outcomes. He didn't like any of them. He was going to end up with at least one, maybe two bullets in him. He slowly lowered his hand and placed his Beretta on the floor.

"Kick it over," Buddy said.

"Well, that was exciting. Get you going better than coffee, hey, Stevens?"

"Harold."

"Excuse me?"

"Getting tired of you saying my name like you're a school principal," Harold said. "Is Michaelson first or last?"

"Why do you want to know?"

"It'll help when I hunt you down and put a bullet in that shaggy-ass haircut."

Michaelson laughed. The goons didn't. He reached his hand out.

"Damien. Good to meet you, Harold."

CHAPTER TWENTY-FOUR

I eased the half-ton to the side of the road. Johnson the Suit had called the guy in the puffy jacket, Larry. I watched Larry go in the small building and pay for his gas. I hung back in case he recognized the truck. I spied a figure in the backseat as the Pontiac pulled out of the gas station. There was no one else in the car. Whoever picked them up must have got dropped off somewhere.

I followed the sedan out of Grassdale, which only took about ten minutes given that it was barely a town, with only the gas station and the shack next to it that could have been a tire shop. For a moment I thought the shape in the back wasn't Theresa, until she turned her head to look out the rear window. She made no movement of recognition. I dropped back further, letting a car pass me, and then another. I scanned the highway, watching to see if they pulled off.

On a long curve, they slowed and turned onto a grid road. If I followed them, for sure Larry in his puffy jacket would know. I didn't want to make a flash judgment, but in my experience guys wearing those kind of jackets weren't the stars of the quiz team. I figured Larry to be more of an assistant goon to Johnson the Suit. Basing my conjecture on fashion choices was dumb, but I'd been right too many times not to think the thought.

I passed the grid where they went in, and then turned onto the next road a mile up. The good thing about grids was that you could usually criss-cross back to wherever you wanted to be. Sure, there were breaks in the system, roads going around sloughs, ending at a T, or just ending. But most of the grid roads lined up like waffle squares on a plate. Gravel spit under the truck tires. I again urged the engine to the max speed before it started to shake, careful not to swim on the loose gravel. I'd fishtailed my share of cars and trucks, even rolled one into the ditch—lucky as hell to walk out of it with only a sore back and a slash across the forehead.

I cut over at the next grid, scanning the horizon for any cloud of dust. If they'd also turned this way, I'd meet them head-on. I wondered how good Larry was at playing chicken. I grew up around guys that drove right up to your grille, forcing you to hit the ditch before you crashed.

I came to the grid they'd driven in on. There were no dust clouds, nor any signs of the sedan in both directions. They could be already far up the road—but the sky had cleared after the rain, so if there was a car kicking up dirt, I'd see it. I turned back in the direction of the highway. Half a mile up, over a small rise, a line of poplar trees appeared. They bordered a small pale-yellow farmhouse. I slowed. I spied the outline of the Pontiac through the poplars, gold color shimmering between the leaves. The driver's door and the back passenger side were open. I pulled the truck to the shoulder, a couple hundred yards from the house. I slid down into the ditch, taking out the 9mm as I walked. I kept low. If Larry was in the house with Theresa, he could see me bobbing along and blast me with a rifle or whatever he was now packing. His shotgun was back on the highway where I'd left Johnson. I swore at myself for not grabbing that before I drove off.

The ditch rose onto the drive going into the farmyard. I slipped into the trees, scanning ahead of me, slowly moving the gun in an arc. I ran to the sedan, crouching as I went, my body tense, waiting for the shot. I bolted from the car to the side of the house, edged around the corner, and up the four stairs to the front door. I checked the door handle, ready to kick it, but it turned easy in my hands.

The living room and kitchen were neat as a pin. I paced down the short hallway, peering into the bedrooms. The place was immaculate—they either had a cleaner come in or were that sort of people. All I heard was the ticking of a too-loud bedside clock. Back in the kitchen, I spied a phone on a counter. There was a pad of paper next to it and a pencil. Some scribbles and doodles, digits but not enough to be a phone number. I pictured Larry calling someone, maybe the other goon who they'd dropped off. I went through a door in the back that led to a mudroom and then the outside. I made out the pair in the distance, wading through the tall grass. She was a couple of steps ahead. Larry was going to kill her. I was lucky he hadn't done it yet. Dammit, I should have followed him when they first turned.

I ran toward them. The wind had picked up, hopefully covering some of my steps on the hard ground, but maybe not. I didn't care. They were still a good eighty yards ahead of me. High above, somewhere unseen, a hawk screeched. I thought I'd imagined it, but it made Larry flinch and he stared into the sky.

I yelled after them.

"Hey!"

The puffy jacket jerked, stopped, and Larry turned. I couldn't make out his expression, he was too far away.

"Don't do it, Larry."

"Get lost," he yelled back.

"Let her go or I'll put you down."

I pointed the Sig. Theresa was a step away. At this range I couldn't be sure I'd hit him square.

Larry raised a pistol at me. I didn't want to gamble on who was the better shot, I had to take a chance. But before I could squeeze one off, he fired. I only imagined it flying past—no idea how close he came. I lunged right. If I fired at an angle maybe I wouldn't hit her. I now saw that Theresa had her hands together, cuffed, or taped. The hawk returned with another screech, this one closer.

Larry startled, looked up to see if something was coming at him. Theresa swung both hands and clocked him in the back of the head. I sprinted toward them. Larry didn't go down, but he was a wobbly top, and gravity was calling. I was about to risk a shot when Theresa brought her knee so hard into his crotch I had to cringe. On his way down, she swung her fists into the side of his head. Larry timbered, out cold before he hit the ground.

"Nice," I said.

She was breathing hard, trying to catch her breath. It took her a second to register my face.

"Come at me, fucker, and you'll join him."

Her left eye was blackened, and a line of dried blood trailed from her lip.

"Theresa," I said her name slow and even.

She closed her eyes, her chest rose and fell. When she opened them again, she shook her head.

"He was going take me out there and kill me like a dog."

She kicked him the ribs. Larry stayed silent, sleeping his goon sleep.

I slid my gun back into the shoulder holster and went to her. She started to shake.

"It's OK," I said.

She collapsed into me, her face wet against my shoulder. I let her do what she needed to do. A couple minutes later, she stepped back.

"That fucker," she said.

I rifled through Larry's puffy jacket and found the handcuff keys. Freed from the restraints, she rubbed her wrists. She spat on the laid-out goon.

"How did you find me?"

"Sheer luck. I saw him pumping gas, figured you were with him. Who picked you up?"

"Some asshole with a big square head. He gave me this." She

pointed at her eye.

"Where did he go?"

"Before Grassdale another car pulled up beside and he got into it. He told this asshole to take care of it."

"Meaning you," I said.

She wound up for another kick and then changed her mind.

"What happened to the other guy. The one in the suit? Did you..." She formed a finger pistol.

"No. I left him back at that farm."

"You think that was a good idea?" she asked. "How about this one? We gonna let him keep on breathing?"

Theresa spied Larry's gun on the ground and picked it up.

"Not my style to kill goons," I said.

"Even if they were gonna kill you?"

She pointed the gun at Larry. Her arm shook.

"You ever shoot anyone, Theresa?"

"Always a first time, goddamn it."

I reached over, tipped her arm down.

"Let's go back to the truck. I don't want to be here when he wakes up."

"Don't you want to question him?" She was still breathing hard.

"Will I find out anything?"

She decided Larry did need another kick. This time he let out a whoof, but it was just a body response. He stayed out.

"Probably not," she said.

The wind whistled through the tall grass, sounding like a prairie ocean. The hawk was gone, off for better hunting somewhere. I took her hand and she let me. We waded back through the field, the long blades shush-shushing against our legs. In the house, I got us a couple of glasses of water. We cleaned up in the spotless bathroom. Again, I wondered who the owners were, and how Larry might have been connected to them. I considered going back out to the field and waiting for him to wake up.

I found a bottle of extra-strength aspirin and we each took a couple.

"While I was running to the barn, I heard shots out in the field. Were you hurt?" she asked.

"Only on the inside."

She gave me a blank stare.

"I hate not knowing what the fuck is going on," I said.

"Not sure I can help."

"I think you should try. Start with Delilah."

She handed me Larry's gun.

"I've never heard of her."

CHAPTER TWENTY-FIVE

Harold was in another windowless room, but this time it was a basement and he wasn't tied to the chair. They didn't lock him down there, but they might as well have. A couple of asshats were guarding the door at the top of the stairs. He considered kicking it open and rapping them on the head, but they'd taken his gun and told him to stay downstairs. He heard them arguing upstairs, trying to figure out what to do with him. A couple of different voices voted for putting a bullet in his head, but this joker Michaelson, or Damien, whatever the hell his name was, said no. More yakking back and forth, somebody yelled *not yet*.

The door upstairs opened and the guy in plaid with a goofy hat came down. He handed Harold a plate with a sandwich and a big-ass pickle.

"Damien said to bring you this. I told him that you could fuck off and starve."

Harold took a bite out of the sandwich. It was a good one, corned beef and some sort of spicy mustard. It burned his guts a bit, but he didn't care.

"You leave your rifle upstairs?"

"Should have put you down earlier," Plaid Guy said.

Harold gave a quick head move, and the guy jumped back, knocking his hat to the floor. He picked it up and dusted it off.

"You'll get yours," he said.

Halfway up the stairs, Harold called to him.

"That's a stupid hat."

Harold wished he could come up with something better than that, but he was pissed off, sore from the punch that the one called Buddy gave him before dragging him downstairs. And he was damn hungry. He wolfed down the rest of the sandwich and left the pickle. Never liked those vinegary things. Waste of a good cucumber.

Upstairs he heard some moving footsteps, a door opened, and a new voice was added to the conversation. It was deeper, had some gravel in it, like the guy needed to clear his throat. He flipped through his memory of the stubble-jumpers he'd run into since getting here. He thought back to the other room where he was tied up. What was that guy's name? Cooze… except not spelled that way.

Harold tried to put it together. Who was dancing with who? Kuz, that's how it was spelled. But it wasn't his voice—and it wasn't the fat dealership guy, Stiltson. He was probably the one that sent the three happy pals after him and Reyna. Harold remembered those weird dumplings she cooked him. They weren't bad.

He figured the tweed one named Taylor who started this whole thing was working for one of them. Stiltson or Michaelson. Or maybe both. It could be Michaelson was running the whole show. *But what was the show?*

Harold wasn't too worried about them coming downstairs and taking him out. They didn't seem the types otherwise they would have done it in the upstairs kitchen and dug a hole for him out back. Reyna had lit out at the first opportunity, so there was no help coming from her. He wondered if she was as tight with Michaelson as she told him. Could be that she was working with Delilah. Harold knew Reyna was keeping secrets.

There was a whole lot of bullshit going on in this big circle of wagons. He thought about it all, and considered who was at the center. They were all looking for Delilah, he knew that much. He started to form another theory, one where this Damien guy was in cahoots with the fat dealership guy. Cahoots. He'd learn that from the last L'Amour he'd read. It was the right word for this bunch.

Harold couldn't quite make out what the new gravelly-voiced guy was saying. But then another voice joined. A woman who must have come in the house with this guy. To hear her voice after all the shit he'd been through gave Harold a jolt of emotion that surprised him.

The door opened again, a different sound of feet on the stairs, lighter. Harold tensed.

"Funny place to run into you," she said.

"I could say the same thing."

"You look rough."

Harold stood, ran his fingers through his hair, did a fake dust-off of his lapels.

"I've had some interesting days," he said.

"So I heard."

She held her distance from him.

"Lot of pissed-off people looking for you," he said.

"Yeah, they all need to settle the fuck down."

"What are you doing for them?" he asked.

"Moving some things around. It's what I do."

"Like money?"

"Sure."

He studied her. She looked a bit ragged, hair pulled back into a messy knot.

"Seems to me you should have stayed out of sight," Harold said.

"That was the plan. Things change."

"The shaggy-hippie guy upstairs seems all relaxed. But he could hurt you."

"I'll handle Damien. I wouldn't have come back at all if it weren't for Macintosh."

"That the guy with the gravel in his throat? He got to you before you could get airborne?" he asked.

"Who told you that?"

She crossed her arms. This wasn't the reunion Harold was expecting.

"You want to explain to me why you lit out?"

"I never planned to stay in Colorado as long as I did, Harold. My business is up here."

"So why did you?"

"Stay?" She cracked a thin smile. She had a light in her eyes, which he thought was weird because there wasn't a drop of sunlight in the basement. "You were interesting to me, Harold."

Delilah stepped toward him and reached out her hand. He took it and brought her in. He felt her heart beating as he wrapped his huge arms around her. She gave a sharp intake of breath. He let her go. She wiped her face and sniffed.

"Dammit. Didn't want to do that," she said.

"So, you lost interest in me?"

"Why are you here, Harold? In fact, *how* are you here? I know you're a helluva tracker, you told me so yourself."

"You mentioned Canada," he said.

"It's a big country. How did you find me?"

"Someone you talked to heard the name of that town."

"Who?"

"Doesn't matter," he said.

The door opened upstairs and a voice called down. It was the gravelly one.

"Time to go. Damien wants to talk."

"In a minute," she called up. "Who told you where I went?"

"You could have told me you were leaving. I wouldn't have stopped you."

Delilah let out a huge sigh.

"Look, I gotta take care of some things. I didn't plan on still being here. After I finish up this deal, I'm getting out. Like way out."

"Yeah, I heard Spain."

"What? Who have you been talking to?"

She gave him a long stare. The light in her eyes was gone. With a look like that she'd make a good hitman. Harold imagined her giving someone dead eyes before she put them down. Then her face softened, she reached out and pulled him close, giving him a long deep kiss.

When she stepped back, there was no dampness on her cheeks.

"I gotta go. Take care of yourself," she said.

"I figure those asshats upstairs are going to do that for me."

"No they won't. Damien told them not to. He just wants you gone. Go back to Colorado. Read some Louis L'Amours. Work the bar, forget about all this."

"Might have a hard time doing that."

"It was good seeing you, Harold. You're a true individual."

She nodded to him. He watched her go back up the stairs. Some more mumbled voices. No one seemed overly pissed. Still, he wasn't too sure she was right. If Michaelson was in charge, maybe he'd let Harold walk. He was a cool customer, what with that shaggy hair. But those other goofballs, especially the plaid one in the hat, would just as soon shoot him as they would a rabbit in the garden.

Harold sat back in the chair and waited. He hoped the next guy they sent downstairs had a gun.

CHAPTER TWENTY-SIX

We stood outside the farmhouse, a wind had picked up and washed through the poplar trees. Marguerite always hated that sound, calling it one of the loneliest sounds she knew. The wheat in the field next to us bent and swirled. The wind and the color of sky gave me memories that slowed my thinking, like I was in a prairie trance. I needed to pull out of it because Larry would be waking from his golden slumber any moment.

I'd put him down if I had to.

"You said we were driving up to Damien's other place. Why?"

"I told you. He said to come up there after I checked on you."

"They were looking for Delilah," I said.

"Who was?"

The quaver in her voice was gone.

"The one who came after me. I had a gun on him and he told me her name."

"Yeah. Never heard of her."

"She's the one Harold came looking for."

"Right. You said."

She wiped her lip with the back of her hand and checked to see if she was still bleeding.

"Maybe they have some ice in the fridge for your eye."

"Asshole punched me right in the face when I wouldn't get in the car. I'm going to go back out there."

I put my hand on her arm.

"You said we had to get out of Dodge," I said.

It took her a moment to remember.

"Right. We better go."

She took a final look out the back door window. We couldn't see Larry, as he was still laid out flat. We went out to the truck.

The Pontiac doors were still opened. I kicked them closed, took Larry's gun and fired into two of the wheels and one through the grille. I emptied it of the other bullets and tossed the gun into a bush.

Theresa revved the half-ton's engine and I hopped in.

"Should have put the bullets into that stupid jacket of his," she said.

"Drive."

We went down the poplar-lined lane and back onto the grid. I listened to the gravel hit the underside of the truck. The thing about a flat landscape like this, I could see miles in every direction. We had the place to ourselves.

"How is that Damien knew people would come looking for me after they saw us at the bar?"

"Damien just knows stuff like that."

"He's some sort of fortune teller?"

"He's a businessman," she said.

"A traveling weed salesman."

"He has more going on than that."

"How about this Stiltson… who is he?"

"Never heard of him."

Theresa looked straight ahead as we pulled onto the highway.

"Johnson told me they were hired by Stiltson to come after us. He has a car dealership in Bennett."

"Johnson?"

"The one in the dark suit who chased us in the field with puffy jacket, Larry, who thanks to you, will be walking funny for a while."

I watched her face for a sign of recognition but got nothing. "You really don't know any of these guys?"

"Nope. I'm as much in the dark as you are." She touched the area around her black eye with her fingertips.

"Should have iced it," I said.

"I'll be fine."

"How far to Damien's?"

"A couple more hours. A place called Stillwater. You know it?"

"I've seen it at the top of the map. Never been."

"We need to stop for some gas. There's a station about ten miles up."

She coughed and swore under her breath. We were behind a semi-trailer, and Theresa suddenly pulled out and gunned the engine. The truck whined in protest. The shimmer of another car appeared, coming toward us. She passed the semi and jerked the truck back into our lane. The oncoming car swerved onto the shoulder as the trucker leaned on his air horn.

"You want to kill me, there's easier ways," I said.

She didn't say anything, reached down and flicked on the radio to static.

"Find something," she said.

I twirled the dial, finding some twangy guitars and a crooning voice. We drove in silence until a sign for a gas station appeared on the horizon. It was one of those forgotten not-quite-a-towns where the only thing still doing business was the Esso. A few worn-down houses dotted the landscape like lost children. The gas jockey was a gray-haired man in stained overalls that matched the condition of the houses.

Back on the highway, Theresa said she grew up in a place like that but didn't offer any more of her story. I couldn't tell if she was shook up from what happened, or what could have happened, with Larry. There was a lot bubbling underneath the surface that had nothing to do with land deals. She knew more about the whole

Damien deal than she was letting on. And she knew who Delilah was. I didn't need to be a detective to figure that out.

"You OK if we don't talk for a while?" she asked.

"You all right? I can drive."

"I'm good. Just need some quiet." She reached down and clicked off the radio.

"Sure thing."

"Thanks, Luke. I really mean that."

There was a skip in her voice. I drifted into thoughts about my weed-growing pal, Damien. There was more to his business than selling pot. He seemed like a nice enough guy. I didn't mind him having my car. I had his gun. Seemed a good trade. But maybe he wasn't as nice as I thought. That kind didn't usually attract goons with shotguns.

The landscape had developed a bit of a roll. There were more pine trees in this part of the province. We crossed some snaky rivers that were spanned by concrete bridges. A large body of water emerged to the east. A squadron of ducks glided toward the bullrushes, and I thought I saw a fish jump. My father had told me that these bigger ponds were stocked with perch. The problem was when the northern pike swam from the river and gobbled them up. I was like one of those perch, swimming in these old waters. I considered that some big-ass jackfish might be heading my way. Eat or be eaten. That adage never made a lot of sense. Some days you had no choice but to be someone's perch. But then who was the jackfish?

***

Overhead, Harold heard scuffling, feet moving, chairs being pulled out. The furniture stopped. A voice started getting louder. It was her voice. Then quieter responses, low mumbling. Hard to make out the words.

"All of it!"

That sounded like the shaggy bossman. Harold hadn't heard him get mad like that yet.

She shouted back.

"I'm doing what I said I'd do. So fuck right off!"

Now shit was getting broken, someone got smashed against a wall, or the floor. Things were being thrown. Harold tried to follow the shouted conversation. She was promising him something, or maybe she already had. For sure her appearance at Michaelson's had stirred up a lot of shit.

Michaelson's voice then, loud and clear.

"Enough."

Lots more shuffling now, a few more shouts, slamming noises. Probably the door. So the group upstairs was heading out. Delilah was with them, probably not willingly. What was her beef with the shaggy man? Who was she working for, or who was she against?

Harold had driven way too many hundreds of miles only to enter a shitstorm of goons in plaid carrying rifles and bags of money. He hadn't seen the money, but he smelled it. Michaelson was in charge, no doubt. The fat car dealer had to be on the other side. Delilah was working for them, maybe both sides of the street like in that old Western. Harold remembered that a lot of people died in that movie.

Now, he just had to get out of this fucking basement so he could rap somebody's head and figure out the rest. She'd kissed him like she wasn't going to see him again. Harold believed she was wrong.

Car engines roared and tires spun on gravel. He wondered if they were going to leave him down here. With all the chaos upstairs, maybe they forgot. It would be no problem to kick the door in if they locked it. But the bastards wouldn't leave him a car. Harold pictured himself grabbing a wobbly bicycle and pedaling to civilization. The image made him even more pissed off than before.

His mood lightened when the door opened and the one in the

goofy hat clomped down the stairs.

"What the hell you looking so happy about?" he asked.

The guy had exchanged his rifle for a pistol that hung loose at his side. It was a Glock, Harold's favorite.

"Everybody leave the party?" Harold asked.

"Huh?"

Harold stood up from the chair.

"Need to stretch."

"You sit your ass back down." There was a bit of shake in Goofy's voice.

Harold bent down and touched his toes. His back cracked and he grunted, appreciating the pull on his muscles.

"Stand back up."

"Uh-oh." Harold let out another grunt, then a higher-pitched yelp.

"What are you doing? Stand up."

"I'd like to. But ow. Shit. It went out."

"What went out?"

"My back. You wanna give me hand?"

Goofy didn't move. Harold pictured him raising his gun, pausing to think about putting a bullet in him.

"C'mon. Help me up," Harold reached a hand out. "You can shoot me after. I promise."

"They didn't tell me to shoot you," he said.

"Even better. Now… a bit of help?"

Harold heard the step. He felt the hand in his, grasped it hard, and yanked.

"Hey."

Harold came up fast and drove his fist into Goofy's face. He knocked that dumb hat right off his head, along with at least one tooth. He followed it with a hard knee to the crotch. Goofy folded and made a sound like air escaping a balloon. Harold plucked the Glock out of his hand on the way down. A boot to the head and he said nighty-night. He kicked the hat across the room.

Harold bolted upstairs and burst through the door. A car engine was running outside. The driver stood next to a rusted olive Mustang. When he saw Harold come out of the house, he reached inside his jacket.

"This is a shitty place to die." Harold drew a bead on him.

The guy moved his arm and Harold shot him in the shoulder. Somehow the bastard still got his gun out, not that his aim was going to be worth shit, and waved it around.

"Fine."

Harold shot him in the head.

"That's what happens when you make poor choices."

He pushed the body away from the car. He thought for a second about the guy in the basement. Probably should clean up loose ends. He heard the door swing open behind him. Harold spun around and took out Goofy.

"Dammit."

Harold looked out to the road. He didn't figure on anyone coming back in a hurry, and he doubted that what passed for the police out here would show up. No one was doing drive-bys in the middle of nowhere. Still, the professional in him said he needed to put the two bodies somewhere. He carried them one by one into the basement. He took the driver's gun, a Browning, and put it in Goofy's hand. Let them Canadian horse-detectives figure that one out. He went back outside to the Mustang.

He circled the yard before he peeled out. The car was a bit beat up, but had some actual juice. Pulling onto the highway, he gunned it and the Mustang responded. Someone had souped it up, but never gotten around to the body work. It was a shame to let that happen to a nice car. Harold was up to eighty, then pushed it to eighty-five. He sailed along the highway, smooth as silk. He hit the buttons on the cassette player, an aftermarket job with lots of fancy red lights that meant it was expensive. A soft trumpet started playing a melody that Harold knew by heart. The horn was followed by those strings, man what he could do with those strings. Harold nodded his head to the music.

"Well, I'll be damned."

CHAPTER TWENTY-SEVEN

"So this Harry guy you told me about. He's the reason you came here?"

After driving so long, listening to the hum of the truck tires and the rattle of the hood, her voice startled me.

"Harold. Yeah, what about him?"

"Right. You gave him a funny name."

"Mostly."

"You catch any sight of him since you've been here? You never said."

"Not yet," I said.

"You said he was a killer."

"Hired gun, assassin, hit man, all those names fit. I haven't seen him, or talked to anyone who has. But there's remnants."

"Like the shooting in the King's. That was him."

We passed a sign for Stillwater, another fifteen miles to go.

"Yeah. Damien described the guy he saw in the King's… it had to be Harold."

"You said he was up here looking for a nephew," she said.

"No. The nephew is dead. I'm not sure why he's up here. Like I said, could be because of a woman."

"Then why's he shooting guys in bars?"

"Haven't quite put that one together."

"You're not much of a detective."

"Never pretended to be."

A prickling sensation crawled up my neck. I felt my jacket for the bulge of Damien's Sig. I wasn't sure what I was entering into, but something told me there was a very good chance I wouldn't like it.

The number of pumpjacks had increased as we drove north, the metal beasts dipped up and down, oblivious to our presence. The Stillwater grain elevator lifted out of the landscape, the red worn exterior pointing into the sky like a giant's toy rocket. We entered the town limits, the sign said POPULATION 700, smaller than Hamel. I knew that farmland up here wasn't as good, some made their living fishing, and there was oil. The town was weathered like the wood on the elevator, though we passed someone slapping fresh paint on one of the lampposts that lined the main drag. Maybe things weren't as bad as they seemed. Those who lived up here had chosen to be further away from the action, and I couldn't fault their desire for a quieter life.

As we drove out of the town limits, the highway acquired a few more bumps and rolls.

"Why does Damien have another place way up here? Another pot farm?"

"I've only been here once before. But no, he does all the growing at the house where you were. I think this was his uncle's place, he takes care of it since he died. Some of his clients like to meet him here."

"Who are all these clients of Damien's? Is there really that many pot smokers around here?"

"Marijuana is only part of the business. Don't ask me what the other things are because I don't know. And I've never asked."

I needed to tell Theresa to not play poker, as she was a helluva bad liar. We passed a set of rail tracks and came to a crossroads. There was a red flag on a stick, a marker of sorts. We turned down a gravel road and drove a couple more miles. We turned into a long drive that cut through a swath of bush. A low-slung bungalow sat in the yard. There were three outbuildings, no barn, and an empty garage.

"Doesn't look like anyone's here," I said. "He must be still cruising the byways in my LeMans."

We parked the truck and Theresa went up the steps. She rapped hard on the door and walked in.

"Damien?"

It was for sure Damien's place, the same crisp lines of Scandinavian furniture, and all the pale wood and stainless steel. A kitchen chair lay on its side, and a door at the back was flung open.

"What do you figure?" I asked.

"He's probably still out."

"Seems that way." I placed the chair upright. "Left in a hurry."

I went to the back door, which led to a landing, another outside door, and a set of stairs. I took a deep breath but didn't smell the sweetness that permeated Damien's other basement. If anything, there was a rotting smell. I went to the kitchen where Theresa was going through the fridge. She brought out a couple of bottles of 7-Up.

"No beer," she said.

"I could use some carbonation."

I joined her at the sleek kitchen table. She popped the caps off the sodas and slid one over to me.

"So we're going to wait for him to show up?"

"Not sure what else to do," she said.

"If we wait here long enough your friend in the puffy jacket will show up with Johnson in his dark suit. Maybe they'll pick up some other goons along the way."

"You shot that car. And I doubt they know about this place. That's why the bunch of them hit Damien's farm."

"You wanna say some more about that?" I asked.

I took a slug off the sweet drink, the acid and bubbles felt good. It would have went perfect with a bowl of Jimmy's Cholula-soaked peanuts at the El Rayo Verde.

"Say more about what? They must have come looking for Damien and found you. The other two were sent out looking for us."

"They were looking for Delilah," I said.

"Right."

"I think it's about time you spill some truth."

"About what?" she asked again.

"Any of it. Start with what's up with Damien's business."

"Getting tired of telling you, Luke. I knew Damien before. I don't know what he's up to, or who he works with. Coming to get you was a favor to him."

"So you keep saying. But how's that saying go… don't bullshit a bullshitter?"

She lowered her head, angling her body away from me. Then she sighed and leaned back into her chair.

"Listen. We'll wait here for a bit, I'm sure Damien will show. Then you can ask him all about it."

"I plan to."

She closed her eyes and massaged the back of her neck.

"How's all this going to help you with the dead nephew and the hitman?"

"Harold wandered into something in Hamel. He didn't drive all the way from Colorado to shoot some guy in a small-town bar. He's bumping against Damien's business, and maybe his competitors. Could be those goons at the farm were actually looking for Harold. And now I'm in the middle of it—complete with a shovel to the head." I felt the back of my head, touching the goosebump, still hot and swollen.

"Damien doesn't have competitors as far as I know."

"Thought you didn't know much?"

She rubbed her hands over her jeans. One of her knees bounced to an unheard beat.

"Could be those two who came after us were looking for Harold just like you are," she said.

"Larry and Johnson? No, I know who they were looking for."

"Yeah?"

It was my turn to sigh.

"The one called Delilah who you keep pretending not to know. Just like you don't know Stiltson. There's a lot of people you don't know... maybe half the province."

I finished the 7-Up in one long pull, got up and went to the window. A dust plume rose up, and the front of Benno's mint LeMans nosed out of the cloud. I reached into my jacket and pulled out the 9mm.

"What are you doing?"

"The weed farmer's back," I said.

I went outside and stood on the step, the gun at my side, watching the LeMans drive up the lane. If Damien was also holding a gun when he got out of the car, I wasn't waiting for some Old West gunfight moment. If you shot first, no apologies were needed after.

The car slid to a stop, the tires grinding on the gravel sounded much louder than they were. The engine shut off. No one got out of the car. Theresa now stood right behind me.

"For Christ's sake. Put the gun away. It's just Damien."

Still no one got out of the car. I raised the gun and pointed it at the windshield. The visor was down. The angle of the sun bounced off the glass, making it impossible to see who was in the driver's seat. Or if they were alone.

"You better have filled it up," I yelled. "You didn't tell me you were driving halfway across the province."

The driver's door opened and a woman stepped out. Her hair was dark brown and she had on a pair of stylish sunglasses that could have been Ray-Bans or some fancy-ass Danish brand. She put her hands on her hips and smiled. When she reached up and took off the glasses, I saw the family resemblance right away. They weren't twins, but they sure could have been sisters. I kept a bead on her.

"Still going to pretend you don't know her?" I asked.

A hard edge of metal pressed against my back. Must have been a small caliber for her to hide it on her person without me noticing it.

"Drop the gun, Luke."

CHAPTER TWENTY-EIGHT

I set the Sig Sauer down on the step. I thought about throwing it, but those things had a habit of going off when they got dropped. I couldn't count on it firing and hitting the woman in the Ray-Bans or Theresa. With my luck I'd put a slug in my ass.

"This the one Damien ran into at the King's?" the woman in Ray-Bans asked.

"Yeah," Theresa said.

"And you were supposed to bring him here?"

"That's what Damien told me," Theresa said.

"So who are you?"

"Just a guy who enjoys the wide-open skies."

"Did he give you that black eye?" she asked Theresa.

"No. That was one of the others. They're also looking for you," Theresa said.

"Also?"

"I think the group at the farm were looking for you."

"Who was it?"

"You know who it was."

"You're about as popular as the Delilah in the bible," I said.

"How do you know my name?"

"A guy in a wheat field told me," I said.

"He told you."

"Well, I did have a gun pointed at his face."

"Theresa? What the fuck?"

"His name is Fischer. He came up looking for Harold. Sent by his boss in Mexico… who sounds like he's also Harold's boss," Theresa said.

"Benno," she said.

"Trust Harold to fall in love and tell all his secrets," I said.

"Nobody fell in anything," she said.

"And so you knew who Harold was all along," I said to Theresa.

She didn't respond.

Delilah pocketed her Ray-Bans and came toward the house. She picked up Damien's Sig from the step. Theresa pushed me inside with her gun. Delilah fished around in the fridge freezer and brought out a blue bottle. She got us some glasses and poured us each a couple fingers.

"What if I don't like gin?" I asked.

"I don't give a shit what you like."

"Why are you driving my car? Where's Damien?"

Delilah ignored me. I wasn't going to get anything that looked like the truth from either one of them. Theresa still had the gun pointed at me.

"Put the gun away. We can always shoot him and bury him later. Sit down and have a drink."

Theresa did as asked. She slid out a chair, and we all drank our gin like we were three pals around a stylish Scandinavian kitchen set. It could have been an ad in a magazine.

"Why are you even here? And yeah, where is Damien?" Theresa asked.

"Things got complicated," Delilah said.

Delilah tapped her fingers on the table. She drew in a long, slow breath. I'd seen Harold do a similar thing. Maybe their romance made sense after all.

"If they found this guy at the farm, why is he still alive?"

"They didn't care about him. They were looking for you, and figured you'd be with Damien," Theresa said.

"It was going smoothly until Macintosh found me."

"The apple?" I asked.

"Shut up. He brought me here yesterday," Delilah said.

"You were here yesterday?"

Delilah nodded.

"Macintosh. I met him," Theresa said. "He's the one that sounds like he swallowed a frog?"

"Yeah, he's Damien's go-to violent thug." Delilah rubbed her eyes, then a fast turn to me "What was your name again?"

"Fischer," Theresa said.

"I prefer Mr. Fischer," I said.

"I don't give a shit what you prefer," Delilah said. She finished her gin and poured her and Theresa another drink. "I told Damien everything was in place. He accused me of trying to leave with the money."

"Which you were," Theresa said.

"Whatever. He wanted some assurance that I'd finish the deal. The plan was I'd go with Macintosh to the main branch in Saskatoon. He'd watch me make the transfer and then call Damien to let him know."

"Did you make it?"

"Yeah, I made it. But the money's not going anywhere right now. Fuck 'em both." she said.

"You moved it again? How? And where's Macintosh?" Theresa asked.

"I took care of it." Delilah waved the bottle at me. "Fill me in, Mr. Asshole."

"I see why Harold liked you. Your temperaments are similar." I downed my gin and slid it to her for a refill.

"Why are you looking for Harold? And how did you know he was here anyway?"

"Someone in Colorado said he might come looking for you," I said.

"That lesbo bitch Alex? Knew I shouldn't have talked with her," Delilah said.

"Who's Alex?" Theresa asked.

Delilah ignored her.

"Still doesn't explain why you're looking for him," she said.

"Benno asked me to find him," I said.

"All the way from Mexico? What's this Benno guy so pissed about?"

"He's not pissed. Or not yet. He's trying to find out what happened to his nephew," I said.

"Oh, I met that twerp. Someone finally kick his ass?"

"Put a bullet in him."

Delilah held up a finger like she was about to fire back a response, but then stopped. She swirled the gin in her glass.

"Benno thinks Harold did it. So you're up here to take care of Harold."

"I don't do what Harold does," I said.

She flicked a finger at her glass, hard enough to almost crack it.

"Good thing. He would have put you down like a—"

Delilah stopped, something went across her face, her eyes flitted. Theresa must have seen it, too.

"Where's Harold?"

"He was here yesterday, too. I came back. Just to see."

"To see what?" Theresa asked.

"It doesn't matter."

Delilah grabbed her drink, got up from the table, and started pacing in the kitchen. She went over to the living room. She banged the wall with her fist, looked around like she wanted to punch something else, maybe me. She swept her hand over a stack of arty magazines perched on a side table, sending them flying.

"Damien's a helluva housekeeper. He's not gonna like that," I said.

She pitched her gin glass across the room, shattering it against the wall.

"Did Damien do something to Harold?" Theresa asked.

Delilah stared at the wall. Nobody said anything. If there were crickets they were afraid to chirp.

"Dammit. It's her. She's the reason Damien sent Macintosh after me. Had to be," Delilah said.

"What? You told me she was getting account numbers for you."

"She was going soft. I saw it. I had to cut her loose. It wasn't going to work."

"Who are we talking about?" I asked.

"Name's Reyna," Theresa said.

"You're gonna make it so I have to shoot this guy?"

"He already knows about Stiltson. Fischer's a nobody. Who cares who he knows? We need to leave, Delilah."

"I'm having a hard time keeping up. Who's Reyna?" I asked.

Delilah came back into the kitchen, grabbed another glass, and poured another two fingers of gin.

"OK, look, Fishman. You wandered into something that you need to wander right out of. I brought your car back, so now you can just fuck off." She reached in her pocket and threw my keys on the table.

"Things were just getting interesting. Who is this third mystery figure?"

Delilah pointed a finger at Theresa.

"I say we kill him. You got an opinion?"

"Luke, drive back to where you came from. I doubt you're going to find Harold."

"Not breathing anyway," Delilah said.

"What?" Theresa asked.

"Shit, shit, shit." She put her Ray-Bans back on.

"I've got the airfield set up. If we go there now, it's done." Theresa said.

"For Christ's sake. You want to draw Fishhead a map?"

Seeing Delilah's anger seethe under the surface again made me think of her and Harold. I'd seen him do the same thing, usually before he put a bullet in someone.

"We need to call Reyna. We owe it to her," Theresa said.

"We don't owe her shit," Delilah said.

I picked up the keys to the LeMans.

"I'll let the two of you figure this out."

"You sit the fuck back down." Delilah slammed the table with her palm. "OK. This is what's going happen. Does that broken-ass truck of yours drive?"

"Of course it does," Theresa said.

"You stay here." She pointed at me. "I'd ask you to wait an hour, but I know you won't. Then you can drive wherever the fuck you want—I suggest going back to Mexico. Forget us. Forget it all. Forget Harold."

"Like you did?" I asked.

"Against my better judgment I'm not going to shoot you. Damien wouldn't make that choice. If you go looking for him, it won't go well."

"We're buddies," I said. "Had a sleepover at his farm."

"You trying to change my mind?" she said.

"Can I have my gun back?"

"Are you for real?"

She finished her gin, slammed it on the table.

"Let's go."

Theresa and Delilah left me sitting in the stylish kitchen by myself. The gin bottle was still a quarter full, but I really didn't like the stuff. It always tasted a bit like the perfume counter at one of those big department stores. I grabbed a 7-Up out of the fridge.

Sucking on a cold soda, I surveyed my situation.

Harold, like me, had wandered into a program already in progress. The question was whether I stuck around to see how it ended. And now there was a third someone. I couldn't piece together the part this Reyna played, or why Delilah had cut her out of the deal she was working with Theresa.

I'd come to believe that Harold had nothing to do with Benno's dead nephew—though, I started to wonder if Delilah did. She said she met him. The bubbles from the 7-Up weren't bringing me much clarity.

My buddy the weed farmer was pulling a lot of strings. Stiltson's name kept popping up. Money was getting shifted around, and that's always bound to piss people off. But who was working for who? This thing had more twists and turns than a Tilt-a-Whirl ride at the Marvelle Fair. If I kept poking at it I'd find out if it was Colonel Mustard with the lead pipe... or I'd end up with a bullet in my noggin, and thrown into a Fischer-shaped hole.

I needed a beer.

I didn't like carrying a gun, but dammit, now I really wanted one. I was getting kind of used to having that 9mm next to my body for comfort.

I searched the kitchen, hoping Damien had a backup piece stashed somewhere. I went through all the cupboards, but came up empty. Nothing in the living room, and nothing in the bedrooms. It was unlikely he'd keep guns in the basement. How are you gonna get a drop on the bad guys from there? Though, I now realized that Damien was the head bad guy.

I was out of options.

The rotting smell was stronger than the first time I'd opened the door to the basement. I hit a switch on the wall, and a thought flashed in my head a second before I made out the bodies.

They were laid out like someone tossed them in there. The only piece of furniture was a chair laying on its side. I knew before taking a closer look that neither of them were Harold. They were nowhere near his size. The relief I felt inside surprised me. In the corner was a plaid deerstalker hat. It must have belonged to one of the dead guys.

I carefully rolled over the one face down. In his hand was a gun. Damned if it wasn't a Browning Hi-Power. Back in what felt like a hundred years ago, Franko had given me his.

I left the dead guys in the basement and headed back to the kitchen. I needed to think, and bubbly sugar water wasn't gonna cut it. I got the gin and decided to forego the glass, swigging right from the bottle.

So which one of the guys in the basement was Macintosh? I knew what Delilah meant by taking care of him. I went through their pockets and yanked out some ID. Neither of them were named Macintosh, first or last. Though, I'd learned a lot of thugs didn't use their real name—like Mostly Harold.

Damn, Harold. Where are you at? Benno had sent me to find him, or to unravel whatever the hell happened in Colorado. So far I'd learned just shy of nothing. Benno couldn't have known about whatever Delilah and Damien were involved in—he wouldn't even know about Delilah. Or would he? My benefactor seemed to have a way of finding things out.

I took another belt of gin. Delilah was right, I wasn't going to wait an hour. It didn't matter how long I waited here. I had no intention in going after her and Theresa.

I pictured a road with three forks. One led to Harold—if he was in fact still breathing. After witnessing Delilah's reactions, I had my doubts. Another fork led to Damien. The prospect of getting deeper into a situation where people ended up laid out in a basement had lost its appeal. If it ever had one.

The third fork had been poking at me since I drove past the sign on the highway. I'd tried to ignore it, but it kept jabbing at me. I grabbed the keys and went out to the LeMans. The tank was still half-full. Driving out of the yard, I heard something go thump in the trunk. Damn. So that's why she left me the car.

CHAPTER TWENTY-NINE

Dragging the very dead Macintosh out of the LeMans trunk, and putting him in the basement with his dead friends, sealed it for me. I was done. I would tell Benno I found Harold. I'd say he had nothing to do with his nephew, and that I didn't know who did. Maybe Benno would accept it. I didn't care if he did. I was out.

The sign said Marvelle was a hundred and fifty miles from Stillwater. That was fine with me. It allowed me time to do the thing I do best: think in a car.

The LeMans cruised the recently worked-on highway. There was nothing like a long stretch of super-smooth road to make me feel like I was floating, or riding a wave on a surfboard. It was an odd image for a guy who had never been on a board in his life. I'd admired the young bucks with zero body fat who rode the crests in Bar Navidad. My wave was made of asphalt, but it cleared my head as much as a Mexican bay filled with corduroy.

I pushed away Harold. I pushed away the two women who threatened to shoot and bury me on the lone prairie. Memories flooded in, and I let them. I'd driven this road, and others just as flat, many times over the years. The lush fields swayed along with the music that drifted out of the car radio. I drove past long rectangles of green, yellow, tan, and then a gorgeous square of blue from a flax field.

If I had stayed here, what would I have become? Farming was

damn unlikely. The jobs that paid above minimum were hard labor, like working for the railway, or putting in long shifts at the wire factory. White-collar around here looked like insurance agencies or real estate. All the towns had bankers, who made money wherever they lived in the world. There was a different kind of banking going on with whatever Delilah, Theresa, and Damien were involved in. In their world, money changed hands like the ultimate shell game and was just as crooked. Come to think of it, what they did was not much different than regular banking.

After leaving the prairies and ending up in Montreal, I'd considered becoming a boxer—not just a sparring partner, but strap on the gloves, climb in the ring and see if I could win a bout or two. I told the gym owner, Hank Harken, that I wasn't interested in becoming one of his hopefuls. It was a lie, as I'd thought the thought.

Hank was full of wisdom gained by watching grown men in shorts knock the hell out of each other.

"There's three people in the ring, Fischer," he told me after I'd knocked another of his boxers out in a sparring practice.

"Yeah, me, the other guy, and the ref," I said.

"Not talking about the ref. The third one is time. And it ain't on your side."

Hank went into a long monologue about the ritual of the ringing bell and the clock ticking down.

"Every second you're in the ring, more of you is getting sucked out." Hank took a deep drag on his Cuban. "It either drains out on the floor in sweat and blood, or it disappears into the other guy."

"Disappears? I don't—"

"Shut up, Fischer. Listen for once. You ever hear of that Einstein guy? He figured it out."

"Didn't think he was a boxer."

"Energy, it don't go nowhere. It gets turned into mass. That formula he came up with applies to boxing, too. Take two humans, strip 'em down naked, so only their souls and will are left. Their energy has to go somewheres. They drive it into their opponent and it becomes part of them. At the same time, they both lose something."

"What?"

Hank stared up at the cracked ceiling in the Montreal gym like he was looking for answer.

"There was a fight once, not sure you ever heard of it, a Latino named Pinto pounded an Irishman into mush. Killed the guy right in front of an auditorium full of lookie-loos, all who'd paid to watch the blood get spilled. And there is blood. Greb hammered Tunney, they say, until two quarts of it spilled on the canvas. It happens, Fischer. More than people like to talk about. The deep right hook that drives a bone into the brain. They don't call the ambulance, they're calling the mortuary."

"But the refs are supposed to stop them."

"That's right, Fischer: supposed to. There was a ref named Goldstein, back in sixty-two, should have stopped the fight. But he just hung on the ropes. Frozen. Lost in it, watching someone die. He didn't know it then. It's about time, Fischer. We're all in the middle of it, we just don't hear the clock. But the fighters, the best ones, they hear it. They live their lives in three-minute stretches. And damned if it doesn't make them aware of it all."

After that Hank sunk into a silence. This gym philosopher knew I'd never be one of his boxers. He wanted to tell me something deeper. Hank often talked about the three-minute hero. He'd seen it happen. A fighter way behind in points, no chance in hell of winning the fight, came out of his corner with a look in his eye. To use Hank's philosophy, the boxer heard that clock in his head. It wasn't ticking, it was booming. Time was being sucked from him. Then, in the scant minutes left before he was totally destroyed, he found a hidden source of strength. Maybe it was desperation. All the pain his opponent had inflicted faded way. Pain didn't mean the same thing to boxers as to regular humans. Then, in a moment of beauty, poetry, and Einsteinian physics, he lets a punch loose into the universe that connects. One of those sciencey cameras would show how the guy's face bent around the punch, and the hero's glove went deeper and deeper until it tapped on the opponent's brain cage. Then all went dark.

I never got a chance to be that sort of hero, I was only a sparring partner. I saw a young boxer do it once. He looked completely spent, depleted of every ounce of energy—they'd invented the phrase throw in the towel just for him. But then, from some hidden place he summoned and launched a punch that no one thought he had. He KO'ed his opponent so fast the crowd thought they'd missed something. It was glorious to watch.

Next week, I laid out the kid in a sparring match at Hank's gym. It was time to go. The owners of the gym couldn't agree more, as they told me I either needed to train as one of their regular hopefuls or hit the road. I couldn't keep laying out their kids, it was bad for their self-esteem.

The hours had slid by as I thought about boxing, Montreal, and all the days before that. A large swath of black birds wiped the sky, fat cows munched away in a landscape dotted with barns, usually deep farm red, and tidy houses tucked against rows of planted trees. A sign came up telling me that my destination was ten miles away. I remembered a lone gas station outside of town, and it soon appeared on the horizon like a desert mirage. I pulled in, filled up the LeMans, and asked to see a phone book.

"Cost you five bucks to make a call. And it's gotta be local."

"What's local around here?" I asked the jockey.

"Marvelle. Grassdale. That's it."

He was the age of a college kid, but his stained hands told me he worked on oil changes and transmissions more than textbooks.

"You used to have a pay phone," I said.

"Not since I've worked here."

I flipped through the Marvelle pages, scanning the names.

"I'm just looking for an address."

"What's the name? I probably know them."

I was about to answer when I saw the one I was looking for. There were two names, no first initial. Even as I scribbled it down on a piece of paper, I knew it was a stretch that she still lived there.

CHAPTER THIRTY

Harold cruised the highway in the stolen Ford Mustang, which turned out to have a decent engine, and a cassette of the best of his boy, Burt. Bacharach's music helped him think, it always had. What the world needed now was love… well, he wasn't so sure about that. What his world needed was to figure out what the fuck had just happened to him—and why he'd driven two thousand miles to find a woman who didn't give a shit about him. Maybe she did. But there were things that were more important to her now. She was working with that shaggy-haired goof, who had to be in charge of things.

The song changed to singing about never falling in love again.

"That's for damn sure," he said to Burt.

Something Harold had learned from all the tracking he'd done over the years was that when you're stuck, go back to the beginning. He read the green sign with three town names and how far it was to each. He followed the arrow south, already picturing the bar where he killed the guy in tweed. If he recognized anyone in there, he was going to take them to the parking lot and rap their heads against the pavement until they spit out answers.

It wasn't much of a plan. But the simplest ideas were often the best. Burt's strings were really going now, and he cranked the sound. Bacharach's music put him back in Colorado, on his deck, looking at the mountains and those puffy clouds. He'd have a Bud in one hand, a Louis L'Amour in the other, or maybe no book—

just sitting and watching the sun go down and the colors change. Harold was no arty-farty, but he loved a good sunset.

The town limits came up for Hamel, and Harold slowed the Mustang. There was a chance he'd run into some goons from the party he just left. They might be surprised to see him still breathing. Or he could run into those asshats from the dealership. He might have to drive over to that other town and chat with that tub of lard that ran away. If none of them were in the bar, he'd ask the bartender some questions. They always knew what was going on.

Turned out that Harold didn't have to worry about a backup plan. Entering the bar, he saw the dealership guy at a table with Suspenders Guy, the one who had tied him to a chair in that room he broke out of. Kuz spied him first and jumped up, quickly reaching for something in his jacket. Harold held out his hand, gesturing for him to sit the fuck down. Kuz took a fast look at Stiltson, who had his back to Harold. Stiltson growled something, then without looking back, slid out the chair next to him. Harold joined them at the table.

"Thought you'd be dead by now," Stiltson said.

"Thought you'd be thinner," Harold said.

"That doesn't make any sense," he said.

"Did you find her? Or the one she's working with—that weed-dealing hippie?" Kuz asked.

"Settle down," Stiltson said. "Let's have a drink together and have a conversation."

"I should have put a bullet in both of you. More than one bullet," Harold said.

"We all regret lost opportunities," Stiltson said.

A girl came over to take their order, the same one he'd first talked to when he arrived in Hamel.

"Oh," she said.

She took a fast look back at the bartender.

"If I see him dialing the cops, I'll shoot him first. Then you,"

Harold said.

"Laura, tell Charles to keep it quiet. And bring us a round of Glenlivets. Scotch all right with you?" Stiltson asked.

"I'll take a Bud," Harold said.

"We don't have American beer," she said.

"Bring us a couple of the scotches, and a Pilsner for our large friend. We'll convert him to Canadian beer."

"Beaver piss," Harold said.

The girl went back to the bar. Harold watched the bartender, making sure he didn't pull out a phone from below the bar or try to make a quick exit.

"I don't plan on being here long. Let's cut to it," Harold said.

"You'd shoot someone in broad daylight?" Kuz asked.

"Right after I put one in you."

"Oh yeah. How come you didn't do it before? And you stole my gun, asshole."

"It came in handy. Thanks. But I had to give it up."

"You have another gun, I'm assuming," Stiltson said.

"Yeah, and it'll blow off your nutsack unless you start talking."

Harold made out Stiltson's Adam's apple bobbing under a layer of fat. The girl brought the scotches and beer. Harold took another look at the bartender, who was reading a magazine spread out on the counter.

"You haven't found her," Kuz said.

"Spill it, fat man. You're the one who knows the game plan."

Stiltson's eyes flitted to Kuz and back, a shake in his hand as he sipped his whiskey.

"What's to say? She screwed us," he said.

"Who's us?"

"There's a group of us who own certain things, let's call them investments. We were looking for someone to help us move them into other opportunities."

"You needed someone to launder dirty money," Harold said.

"A crude way to put it. But sure."

"Drugs, guns, what?" Harold asked.

"Does it matter?"

"Hang on."

Harold left the table and went over to the bartender, who had left his magazine and had a phone in his hand. Harold pushed his finger down on the cradle.

"You ever try to swallow one of these?" Harold grabbed the handset out of the bartender's hand.

Harold took the rest of the phone and yanked the cord out of the wall. He handed the phone to the bartender and went back to Stiltson's table.

"I doubt he was calling the Mounties," Stiltson said. "Laura would have told him not to."

Harold took a long swig of beer. It wasn't half bad, not a Budweiser, but it was drinkable.

"So Delilah screwed you. Took your money and headed out for parts unknown. It was dumb to give it to her in the first place."

"We didn't give it to her all at once. She delivered on a couple of things, moved some money stateside. We even picked up some profit in the exchange. She's very good at what she does."

"Where in the States?"

"Southwest. She bought and sold some properties in New Mexico, and I think, Colorado."

"Why do you care?" Kuz asked. "You got a deal with her?"

Harold ignored the question, still wanting to wrap those suspenders around Kuz's head.

"What about the other guy?" Harold asked.

"Ah. You met Michaelson."

"Said his name was Damien."

"He goes by Damien Price in some circles," Stiltson said.

"What kind of circles?"

Kuz gave a fast nod. Stiltson grinned.

"Ask him yourself."

Harold pushed his chair back and spun around. Damien came through the front door followed by a pair of goons, all striding fast and hard. Harold grabbed Stiltson and pivoted him, chair and all. He took out his Glock and jammed it where he thought Stiltson's ribs might be.

The whole place erupted into a funky dance. The bartender rushed over, carrying a bat. The goons on either side of Damien pulled out pieces and Kuz pulled a knife the size of a crosscut saw. Lucky the asshat didn't cut off his nuts getting it out.

Harold took Kuz down first—one right between the suspenders. Enough of that shit. Someone screamed. He put the gun back against Stiltson. Half a dozen folks ran out the bar doors. The bartender was at the table now, bat arched, ready to swing.

"Put it down, Babe Ruth," Harold said.

"Thought you'd be dead already," Damien said.

"Yeah, I get a lot of that."

Damien pointed to the few people who'd remained in the bar and then pointed to the door. If they were too scared to move before, they took off like rabbits now.

"Seems we've been here before. You're not big on odds, are you?"

"Go easy," Stiltson said.

Kuz was laid out on the floor. His knife clattered a few feet away.

"Charles, we're going to be done here in a minute. Call an ambulance," Damien said.

"Phone doesn't work," he said.

Harold stood and pulled Stiltson to his feet. Using the fat car salesman as a shield, he walking backward to the door behind the bar. The goons tried to get a bead on him.

"Tell them to stand down or they'll join Suspenders on the floor," Harold said.

"Aren't those the stupidest things? Who still wears those?" Damien asked.

"You too, slugger."

The bartender shifted his feet.

"Put it down, Charles," Damien said. "This has all got a bit too intense, my man. Let's all ease down, we don't need more violence."

"We'll do a group hug later." Harold was by the doorway behind the bar now.

"Before you go..." Damien started. "You want to tell me what your deal was with her?"

"Who?"

"Delilah told me she got to know you down in Colorado. Something in her voice, not sure, almost seemed like she really liked you. What happened down there?"

"Still trying to figure that out," Harold said.

He pushed Stilton forward, who tumbled to the floor like a bag of grapefruit. Harold spun through the door. He waited for the shots from Damien's goons, but they never came. An old skinny guy with an apron stood over a sink of dishes. His mouth hung open. He lifted a sudsy hand and pointed to the door that Harold was already headed for.

That was it. He'd had enough. Harold made a quick plan: run until he found a car with a driver, flag them down, rap them one, take their car and drive right the fuck back to the Springs. He didn't care what Delilah was doing. Whatever he thought was between them was done—if it ever was anything. He was putting some miles between Damien, Stiltson, and the whole damn party patrol. He would never set foot in this bullshit excuse for a country again.

All of this rifled through Harold's head in the seconds he cranked open the back door and stepped outside. A group of six men—all thick, half in plaid, half in suits—formed a ring in front of them. Each of them pointed a gun at Harold.

CHAPTER THIRTY-ONE

The road into town was a lot rougher than the highway. It was that way when I lived here, so I guess the town council never did get around to repaving it. I drove to the first address I'd written down, passing the street where we used to live. I parked outside a squat apartment building with six suites. I buzzed and waited.

"Yes?"

"I'm looking for a Miss Hubert."

"That's me. What do you want?"

The speaker garbled the voice and I couldn't be sure.

"Delivery."

I didn't say what kind. And there was a long pause.

"Hang on. I've gotta get dressed."

Through the thick glass, I saw the jeans and sneakers come down the carpeted stairs. When the rest of her followed—a woman maybe in her thirties, sandy hair tied back—my body let go of the tension I'd been holding. She opened the door and extended her hand. The woman looked like she just woke up.

"Where is it?"

Noticing that I was carrying nothing, she took a fast step backward and started to close the door.

"Sorry. I left it in the car. It was too big to carry. Wanted to make sure I had the right address."

She eyed me.

"And do you?"

"No, I guess not. Or were you expecting something from Texas?"

"I don't know anyone from there." She rubbed her eyes and yawned.

"I saw there was another Hubert in the phone book," I said.

"No relation. Doesn't the package have the address?"

"Sorry. That's the weird thing. Just the last name and Marvelle. Postmark says it came from Texas."

Before she could challenge me on why a delivery person was driving a LeMans and not wearing anything like a uniform, I gave her a wave, said sorry again, and walked quickly back to my car. I hoped she was too sleepy to phone the cops.

The other address was across town, which I could drive in seven minutes. It was a square, wartime build, with a neat yard, some healthy-looking shrubs and a row of tall daisies brushed up against the house. My mom always said strangers ring the bell and friends knock. I gave three quick raps on the door. As I tried to put another story in my head, one better than the delivery one, she opened the door. It took a second before her eyes widened.

"Holy shit."

"Nice place," I said. "Kind of surprised to still find you here."

Her whole body stiffened and she flinched like someone threw a fastball at her head.

"What the hell do you want, Luke?"

"I'm not sure. Can I come in?"

The next ten seconds stretched into a week-long silence. I was about to pivot and go back to my car when she said, "OK."

Her place was simple, neat, very little of the usual clutter you see when you drop in on someone. She sat in wide wicker chair with a striped cushion. I took the overstuffed chair across from her. It had the Queen Anne legs that she always liked, wide enough for two people to sit.

"How've you been?" I asked.

"Cut the bullshit. Tell me where."

"Mexico. Last thing you told me was to get it figured out."

"Did you?"

"Working on it, Marguerite."

I just wanted to say her name. It hung in the air. She crossed her arms. There was the smallest of quaver in her chin.

"I want to smack you right in the head."

"You always were a good smacker," I said.

Not a smile, but a release of tension, her shoulders dropped.

"Fine." She looked past me, through a window to the street. "Why are you back? If it's to—"

"It's not."

I wanted to go to her, hold her close to feel her skin against me, inhale her scent. Chances are she'd knee me right in the balls.

"So you had some vacation time and decided to spend it in Marvelle? Why Mexico?"

"It's where I ended up."

"Maybe you should have stayed there."

"I've had some rough years, Marguerite. But I'm not here to try some sort of restart. The man I work for sent me to look for a guy."

"What do you mean look for a guy? Are you some sort of…" She trailed off without finishing.

"I find people. I know that sounds weird, but it's the work I do."

"They pay you for this? Or this man does?"

"I'm good at it. My stubbornness finally has a purpose."

"This guy you're looking for is in Marvelle?"

"No. Pretty sure not."

"You're keeping something from me. He's dangerous?"

"I've seen him shoot people and walk away like he just stepped on a bug."

"Quelle horreur."

Her face blanched, but then almost immediately softened. She was open to me now, the corner of her eyes were wet. She gave a look that always broke me in half.

"Have you eaten? You look rough, Luke."

"I could eat."

I followed her into her neat kitchen. It was soft gray surfaces and a few brushed-metal appliances.

"Is that a German toaster?" I asked, recognizing the brand. "Not the sort of stuff we could afford when we had our place."

"I like well-made things," she said.

Marguerite made us simple omelettes, one at a time. She snipped spring onions and grated hard cheese over them. We had bread she told me she'd baked, toasted in that well-made toaster, and served with a raspberry preserve she'd also made. I forced myself to eat slowly, savoring the taste. My body reminded me I hadn't eaten anything decent in what seemed like weeks.

As we ate we talked about the things we'd been doing, the people we'd run across. It started out as small talk, just trying to fill the space without talking about the past. She had been taking some classes by correspondence and had a good gig with a lawyer in town.

"I missed you," I said in the middle of her story about the work she was doing.

She gave me a long look, searching for something in my face.

"You could have killed him."

"But I didn't," I said.

"He could have killed you."

I thought back to Scarecrow Norman, wondering again about why he never pulled the gun on me. We were both visiting that time in our minds, like a movie shot from two different angles, each of us creating a different story. So who held the true one?

"I'm really tired, Marguerite."

"There's a small room with a cot. I use it as my office."

"Would it be OK?"

"Yes. I'll get another blanket. It is supposed to be cool tonight."

We said our polite goodnights, like we were strangers in a bed-and-breakfast. A deep fatigue came on me as I lay in the narrow but really comfortable, bed. I was tired from the great meal she'd given me, tired from the road, tired of dragging bodies from trunks, but mostly tired from the sadness that had welled up within. Marguerite was the past that I'd run from. I didn't kill Scarecrow Norman, but I could have. Before I left, Norman got out of the hospital, and I'd heard he was eating solid food again. If I'd stayed in Marvelle, there'd be other Normans. I might have killed one of them.

There was a part of me that wanted to look up Norman and see if he was still kicking and if he'd stopped being an asshole. I guess I'd have to apologize for almost killing him. Maybe we'd have a beer together. Or maybe I'd punch him in the head.

That river, hell, that ocean of violence still lived inside me. The last few years, I'd buried it deeper. Any good therapist would tell me I was denying the very thing I needed to work on—how I should embrace my shadow or something Jungian like that. What the shrinks should realize is that me and my shadow do hang out, usually after a table full of Pacificos, and a Mexican moon shining through the El Rayo Verde's glassless window.

I tried to imagine the smell of the Pacific and bring it into that small room in Marvelle. I drifted off with an image of a pelican dragging its briny catch across the white sand.

I was awakened by footsteps in the hall. She came in the room, laid next to me, and buried her face into my shoulder. Her soft body pressed into me, I felt her chest rise and fall, her tears were wet against my skin.

"I thought you were dead," she said.

"Why?"

"I dreamed it."

She pulled back, eyes reddened, cheeks wet, and kissed me deeply. A prairie moon shone in the window, cooler than the one over the Pacific I'd been imagining but casting a bright light on our barely dressed bodies. She ran her fingers over my scars, stopping on the one that almost ended my life. She studied my face, wordlessly probing for answers. Tiny goosebumps raised on her skin as I undressed her and explored her body. My desire wanted me to move quickly. I again forced myself to slow down. I wanted to experience every moment so that I could call it all back to memory in the lonely nights ahead of me. We made love like we were both strangers and the best of friends. At my climax, I felt close to tears. I relented and let it happen.

"Luke."

We held each other in her small bedroom, breathing together, until she lay back on the bed. We both had a choice on how to fill the silence. We could go back to our time together, talk about the things that pushed us apart, all which led to my leaving Marvelle. I had no intention of ever returning. The other choice was to think of the *what now*? Or we could say nothing. We made the same choice.

Marguerite left the room and padded to the kitchen. I heard her run the sink and soon a kettle started to hiss. I joined her as she poured hot water into two cups.

"Chamomile. I don't do caffeine anymore."

"Works for me."

The smell of the tea reminded me of the fields I'd passed, the blue flax and the bright yellow canola. We finished the tea without any more words and went to our separate bedrooms.

I met her in the kitchen early the next morning. She wore a pastel blue robe with birds on it.

"More tea?" She had a steaming cup in front of her.

"You don't have any coffee?"

"Gave it up shortly after you left. I gave up a lot of things."

"Marguerite, I—"

She cut me off. "You going to keep looking or go home?"

I ignored the twinge in my chest when she said *home*.

"Not sure."

"Yes you are," she said. "You can't let something be. I know you."

The floral scent from her tea drifted across to me.

"Maybe I've changed."

"Have you?"

I laughed. She wasn't smiling.

"There's no telling where Harold is now. Or if he's still alive," I said. "Or if he's even the one I should go after."

"That's a funny name. Tell me about Harold," she said.

We sat in our places again, she in the wicker and me in the Queen Anne. I told her more about Harold, and how he'd almost killed me before. I told her what I'd learned in Colorado, and since. I told her about Theresa and her sunglasses-wearing sister with an anger management problem.

"They are sisters?"

"I think so," I said.

As I spilled out the story, I realized that I didn't know much. I'd wandered into a web of corruption, bad guys with guns, and likely suitcases of money. There was always a suitcase of money somewhere.

"There are drugs?" she asked.

"A guy named Damien is a weed grower—but I think more than that. Delilah has pulled some sort of double-cross on him."

"She's the one in sunglasses… the one with Harold?"

"Yeah, but I don't think she's really with him. Harold came up here looking for her. But he found himself in the middle of the same thing I did."

Marguerite didn't say anything for a while. It was bright outside, a fine June day, one where some couples would go for a long walk in the sunshine. They'd hold hands and feed the birds.

"You still haven't told me why you are here."

"The guy I work for, Benno. He's the one that wants me to find Harold. He wants to know what happened to his nephew, and if Harold is connected."

"You already told me Harold's not in Marvelle," she said, turning from the window to look at me. "Why are you here, Luke?"

There were a couple of faint lines on her face, the start of laugh lines or wrinkles. When they emerged they'd only make her more beautiful.

"You don't need to answer. I'll tell you what I see. You're lost." She leaned back in her chair, widening the space between us. "You were lost before, and that's why you left. I don't know what I hoped for you. It hurt like hell when you were gone, but it may have hurt more if you had stayed."

"I understand."

"No, I don't think you do. You've come up in my mind a lot less lately. I hadn't even thought about you for months. Until you showed up at my door like you're delivering the mail."

"I was in the neighborhood," I said.

"You don't always need to be a smartass, Luke. And whatever your life is down in Mexico, it isn't home."

"It's home enough," I said.

"I think you need to leave now."

"OK."

"I don't mean leave for Mexico. Luke, go find this guy. Put it all together."

I finished the dregs of my tea, then stood to leave. She came to me, wrapping her arms around me.

"It was really good to see you," I said.

"If you get killed doing this I don't want to know about it."

Driving away from Marvelle I promised myself that I'd honor her request.

CHAPTER THIRTY-TWO

As usual, Marguerite called me on my bullshit. I wanted to go back to Mexico, to escape to my pretend home, forget this whole rambling circus of violence and disappear into long afternoons in the El Rayo Verde. What I needed was a bucket of Pacificos, Jimmy's Cholula-soaked peanuts, and a perch to watch the pelicans dive into the bay under a flame-orange sunset.

I didn't want to be here anymore.

Was I lost? I'd put together a decent life down in PV I didn't have to think much about anything— except for what Benno wanted me to do. If I went back without answers about his nephew, he'd understand. Wouldn't he?

Marguerite knew that unfinished things ate away at me. *Put it together*, she'd said.

Damn.

"Can I use your phone?"

The gas jockey was reading the sporting news. He had it open to a spread of baseball players in green uniforms brighter than the grass they stood on.

"Local calls are still five bucks," he said.

"How about not so local?"

"Where?"

"Mexico."

He flipped a page, more players, most of them in beards or bushy mustaches.

"No way. Wouldn't even know what to charge you for that."

"I'll make it collect," I said.

"Nuh-uh. I'll get in trouble."

I plucked a chocolate bar off the rack, unwrapped it, and chomped down.

"Two bucks," he said while flipping the page again.

"You like the A's?" I asked.

"They're cool. It's like a bunch of hippies play baseball, and they're really good at it. You like 'em, too?"

He looked up at me and the Browning Hi-Power pointed at his forehead.

"They got some good pitchers, but besides Reggie they can't hit for shit," I said.

"Th-there's like twenty bucks in the till. You can have it. And the candy bar, too."

"Just want to use the phone. You go back into that little room of yours and lock the door. When you hear me stop talking you can come out."

The gas jockey murmured something under his breath. I didn't want to scare the kid, but I didn't know where else I could make the call I needed to make.

Behind the closed door he called out.

"You better make it collect."

I dialed zero, gave the operator the number and waited. The person on the other line answered in Spanish. I was about to interrupt the operator when she smoothly responded in the same language.

"Aceptas los cargos?"

"De quien es eso?"

"Luke Fischer," I spoke over the operator.

"You'll need to let me do the speaking, sir," she said.

"Un momento."

I heard music in the background, a guitar strumming. I pictured the old guy in the straw hat and faded jeans who played most afternoons at Benno's place.

"Yes, I'll accept."

We waited as the operator disconnected. The guitar got louder, joined by another, and what sounded like brushes on a snare. Benno said something in Spanish and the music stopped.

"Mateo get himself a band?" I asked.

"Luke, my friend. Good to hear from you. But where are you?"

"Right where you thought I'd go, Benno."

"Hmm. Yes, I heard from my friends in Colorado that you were headed there. And have you found our mutual friend?"

"No. Not sure where the hell he is. But he's up here."

"How do you know?"

"Mostly Harold makes an impression."

"Very true. I've noted that as well."

"I don't think he had anything to do with what happened to your nephew."

"I believe you are right," Benno said.

"I'm not sure. But something might have happened to him."

A crackle on the line, and I thought I'd lost him.

"You still there?" I asked.

"That would be unfortunate if harm has come to Mr. Stevens," Benno paused. "I'd like you to look into something else while you're up there."

"Oh. OK."

"Do you need me to wire some funds?"

"That would help," I said. "I still want to find out what happened to Harold."

"That is fine. Arkin talked to some people who were present when Benito was killed."

"Where were these people before?"

"They were unsure they wanted to come forward. When Arkin found them, he convinced them to tell what they saw."

I was about to ask how he did that, but I didn't want to know. Another crackle and the line went dead. I hung up, got ahold of the operator again, a different one who didn't speak Spanish. After a few frustrating minutes, Benno was on the line again.

"Who was responsible for Benito?"

"There was a woman. She'd been seen around the bar."

"Did she wear stylish sunglasses?"

"This was not part of the description. She has long dark hair, an attractive face and figure. I believe she knew Harold. She knew him well."

"Right."

"Arkin learned that this woman was seen talking in a heated fashion with my nephew. They left the bar together, but on her return she was alone."

"So what's the connection?" I asked.

"This couple, a man and a woman, had seen her leave. When they walked out of the bar they found my nephew lying in the passageway between the buildings. Afraid of getting involved, they said nothing."

"That still doesn't say much about the woman, Benno. It could have been a coincidence."

"On further searching, Arkin came across a man who had dealings with this woman. He came to the bar asking for her."

"Her name?"

"Delilah. As in the old story, you know it?"

The gas jockey knocked on his door and called out.

"Hey. You better be done soon!"

"What kind of dealings, Benno?"

"The woman had been buying property. And then turning around and selling it quickly. Sometimes for the same price, which was odd. The man Arkin spoke with had recently purchased property from her. That's why he wanted to find her. He also knew my nephew."

"So this Delilah was collecting from your nephew and something went bad?"

"I hear the doubt in your voice, Luke. There is some uncertainty. I do know this woman traveled north. It is the most probable reason that Harold is there. Perhaps you could track her down for me? I'd like to ask her some questions."

"So would I."

"Ah, you are always a surprise, my friend. You've come across her already? And you know some of this story?"

A car pulled into the station and a large man got out. He waved at me, thinking I was going to pump gas for him.

"I've gotta run, Benno."

"You will put me in contact with the woman?"

"As soon as I find her again."

"Again. I see. Do you have an idea where to look?" Benno asked.

"I think so."

The man waved again, and then began walking toward the door.

"Where should I wire the money?"

"There's a post office in a place called Hamel. Send it there."

I put the phone down and strode past the man who'd just entered.

"Fill it up with regular," he said.

"Sorry. I don't work here."

"What? Well, who does?"

"I was wondering the same thing."

CHAPTER THIRTY-THREE

It was another hour and a half to Hamel. Nothing told me that Delilah and Theresa would be there. But I had a feeling. Theresa mentioned an airfield. If they were flying out of here, they wouldn't be at one of the big ones. There were a couple of farmers that had air strips for their dusting planes.

Benno sounded surprised that I'd came across Delilah. I wasn't. Paths have a way of intersecting. Of course, she was the reason Harold came up here. If she gave Harold the hard pass, and it looked like she did, then he could already be driving across Wyoming on his way to his place in the Springs. Or he might be still here… but no longer breathing, like she said.

Benno had given me a new task. But he didn't need to ask me to find her. I'd already made that decision when I'd left Marguerite's house. It was the fourth fork, or tine, or some kind of utensil. It didn't matter because I'd follow it if it was a goddamn pizza cutter.

I passed a dog, a shepherd, running in the ditch and barking.

"Guard your territory, buddy. Don't let anyone tell you different."

The farmyard and house behind the dog had seen better days. It was badly in need of a paint job and one of the windows was boarded up. I remembered a house like that one growing up in Marvelle. A family had lost a son in a farm accident, something that happened way too often around here. I remember seeing the dad coming into the lumberyard in Marvelle, maybe to buy wood to board up his windows. He had a vacant look in his eyes, going through the motions of a life he didn't want to have.

Driving into the Hamel limits, the dog's barking echoed in my mind. I drove down the main drag, past the King's, keeping an eye out for Theresa's truck, or any other vehicle I might recognize. I'd shot up Puffy Jacket Larry's Pontiac, but maybe Johnson got himself patched up and drove his Ford sedan here.

Nothing looked familiar in the King's lot. I decided to drive out to Damien's place. If his place was crawling with goons, I'd go in blasting. It was a dumbass plan. One of my dumber ones. Like the dog barking in a ditch thinking he might catch the car, it wouldn't achieve much.

Damien's house came up on the horizon. The yard looked empty. Still, I didn't want to announce my arrival, so I drove on past. A mile up the road there was a crossways. I turned onto the northern road and dipped the LeMans into the shallow ditch. There was a straggly group of trees and a line of bush between me and Damien's place. It was enough to obscure the car. I walked back and kept low.

No cars or plumes of dust appeared on the gravel road. Reaching Damien's yard, there were still no signs of life. I made out tire tracks in the dirt, but no telling when they were last here. I was no Kit Carson, able to track folks based on broken twigs and turned-over rocks. I took out my gun and went up the porch stairs. I gave the door a rap. Nothing. Then I banged on it and waited. I listened for movement— still nothing. I twisted the knob, then backed up and gave a hard kick. It took a few boots before I split the wood.

No one was sitting on Damien's fancy furniture. Everything was neat as a pin and not a magazine out of place. There was a half-full bottle of 7-Up on the kitchen counter. It was warm.

I roamed around the place, confirming that I was alone. I discovered one surviving beer in the fridge, popped the cap, and plunked down on the couch in the living room. I checked the magazine in the Browning. Thirteen rounds. Full.

It made Columbo-sense that even if no one was at the King's

someone would head back to Damien's house. When in doubt, go back to the beginning for that one more thing. But TV detectives aside, the question was, who was going to show up first? Theresa and Delilah were heading for an airfield. If Damien showed up with a clown car full of goons... well, I wasn't sure what I'd do with that.

I stopped mulling over my non-plan and went to Damien's impressive record collection. He had some vintage rock and blues, a lot of jazz, country including about ten Johnny Cash albums, and some newer stuff. I plucked out one with a black-and-white checkered cover. It was the ska that Damien asked if I liked—a band called The Selecter. I'd never heard of them. I put it on the turntable and cranked the volume.

I pictured young people bopping their heads to the beat. The music had an edge of violence, stirring up aural memories that took me back to the gym in Montreal. My feet shuffling around the ring, my opponent dancing, like this bopping music was in both our heads. Come in close, take a jab, bounce back, watch for an opening. Bop-bop-bop. Then it came, the hard right hook, the sweeping uppercut, and the guy timbered. It was a good feeling.

Tires spun on gravel. I almost didn't hear them over the music. I turned up the volume and scooted to the kitchen window. A long black sedan barreled up the drive. It wasn't Johnson's Ford. And Larry hadn't gotten his Pontiac running.

I ran to the bathroom, threw the rug off, searching for the button I'd seen Damien press. Car doors slammed. Still looking. Shit. Footsteps clomped up the stairs. Got it. I went down the stairs as quickly and quietly as I could, pulling the door down with me until I heard a soft click.

The thick aroma of pot plants filled the basement. I moved down and in behind the thickest row of them, crouching low and peering through the patterns of foliage. The ska beats softly pumped, the floor creaked above me. Feet scraped as they searched the main floor. The music told them someone was here, or had been. If Damien was with them I was fucked anyway.

Footsteps sounded in the bathroom. Someone walked right onto the hidden door. I took a bead on the stairs coming down from the hatch. The rug was out of place, there was no way to do it otherwise. But I knew the seal was perfect and the tiled pattern further hid the seam. Damien was right: if you didn't know the hatch was there, you wouldn't find it. I pictured the goons scratching their heads.

The music stopped abruptly. Voices murmured. Damien's thick floor and insulation made it impossible to fully hear what they were saying. There was more banging, moving of furniture, glass breaking. They were getting pissed. Another voice was distorted by an electric hum, a click, and what sounded like static. It could have been a radio or walkie-talkie-type thing. I didn't think it was the sort of thing Damien's guys would have. Who the hell was this group?

The footsteps left the bathroom. They creaked across the floor, and then the sound of ripping wood. They must have put the door I kicked out of its misery.

I went to the box Damien had shown me, slid open the panel, and peered into the peephole. There were two of them, both wore thick belts. One had a radio clipped to it—hard to say if they were unmarked RCMP. They both wore black lace-up boots and matching black jackets. Damien had said the Mounties questioned him about the King's shooting. This pair obviously didn't know about his basement farm.

I followed the plumes of dust down the road. The peripheral vision of the peephole was limited, so I couldn't see if they turned toward where I'd left the LeMans. If they found the car, would they come back? Benno's Texas plates were bound to arouse some suspicion.

I waited in the basement for almost an hour, listening for movements and checking the peep hole. When I was finally sure they weren't coming back, I went upstairs. On the porch, I squinted in the direction of the LeMans. Like I thought, the bush and trees had obscured it.

It was almost four miles to Hamel. The sun had moved behind a rack of clouds, and a slight breeze had come up from the west. It was a good day for a run. I hope my body agreed.

CHAPTER THIRTY-FOUR

Harold was in a barn. It smelled like animals, which wasn't a bad smell, he kind of liked it. There were no cows in the barn, a couple of chickens clucked and pecked at the ground over in a corner. There was a square table in the middle. It looked out of place, more like someone should start dealing cards for a game of stud. At the table were the two jokers who he'd been chasing. They held all the answers, and at this point all the cards. Damned if they weren't sitting at the same table like they were poker pals.

Harold sat a few feet away from them in a hardbacked chair. He wasn't tied to a chair this time. He had to take a few punches to the gut and several to the head before Damien told the welcoming crew to cut it out. They'd shoved Harold in a car, a big Olds the color of dirt. They drove him to a farm. The ones that had been beating on him sat outside the barn. They were keeping watch, but he didn't know for what—maybe a sudden stampede of chickens.

"So you don't know where she he is?" Stiltson had taken off his hat, exposing a band of sweat on his fat forehead.

"Already told you that," Harold said.

"He already told you that," Damien repeated.

"Shut up. This musclehead shot Taylor and now he's killed Kuz, too. I liked both of those guys."

"Kuz is a really stupid name," Harold said.

Damien chuckled. He took a swig from a soda bottle he'd brought with him.

"You're quite a guy, Harold. You should stick around, work for me. I could use someone like you."

"First chance I get I'm getting the hell out of this backassward country."

"Except you didn't get out. But you had the chance, didn't you?" Damien asked.

"What do you mean?" Stiltson asked.

"I'll be adding a few names to that list of dead guys, won't I, Harold?"

Harold grunted.

"Down there in Colorado… what were you and her hatching up?"

"Chickens hatch. I shoot people."

One of the birds in the corner gave a loud cluck like she knew she was being talked about.

"So I've heard," Damien said.

"Besides, you were the one that let her go. That wasn't the brightest idea, was it, Shaggy?"

Damien laughed.

"What's he talking about?" Stiltson asked.

"Harold was in the basement when she showed up. We were trying to come to a decision about what to do with him. The votes were leaning heavy on burying him in the back forty. But then we got interrupted."

"By who?"

"To be honest. I never expected to see her again," he said.

"Delilah showed up? And you let her go? What the fuck, Damien? We had a deal."

Harold snorted.

"You guys are better than the Smothers Brothers. You should have a show," he said.

"I sent Macintosh to find her. He's good at what he does. He brought her back."

"So why isn't she with you?" A vein was throbbing on Stiltson's forehead.

"We needed the transfer finished. Delilah said it was being routed down in some Caribbean island. She had all the account numbers. Then it would come back squeaky clean. Macintosh went with her to finish the transfer. Then he was going to call me when it was done."

"Except he didn't," Stiltson said.

"Haven't heard from him," Damien said.

"What about the money?"

"I called one of the banks I deal with. It was there in the account. And then it wasn't."

"Son of a bitch. What happened to Macintosh?"

"You got anything on that, Harold?" Damien asked.

"What's he, some kind of Scotsman?"

Damien laughed again.

"Why in the hell did you let her walk? You should have put her in the ground," Stiltson said.

"Then where would we be?" Damien finished his soda and went to throw it across the barn, but stopped himself.

"Somebody fucked up," Harold said.

"Where's the money, Damien?" Stiltson asked.

"There was some ghost in the machine, I don't really understand it. The transfer was there. I checked with our bank guy, and he said it registered. Totally clean. And then it was gone."

"How much of it was gone?"

"All of it."

"My share too?"

"You don't understand the word *all*?"

Stiltson banged the card table and got up quickly, his belly jiggling like an underdone pudding.

"How did this happen?"

Damien shook his head.

"Damned if I know. That's why we hired her in the first place. She does stuff with money. She can move it around without anyone knowing."

"Including us," Stiltson said. "What now?"

"I've got one last shot. A couple of guys I've hired before. They're mean, and maybe not the brightest, but they always get the job done."

"Names?" Stiltson asked.

"Yeah, they've got some," Damien answered.

Stiltson looked over at Harold. "OK, *you*. You shot Taylor at the King's, and then somehow you ended up with whatserface. What was that bitch's name, Michaelson?"

"Reyna."

"Yeah, her. So where the hell is she?"

Harold shrugged.

"I've got some people on that," Damien said.

Stiltson's vein throbbed.

"What people?" Stiltson shouted his question.

"Does it matter? They're good, they'll find her."

"Same guys as you mentioned before?"

"Oh, not them. No, they can be hard to predict. Like I said, mean. Like Bluto-mean." Damien said.

"Who the hell is Bluto?"

"You don't read the comics?"

"Shit's sake, I never should have partnered up with you and your goofy-ass ways. Things made more sense when it was just my guys," Stiltson said.

"We get the money back, we can split it and never have to work with each other again."

"That's the only thing you've said that makes sense. All right, you sent someone after Reyna, who did these Blutos go after?" Stiltson asked.

"Delilah. They'll find her. Guaranteed," Damien said.

"You two should put up some signs on poles. Lost: two women and a barrel full of money," Harold said.

Stilton stepped toward him.

"Listen, you overgrown ape—Hippie Dippie over there is all peace and free love and shit. I'm not like that. You better start talking or I'm calling in two of my guys with tire irons and we'll get some answers."

Harold tightened a fist. He couldn't wait to pop the guy right in his fat pie hole.

"Settle down." Damien's voice was flat. He put his hand out like he was trying to calm a large bull into not charging. "You're gonna have a heart attack. Then I'll be stuck digging the hole."

Stiltson sat back down at the table, his breath short, a band of red glowed across his forehead.

"How about the other guy? What do you know about him?" Damien asked.

"What other guy?" Harold asked.

"Tall, lanky one with that hungry-dog look about him. He was at the King's looking for you, so I took him to my place," Damien said.

"To your place? I sent guys there looking for Delilah," Stiltson said.

"What other guy?" Harold asked again. "This asshat gotta name?"

"Fischer," Damien said.

Harold jerked his head back.

"You've got to be fucking kidding me."

"So you do know him?"

"What the hell is he doing up here?"

"Why do you 'mericans always think of Canada as 'up here'? Is it because you're below us in a toilet of a country?"

Harold stared at Damien and got up from his chair.

"Easy," Damien said.

"I've had enough of your circle-talking bullshit. Why is Fischer up here?"

"You tell us."

Harold, now at the table, spied Stiltson reaching for something. He shot out his arm and grabbed the fat wrist and twisted. He let out a yelp. Damien laughed.

"Hey, you assholes, get in here," Stiltson talked through clenched teeth. "Are you going to pop this guy or what?"

"Ha! I kind of like him," Damien said.

Two goons ran in from outside the barn and pointed guns at Harold.

"Let him go," one shouted.

Harold ignored them.

"You jerkwads are giving me a headache. Neither of you could find your ass with a road map and a compass. I told you I don't know where she is. But sure as shit, Fischer does."

"Why?" Damien asked.

"Let him go or we will put you down," one of the goons squeaked.

Harold let Stiltson's wrist go and pushed it away like it was a bad piece of fish. Stiltson rubbed where Harold had grabbed, the red on his forehead got redder.

"Who's Fischer?" Stiltson wheezed out his question.

"Me and him work for the same guy. He's kind of a dope—but he keeps on stuff. I wouldn't doubt that he's already run into her."

"Her sister probably introduced them," Damien said.

"She's got a sister? What the fuck, Damien?" Stiltson asked.

"Theresa. She was the one who introduced me to Delilah. Said she was someone I should know. I asked Theresa to check on the farm and if Fischer was still there to bring him up to Stillwater. She must have got there after your crew."

Harold snorted again.

"Sisters… what's next, cousins and nephews? You guys are

perfect for each other. You really don't have a sniff."

Stiltson had been bouncing his eyeballs back and forth between Harold and Michaelson. The two goons hadn't moved from where they stood, still pointing their guns at Harold. A rumbling car engine sounded and a half-ton pulled up in front of the open barn door. Another goon got out of the truck and went across to pull out the passenger.

"Get your hands off me. I'll get out myself," she said.

One of the goons took their guns off Harold and pivoted to the truck.

"Oh, put them away," Stiltson said.

She yanked herself away from the one holding onto her and walked into the barn.

"Thought you'd be in another country by now," Harold said.

"I thought you'd be dead."

CHAPTER THIRTY-FIVE

I ran along the grid road for a couple of miles, a light jog only—I didn't want to arrive in town a sweaty mess. The road was empty of traffic. I thought about what I might say if the RCMP showed up and asked what I was doing. People didn't go for runs out here. If the undercover guys at Damien's place picked up the LeMans, Benno would have made sure the car traced back to the middle-of-nowhere Texas.

A car came toward me, spitting gravel. I dipped down into the ditch and came up the other side to a grassy field. It was a cattle pasture, but none of my bovine friends were about. I crouched down as the car, a late-model Buick, buzzed by without slowing.

I decided to keep running in the field. The softer ground was easier on the joints, though I had to keep an eye out for gopher holes. All I needed was to limp into town with a twisted ankle. Despite the slow pace, the back of my shirt was starting to soak through. I turned back and looked at a dust cloud coming from the same direction as Damien's house. It was a grain truck, a two-ton, so I figured I'd give it a shot. I ran through the ditch and stood on the side of the road waving. I heard the driver shift down, grinding gears. The truck slowed, passed me, and then stopped up the road.

I went to the driver's side. He cranked down his window—an older guy with gray stubble wearing an International Harvester hat.

"Where you coming from?"

"My car broke down a few miles back. Going into Hamel to get someone to come out and tow me."

"Whereabouts? I didn't see any car back there."

I gestured quickly to the north, hoping that wasn't where he was coming from.

"It's quite a ways back. I've been running for a while," I said.

"Running? That's a good way to get heat exhaustion. Hop in."

He shoved some papers, a box of spark plugs, and a pair of work gloves out of the way to make room.

"Appreciated. You headed into Hamel?"

"I'm driving through. Need to pick something up at a buddy's south of there. You family to somebody in Hamel? I know some folks there. You don't look familiar."

"I'm up from the States. Wanted to visit the Motherland."

"Whose Mother?"

"I grew up in Marvelle. That was some time ago. My folks are gone now. I just felt like paying a visit."

"I know some Marvelle folk. What was the family name?"

"Dumas."

"French name. I think I recall them. All gone, you said?"

"Mom passed just last year."

"Sorry to hear. Helluva damper on your trip. Breaking down, I mean."

"I'll get it figured out. Thanks."

The driver gave a few head nods and adjusted his hat. He glanced at me and gave me the once over.

"So you're a Dumas, then?"

"My mom's name. She left my dad and raised me by herself."

"That's a hard task. What's your name then?"

"Swanson. Fred Swanson," I said.

"Uh-huh."

He didn't say anything after that. Hamel came up on the horizon. Pulling into town, he geared down. The grain truck lurched and groaned.

"Gonna need to get that tranny looked at." The truck made another painful sound. "Where can I drop you?"

"Do you know the King's?"

"Uh-huh."

"Didn't catch your name," I said.

"John Smith." He gave something between a smile and a sneer. "Tell you what, Mr. Swanson. I'm gonna drop you off by the gas station. Locals don't appreciate a big rig like this barreling down their main drag."

He slowed the truck down and we rumbled to a stop. As I got out, he pointed a finger at me.

"To tell you the actual truth, I never heard of any Dumas or Swansons being from Marvelle. You want to stay under wraps. that's no skin off my nose." The truck driver scratched his stubbled chin. "Piece of advice for you. Someone picks you up and offers you a ride, you give them the straight goods or keep your damn mouth shut."

I nodded and closed the truck door.

Before I started the walk toward town, I took a fast look to see if the gas jockey I'd locked in his office was on shift. I didn't need him calling the cops. I'd lied to the grain truck driver because I didn't want any record of me being here. If the undercover RCMP came upon the driver, I didn't want my real name known. There was a damn good chance that someone was going to jail… or get shot.

There were a few cars parked outside the King's. I picked out the black sedan right away. I decided to face my demons, the undercover guys, as I was out of other ideas. I never had that many to start with.

The pair sat at the bar in their black boots and jackets. They had to be some sort of cops. They didn't have undercover detectives in these small towns, so something was brewing that made them drive out from the city. One of them looked over at me when I walked in, but went right back to his conversation with Charles the bartender. I took a seat in the corner by the dusty window.

"Get you a Pilsner?"

It was the blonde with the ponytail.

"Good memory. I'll take a couple. No, wait. Sorry. I think I'll only have time for one."

Charles had pointed me out. One of the undercovers was coming in my direction. The server quickly side-stepped the guy making a beeline for me.

"Need you to answer some questions."

He was more than a few inches over six feet, looking taller as he loomed over me. A well-trimmed mustache hung over a jaw that could break boards.

"I said I need you to answer—"

"Questions, right. Have a seat."

"Don't want to cause a commotion. I'm Constable Van Dyck."

"You a painter?"

"Excuse me?"

"Whattya want to know?"

"Are you a friend of Damien Price?"

"Never heard of him. I'm passing through on my way to Calgary."

"The bartender said he saw the two of you talking in here. Says you left together. That was last Friday, five days ago."

"Must be another guy. I just drove in."

The undercover stepped around the table and put his large hand on my shoulder.

"I'm going need you to come with me."

"For what? You have a warrant?"

"You watch too much TV. Let's go."

He grasped hard on my arm and yanked me up. He pulled me with him toward the bar. He nodded to his partner, who stood stone-faced next to the bartender.

"I guess I'll be taking my business elsewhere, Charlie."

"Good luck, asshole. There is no elsewhere. And you won't be welcome there, either."

The square-jawed cop with the Dutch-painter name pushed me through the doors behind the bar, walking me through the kitchen to the outside. His partner followed. Not sure why we went out the back, as he still walked me around to the black sedan I'd seen in the lot. He pushed my head down as they jammed me in the back of the car.

"You boys taking me downtown? Might be kinda hard out here. Is there a downtown?"

"Shut up. asshole, and listen."

The stone-faced Mountie was at the wheel.

"You guys are RCMP, right? Last time I was up here you were all polite and such. Someone fall off their horse on the musical ride?"

A huge hand swept back and caught the side of my head. I used to play the bob-and-weave with my dad on road trips. He never connected one like this. My ears rang.

"Drive," Van Dyck said.

"Where?" the driver asked.

"I don't care."

Stone-face gunned it down the alley, a slight fishtail, before he gained control.

"Sirens?"

"No, just drive. Go out on thirteen. South."

"Damn that hurt," I started. "Wanna give me a warning next time you—"

Whack.

Shit. It felt like my ears were bleeding.

"Where is she?"

"Who?"

The whole car was chiming like church bells.

"You know who. Damien sent us looking for both of you," Van Dyck said.

"No idea who you're talking about. Who are you guys? No offense, but this seems a bit off the Mountie books."

I swerved back in my seat waiting for another blow, but it never came.

"When did you last see her?"

I swallowed. Trying to block out the bees that had taken refuge in my ears.

"Look, I met Damien in the bar, he offered me a place to stay so I didn't have to rent a motel room. I don't know the *her* you're talking about."

"You a homo?" Van Dyck didn't hide the sneer in his voice.

"Damien took my car. I haven't seen him since," I said.

"You gave him your car?" Stone-face asked.

"He said he'd be back."

"This was a Pontiac. What was it, Marlon?"

"LeMans," Van Dyck said. "Color of ghost snot."

Stone-face made a sound that could have been a laugh.

"Well, if you officers have found my car, I'd like to get it back. I'd like to go home."

"Where's home?"

"Lately it's been Mexico. Puerto Vallarta."

"My sister goes there in the winter. Drinks beer right on the beach. You do that down there?" Van Dyck pointed a fat finger at me.

"You said Damien sent you to find me. Why?"

"He thinks you know where she is," Stone-face said.

"Delilah," Van Dyck said.

"Smack him in the head again, Calvin."

Van Dyck let another blow fly. I tried to dodge it and failed. Clipped me hard on the cheek, stung like hell.

"Marlon and Calvin," I said through gritted teeth. "Didn't you two have a TV show?"

"You don't know shit, do you? Damien was wrong and that

bartender was stringing us a line."

"What did Charlie say?" I asked.

"Who?"

"The bartender."

Calvin looked like he wanted to hit something, probably me again, but settled for smacking the dashboard. Marlon sped up the sedan. The car was a prairie boat with a helluva engine. The needle climbed over a hundred and except for the landscape that zipped by, it felt like I was on a cruise ship.

Something occurred to me.

"You guys aren't RCMP… city cops or—"

"Marlon used to be on the force."

Marlon sighed.

"Look. I can pull off down one of these grids. We can take you out and lay the boots to you. Leave you broken up on the road. Maybe someone will pick you up, maybe they won't."

Marlon stopped talking. Another farmyard zipped by.

"Is there an *or we could do this* that you're not saying?" I asked.

"Or tell us where she is."

It was my turn to sigh. My ears were still burning, though the ringing had stopped. I couldn't figure out these guys. They were obviously working for Damien, and given orders to do what it took to get me to talk. I wasn't too keen on being laid out in a prairie ditch, so I needed to try something else.

"Where's the nearest airfield?" I asked.

"There's airports in Regina and Saskatoon. Why?"

"No. I'm thinking something smaller. Prop planes."

"What does this have to do with anything?" Calvin asked.

"Delilah. I think I know where she's headed."

"You said you didn't know her."

"And she's with her sister," I said.

"She's got a sister? Damien didn't say anything about that."

"Her name's Theresa. They look a lot alike."

"So you do know Delilah. And her sister. Maybe you're not a homo after all." Calvin snorted.

"What about these airfields? There's nothing like that around here," Marlon said.

"Hey, what about that guy who does crop dusting out on the thirty-nine, south of Loren? He's got a strip in his field that he takes off from."

"Oh yeah. I know that place. He's got quite a setup," Marlon said.

"Why the airfield? She gonna dust Damien's house?" Calvin snorted again.

"Delilah and her sister are taking Damien's money and getting the hell out of Dodge," I said.

Neither of them said anything. Marlon eased the sedan to the shoulder and then made a wide U-turn.

"There's no Dodge around here," Calvin said.

"It's a metaphor, you dummy," Marlon said.

"Then why didn't he say that?"

Marlon gunned it and the car took off like we were launched at Cape Canaveral—except a helluva lot smoother.

"Delilah screwed over Damien?"

"Figuratively or actually?" I asked.

The two in the front seat looked at each other.

"Never mind. Just drive to the airstrip near Loren. It makes the most sense," I said.

"Why?" Calvin asked.

"You got another idea?"

Calvin looked at Marlon.

"Listen, asshole. We get to that airfield and nobody's there, we're gonna lay the boots to you… what'd you say your name was?"

"Fischer."

"You'll be a fish, all right. We're gonna hook you and split you into fillets. No tartar sauce. How's that for fucking figuratively?"

Spittle shot out of Calvin's mouth and sprayed the inside of the windshield."

"Dammit, Van Dyck, that is gross. You're cleaning this up after."

Outside my window the fields had turned into a long golden blur. At this speed we'd be in Loren in no time. I hoped we'd find somebody there.

CHAPTER THIRTY-SIX

"Have a seat, Reyna." Damien signaled one of the half-ton drivers to grab a chair against the wall and bring it near.

"I don't know where she is, Damien." Reyna stood next to the table.

"Where did you get off to after you scooted away? Let's start with that." He pointed at the empty chair.

Reyna sat down, eyeing Harold. The half-ton driver went and stood back by the barn wall.

"He probably knows where she is," she said.

"No. I've discovered our large American friend doesn't know jack shit. I think you're the one with the inside track." Damien turned to the half-ton driver. "Where did you pick her up?"

"Carrington. Almost at the border," he said.

"Headed south, Reyna? Thinking of taking a trip?"

"Fuck off."

"We don't have time for this shit," Stiltson piped up. "Have one of your boys lay the boots to her. We'll find out what she knows."

"Hmm. That'd be a bit more direct. What do you think, Harold? You were driving with her for a while. Is she the type to kiss-and-tell?"

Harold opened and closed his fists. They'd taken his Glock outside the King's, but right now there was another in his sight line.

"Her and Delilah were planning on screwing you. If they weren't already," Harold said.

"Ouch," Damien said.

"But if Delilah is in the wind, then this one is in the same rowboat as we are," Harold said.

He pointed at Reyna, but also eyed the half-ton driver wearing a side holster. The driver was a big as Stiltson, but with more muscle than flab.

"In the wind… that's a good word for it, Harold. I thought she was gone for good the first time. I sent Reyna here to find you, thinking you might flush out our money-moving friend." Damien turned to Reyna. "So how about it… is our friend telling the truth about you working with Delilah? A little friendly double-cross?"

"Get ripped," she said.

"Come on. Do we need to follow up with old Stiltson's plan here? I'm running out of options."

Harold saw a shake in her lip. Something in Shaggy-hair's voice was getting to her. He wasn't as direct as Stiltson, but Harold knew he could do some damage. She knew it, too.

Was that a Glock on the half-ton driver?

"I think she—" Harold started.

"Let me hear it from her."

Damien waved over the half-ton driver. He stomped over to the table.

"I haven't heard a peep from Delilah. She's gone. With all your money," she said.

Reyna pressed her elbows to her sides. She looked over at Harold. He quickly shifted his eyes away from the half-ton guy.

"Hmm. Sounds like you two were together… but then she cut you out. Did she cut out her sister, too?" Damien asked.

"Don't know her sister."

"Oh sure you do. I've talked with Theresa. The three of you were in cahoots. That's a good word you never hear anymore. Cahoots." He looked to the half-ton guy. "Break two of her fingers."

"Delilah was driving the scams. Theresa and I were making money, too. But she kept pushing and things started to get too hot for me. I was getting out." Reyna's neck pulsed.

"Hot?"

"Delilah killed a guy. Probably more than one. It bothered Theresa, too."

"Son of a bitch," Harold said.

Stiltson stood up fast.

"I don't give one good goddamn about any of this. We made a deal, Michaelson! You said it was all figured out. And now that two-timing bitch has our money. All of it, Damien! Let's beat a goddamn answer out of these two and go get what's ours."

"Settle down, my corpulent friend. We'll get there. Let's hear the whole thing." Damien moved his hand like he was trying to get a dog to sit.

Stiltson hit the table with his fist. While everyone was looking at him, Harold leaped up. He grabbed Stiltson and spun him into the half-ton driver. It was like a collision at the Indy 500, except with fat people. On the way down, Half-Ton Guy reached for his holster but Harold got there first. He grabbed and slammed the gun into the owner's head. Then he slammed Stiltson with it. Harold spun around and put two bullets in the knees of the other guy by the half-ton. The man let go a scream and slammed his head on the truck on his way down.

Someone yelled *hey*.

It might have been Damien, but he was in the middle of taking a punch to the head. Reyna had clocked him one while he had his eyes on Harold's attack. Two other goons rushed in from outside the barn. Harold put a bead on one and then pivoted to the other. Neither of them had drawn a gun.

"Throw down or you'll be joining the ones on the ground."

"Damn, Harold. You move fast for a big guy," Damien said.

Damien was also on the ground, gingerly touching his face where

Reyna had punched him. She'd relieved him of his gun and now had it pointed at the back of his head.

"Throw down," Harold said.

Damien gave a nod. And Reyna rapped him one.

"Easy!"

The two by the truck looked down at the one Harold had taken out at the knees, who was groaning, but still breathing.

"Spin 'em around. Butt handle first. Don't want one going off and putting a bullet in your boss's fat ass."

The goons tossed their pieces in front of them. Stiltson moaned.

"What the fuck? I told you we should have—"

"Uh-uh. You stay down there, fat man."

"You're a rude son of a bitch," Stiltson said.

"Stop making fun of his weight, Harold."

"What?"

"My dad was big like him," Reyna said.

That made Harold take a step back.

"Are you fucking serious? Did I just walk into an after-school special? What did we learn today? Well, I'll tell you what the fuck we learned. You're all a bunch of sorry-ass amateurs. You couldn't find a target or your ass with both hands and crystal balls."

"That doesn't make any sense," Damien said.

Harold spun and fired into the dirt inches away from Damien.

"Fuck, Harold. You could have hit me," Reyna said.

"Not unless I was aiming there." Harold walked over and picked up the two pieces. "If someone goes for me, do you mind shooting them? Could you do that?"

"I could do that," Reyna said.

He bent down, placed two fingers on the half-ton guy's neck. He'd have a helluva headache when he woke up, but he was still amongst the living.

"Everyone up against that hale bay," Harold barked.

Stiltson got up and moved there, muttering to himself. Half-ton

Guy regained consciousness just in time to see that he was fucked. The other pair joined them. Reyna nudged Damien.

"Get going," she said.

Damien joined the others, rubbing his jaw.

"So what now?"

"Well, if I had a camera, I'd say this is a perfect shot for your Christmas card. But seeing that I don't, I'm just going take this half-ton here… and wait a sec."

He stepped to the side and fired a bullet into the engine of the Olds that brought him there.

"Hmm. Nine-clip, right?"

Harold fired into two of the tires.

"I'm thinking you got more cartridges in the truck. Now, after I leave you might wanna call somebody to get some medical help for Gimpy here. Or I could end it right here," he said.

"Stick around. We could use a guy like you, Harold," Damien said.

Reyna kept Damien's gun on the group and backed her way to the truck. Harold moved to the driver's side.

Damien called out to him.

"Next time I see you, I won't be so nice."

"Next time I see you I'm putting a bullet in your forehead," Harold said.

Harold slammed the door, gunned the engine, and spun out of the yard.

He didn't say another word until they'd made it to the highway.

"Now, you wanna tell me where the fuck she is?"

CHAPTER THIRTY-SEVEN

The kids called it spidey-senses. It was Edgar Cayce stuff—except I wasn't predicting blackjack cards. Dark clouds moved into my head, parked right over my cerebral cortex, and started sending bolts of lightning telling me to watch out. Something bad was coming.

The bolts were picking up in intensity as I drove with Calvin and Marlon, the pretend Mounties, to a crop duster's airfield. Not sure why they were pretending in the first place. Maybe they had some authority complex, or just liked playing cops. Damien had sent them after me, thinking I could lead them to Delilah. I didn't feel like I could lead anybody anywhere. But these were serious guys, and I took their threats seriously.

Someone I couldn't lead them to was Mostly Harold. As hard as it was to wrap my head around, Harold followed a romantic lead up here. He was very good at what he did, and knowing his methods he'd have rapped heads to get answers. Someone probably ended up with a bullet in them. Maybe several.

But it wasn't Harold's plight that moved the danger cloud into my head. A guy as tough as Harold didn't go down easy. I sensed that Delilah was capable of as much violence as Harold. He did what he did because someone hired him. As of late, we even shared the same employer. Delilah was a different bird. She was an angry one, driven by what she saw as hers, and hers alone. Anyone who got in the way was going to get shit on. And by that I meant dead. Could be she had some restraint when it came to family. But Theresa shouldn't count on that. Watching the two of them at Damien's other place in Stillwater, I saw how carefully Theresa stepped with her sister.

Marlon drove over a very dead raccoon and swore.

"So. Fischer, how do you figure in all of this? You boinking this Delilah chick?" Marlon chugged his arm.

"How far to the airfield?" I asked.

"The turnoff is up ahead. It's more a long straight road, not like at an airport," Calvin said. "Might not even be the place. Could be no one there."

"I think it's the place," I said.

"How would you know? And you still haven't said your part in all of this."

"I don't have a part. I came here looking for someone."

"What, like a relative? Some great-uncle leave you a bunch of money?" Marlon asked.

Marlon eased the sedan to the shoulder and made the turn onto the grid. Thick clouds had moved in to match the ones in my head. They didn't look like storm clouds, but appearances can be deceiving. The smattering of cows in the field didn't seem bothered, nor did the few calves that pranced about, one sucking at their mother's teat. Just another afternoon of munching grass on the prairie. These girls didn't have to think about driving into situations where people had guns and bad attitudes.

"Who were you looking for?" Marlon asked again. "They going to be at the airfield with all the others?"

"I doubt it." I paused, thinking maybe Marlon's prediction wasn't that far off. "Like me, he came up here looking for someone. He knew Delilah from down in Colorado."

"What, like a romance thing? What was this guy's name?"

"Mostly Harold."

"What does that mean? He has other names?"

"Probably. But yeah, the two of them were together. Until she lit out," I said.

"Why did you want to find him?" Marlon asked.

"You're as dense as tar. Fischer wanted what the other guy had. The woman. I'm right, right?" Calvin chuckled.

"Sure."

I made out a couple of long buildings on the horizon, big enough to hold planes. They could have just been huge barns, but as we got closer, I saw a yellow plane parked on a paved road that connected the homemade hangers and led to the strip.

"Why do you figure they came out to a piddly air strip like this one? If they're planning to escape in one of those it's gonna be a tight fit. Doesn't look like that cabin would fit more than the pilot."

Marlon pointed at the duster just as another plane eased outside the hangar.

"No, but that one would," I said.

The other plane was bigger than the duster, bright white with red-and-black racing stripes.

"I'll be damned, a Skyhawk," Calvin said.

"A what?" Marlon asked.

"Cessna Skyhawk. Four-seater. How in the hell does a guy afford one of those?"

"Since when do you know about planes?"

"How far could you go in that?" I asked.

"Ground miles or nautical miles?" Calvin asked.

Marlon gave him a look.

"What, so I can't have hobbies? I got a subscription to a couple magazines. Was thinking of taking some lessons."

"How far?" Marlon repeated my question.

"Seven hundred nautical, which means just under thirteen hundred K on the ground."

"That'll get you to an international airport," I said.

"How are we supposed to know if Delilah is there?" Calvin asked.

"Cruise up and ask them nice," I said.

The Cessna pulled ahead, and then swung past a pair of cars parked on the small runway. One of cars did a fast U-turn and headed toward us.

"Shit," Marlon said.

A cherry red car, a foreign job, kicked up dust as it raced toward us. A figure popped his head out the window, and then the top of his body, and then a shotgun.

"Hit it," Calvin said, rustling in his jacket and pulling out a gun.

Marlon gunned the car while Calvin rolled down the window and popped his own head out. The sensations crawling up my neck were gone and replaced with a tangible fear that I was going die in a game of prairie-road chicken. There was no way I'd make a jump from the car at this speed. I'd tumble and be roadkill just like the raccoon that Marlon drove over.

The car swam on the road toward the nonexistent shoulder, spraying gravel. Marlon steered out of the fishtail.

"Easy," Calvin said. "I got a bead on him."

"If you got a bead then shoot the bastard. Don't tell me about it."

Calvin fired off a shot. Marlon braked, slid off the left side of the road, onto the grass now. I felt the car lift, up on two wheels. Shit, we were gonna roll. But good old Marlon handled it. Calvin fired again. Tires chugged through the grass. Dust and smoke rose from the gravel road. We rode the corduroy of the ditch, my head banging against the roof. The cherry car was sliding in an arc, smoke steaming from the hood where Calvin must have hit it. The guy with the shotgun was nowhere to be seen.

"Did you get him?" Marlon asked.

We slammed into something underneath—a rock or a stone raccoon. There was a huge chunk, a grind, and we were airborne. Bouncing like a wounded frog, the car slammed back onto the ground. A blast filled the air. I heard the pellets spray against the corner panel.

"Fuck this," Marlon said, hitting the brakes.

We lurched to a stop. I ducked down just as another blast took out the passenger window where my head used to be. I kicked at the door, rolled out of the car, and scrambled on all fours.

Someone, hard to say if it was Marlon or Calvin, emptied their clip in the direction of the cherry car. I had to make a quick decision, keep doing the dog-walk, or risk moving into a crouch and running toward a small shack about a hundred yards away. I got up, turning quickly, in time to see Marlon go down. Calvin shouted at him. Calvin fired until his gun was empty. He reached in his jacket for what I guessed was another clip. Or maybe he had the Browning he took from me. When he pulled out a round shape, I couldn't be sure what I was seeing.

The air around me stopped. The birds held their breath. *Where in the hell did he get one of those?* I asked it aloud to no one. I dived to the ground as the prairie erupted. The explosion swallowed all the other sounds. When I got to my feet again I did a quick touch for any cuts or pieces of goddamn shrapnel. I bolted across the field without looking back.

I didn't know who was still alive, or if I was one second away from taking a shotgun blast in the back. I chugged my legs like I was running for the end zone—except I wasn't waiting for the Hail Mary pass. I was trying to make it to the shack with all my vital parts still attached.

The door was open a half inch. A small rusted padlock held it in place. I wrenched it hard, splintering the wood. Once inside, I peered back at the road. The cherry car was engulfed in flames and smoke. Nobody was moving. Then from Marlon's sedan, I saw Calvin rise. He seemed to be the last one standing. I looked over to the Cessna and the other duster. The other car was gone, but nobody was on the road.

So where did it go?

I never liked carrying a gun. Recently, they kept getting taken away from me. Right now I really wanted one, preferably one with a lot of bullets. I turned to scour the shed but found only garden tools. A long cupboard looked promising. I knocked off another rusted lock with a spade and opened it up. My heart lightened and fell again as I discovered that it was a pellet gun. They're great for taking out gophers. But unless I got someone to stand still while I shot them in the eye, it was useless.

I looked outside again. Out in the field Calvin walked toward the air strip. I might have imagined it, but it looked like smoke rose from his body. I couldn't stay in the shed forever. Though, the idea was not unappealing. I grabbed the spade and moved outside, at first in a crouch, and then moving into a full stand-up jog. Glancing back to the smoking sedan, and seeing Calvin confidently stride ahead of me, I figured I was safe in the field. All eyes would be on him. At least until he ran into whatever was waiting for us.

CHAPTER THIRTY-EIGHT

The highway stretched out in front of Harold, miles and miles of it with nothing that looked like a bend. Damned if she wasn't right about seeing the curve of the earth. He couldn't figure why the hell people would live in a place like this. Back in Colorado there was actually stuff to look at. Roads went up and down, and around things. This was like living on a pancake. The thought made him hungry.

He didn't know why he was still looking for her. After finally seeing her in the basement, he saw the writing on the wall, and it wasn't good. Still, there was something in that kiss. And she was crying, wasn't she? Dammit, she was.

"You're still not talking."

Reyna hadn't said anything since he asked her the whereabouts of Delilah. He had let her stew in her thoughts while he drove on the pancake. Dammit, he could go for some right now.

"I already told Damien I didn't know where she was. You were there in the barn, remember?"

"Yeah, and I know bullshit when I hear it." Harold sighed. "Look. I don't want to be here any more than you do."

"So why don't you leave? What's keeping you?"

"I have some unfinished business," Harold said.

"With Delilah? What is it with you two?"

"Where is she?"

"You got a hearing problem?"

"Jesus. You don't believe me when I say that I will stop this truck, walk you out to the middle of the field and put three bullets in your head?"

Reyna didn't say anything, but Harold heard her swallow.

"OK, fine. I'm finishing this." He pulled the truck onto the shoulder.

"I already told you she was leaving."

"Yeah, to Italy or some European place."

"Spain."

He slowed the car to a stop.

"Let's get this done." Harold took his gun out and pointed it at her head. "I don't want to get this truck all bloody."

She stared past the gun and held his gaze. She was a tough one all right, but he saw the shake in her lips.

"Get out."

"I know where she is," she said.

"Here's the thing. You ever hear about that boy who cried wolf?"

"She's going to leave the country."

"Yeah, yeah, yeah. Get out. Start walking."

Harold pulled her out of the car. He looked to the farmer's field. One of those big green machines was off in the distance, chugging through the wheat or whatever the hell it was. He didn't want to shoot her, but he was done pissing around.

"I talked to Theresa," she said.

"The sister. You knew her, too?"

"I've known her for a long time. I helped her through some bad shit. She introduced me to Delilah."

"All right, the two of you talked. So what?"

"She's going to Spain with Delilah."

"Right. I heard they got direct flights from here right to the capital of Spain. Or maybe that guy on the combinator will just drive her there." Harold sighed again. "You know what? Just get walking. I'll shoot you and then go find her myself."

"After I left Stillwater, I got a hold of Theresa. She said she was sorry it didn't work out."

"What didn't work out?"

"The three of us were going to leave together. But Delilah cut me out. I already told you that. Theresa said they found someone that could fly them to an international airport. Toronto or Calgary, I'm not sure. Someone with a small plane."

"I don't know the crazy-ass geography of this country, but I know we're not close to either of those. And Jesus, who picks those names anyway?"

"Theresa said they hired some guys to protect the field. Delilah knew people would come for her."

"Damien and Stiltson. I doubt they're going anywhere right now."

"Damien has other people working for him. Including a pair of guys I met only once."

"Names?"

"One is Marlon, I didn't get the other one."

"Like the acting guy?"

"Not nearly as good-looking. But both of them are a bit crazy."

"Everybody's looking for the treasure," Harold said.

"Delilah or the money?"

"Sure."

Harold scratched his chin. He was in need of a shave. The fact that his grooming was slipping was just another sign that this job was getting to him. Hell, this was a job he sent himself on. He could stop doing it.

He looked out at the guy on his green machine. Maybe it wouldn't be so bad, driving all day like that, the machine doing all the work. Harold wondered if he had a radio in there. Could be he was a Bacharach fan, too.

"How do you figure we find a place with a small plane?" Harold asked.

"An airfield?"

"Yeah. Are we supposed to drive from farm to farm and ask these bozos if they have any place to land planes?"

"Dusters," she said.

"What?"

"That's how we find out. Crop dusters will have small strips to take off from. Some of the duster guys have other planes. Bigger ones. Let's drive to the next town, look them up in the Yellow Pages and see if any are close by."

"Theresa tell you the place?"

"No. But I got the sense they were leaving today. It's gotta be around here."

"Long shot," he said.

"You got another idea?"

Harold got quiet. The machine in the field had turned around and was going the other way. He didn't feel like shooting her. He was bullshitting about that, anyway.

"Well?"

"I'm thinking."

"Delilah's not going to be here long, Harold. The two of them could already be airborne."

He scratched his chin again, then put his gun away and walked back to the car. He checked the bed of the truck. There were a couple of large containers that he'd been interested in. He went through them, surprised at what he'd found.

"Are you still going to shoot me?"

"Get back in the truck."

Reyna climbed back in the cab and cranked the window down. A warm breeze blew through.

"What time is it?" Harold asked.

"I don't know," she said. "Around four or five. Why?"

"Because when we get to the next town and find where they fly the dusty planes, then first I'm going to a pharmacist, and then I'm going need to eat some pancakes. So there better be a place serving them."

"You're an interesting guy, Harold. Why the pharmacist?"

"Isn't medicine supposed to be free up here?"

"Some is, yeah. But you need a doctor's prescription."

"We'll see about that."

Reyna gave him a cold-eyed stare.

"OK. We'll get you some pancakes and some drugs. But after that, I'm driving."

"Fine."

CHAPTER THIRTY-NINE

Calvin had picked up his pace. He wasn't quite jogging but he would be soon. He was a man with a purpose. Damien had sent these guys after Delilah, and probably me, but right now I don't think Calvin cared about the initial job. I'm thinking he's thinking these people killed his partner. He was going to lay some people out.

I made my way through the wheat field, shush-shushing through the stalks. I held my weapon of choice, a rusted shovel that had a point as sharp as a kid's playtime fork.

The car that had disappeared swung back and parked on the air strip. A few figures stood outside the duster plane and the Cessna. I scanned over to the hangar where the planes had come out. Further to the south was a farmhouse.

Calvin started to run. There was a shot, but I couldn't tell if it came from him or someone on the strip. I suddenly felt naked—like one of those dolls you shoot at the fair, or targets, or fucking milk bottles. I needed to move. Now.

I peeled off to the right, heading for the farmhouse. I glanced toward Calvin, who for sure was firing now. He was also yelling. It was mostly a string of fucks. I cranked it. My body resisting the sprint until I told it to shut up. My calves burned and lungs were bursting. More shots, but nothing in my direction. Or so it seemed. I reached the yard just as someone came out of the house. The guy was my size, wearing a tan suit and eating a sandwich.

"Who the hell are you?" he shouted at me, spitting bread and meat. "And who's doing all the shooting out there?"

I ran up to him and beaned him right in the head with the shovel. He hit the ground. I thought I'd put him out until he groaned and swung an arm at me. He grabbed my leg and took me down with him.

"Come here, you fucker," he growled. "I'm taking you to the boss-bitch."

I'd dropped the shovel, and now scrambled back to grab it. He got up on all fours and came at me like a rabid dog. Instead of foam at the mouth, he had a long streak of mustard across his face. There was a line of blood dribbling down his forehead below where I'd nailed him. I grabbed the shovel and bounced up. Taking a step back, I wound up and this time I swung for the cheap seats. The metal clanged against his head and he went down for good.

A half dozen more shots rang out. The farmhouse was behind the hangar and I couldn't make out what was happening. I rifled through the unconscious mustard guy and was surprised to find he wasn't packing.

"What kind of goon are you?"

Someone yelled out or screamed, I couldn't tell. I moved to the porch of the farmhouse, scanning the windows. It didn't look like anyone was inside. I opened the front door, holding my shovel out in front of me. I walked to a table in the kitchen. Dirty plates and cups were scattered on a checkered cloth, and a pot of coffee burbled on the counter.

Out of nowhere I was tackled by a Saint Bernard. Or that's what it felt like. The goon knocked me to the ground and the shovel flew out of my hands. I scrambled back out of his grasp. He was the size of a fridge. He put his dukes up, old-style, and came at me.

"Gonna bash your head in. I saw what you did to Clyde."

He fanned a punch, and then another. He wasn't too quick, but I knew if he connected I'd be seeing stars. I moved around him, a pain jolting in my back from where he'd driven into me. The next punch was inches away from my nose. I rocked back, swerved, and went low. I hammered him in his fat gut, making him gasp for air. As he lowered his head, I drove one up and into his jaw. It wasn't pretty, but I wasn't at the Montreal gym, and no one was scoring us. I knew he was out cold before he hit the floor.

I stepped over the now-unconscious goon, and considered how long Calvin might last out there. I came up with a small number of minutes. The two guys I put down were likely supposed to be joining the group by the hangar. Someone would wonder where they were. I didn't have much time.

I rifled through the drawers and cupboards, a cabinet in the hallway, before moving into the bedrooms. There was nothing that even looked like a gun. I picked up a large kitchen knife that looked like it'd come with the wagon trains. I had no place on my body to carry it. I considered dropping the shovel. But it had been good to me so far. I put the knife back.

I gave up the search and went back outside. On the porch I was met by an attractive woman in Ray-Bans. She pointed a gun at my forehead.

"Doing some gardening?"

"Burying bodies in the backyard. Wanna come see?"

"Drop it."

I hesitated, wondering on the age-old question: who wins in a revolver versus shovel fight? I decided I couldn't swing it fast enough. It landed on the porch with a clang. Delilah took a step back, while keeping a bead on me. Down the porch steps in the yard stood a pair of thick goons in plaid. One cradled a shotgun, the other had his hand jammed in his pockets.

"You forget your gun?" I called over to him.

"If you would have headed south like I said, you'd be sipping margaritas at one of those beachside bars." Delilah pocketed her sunglasses.

"I'm more of a straight shots of tequila guy."

We stood there for a while. We'd both run out of clever quips.

"If I shoot you now, can I borrow your shovel for the grave?"

I was wrong. She had one more.

"How did Calvin make out? Last time I saw him he was smoking," I said.

"That his name? Not so good. Who were those guys anyway?"

"Damien's hired goons. They found me and figured I'd lead them to you."

"Theresa shouldn't talk so much," she said. "But why this airfield?"

"Got lucky. Well, maybe not so much for Damien's guys."

She waved her gun toward the airstrip. "Let's go… what was your name again… Trout?"

"Bond. James Bond."

"Walk ahead of me, smartass."

I went past her and the goons, walking toward the hangar. I had the thought that she might put the bullet in the back of my head before I got there. But she probably would have already done that at the farmhouse.

Out on the airstrip, two men were dragging Calvin's very dead body across the tarmac. They popped the trunk and put him in it. He was no longer smoking. Next to the Cessna was a guy in a black flight jacket and matching hat. Standing next to him was Theresa. She was pale, like she'd just thrown up her breakfast, and maybe lunch, too.

"There's been enough killing today, Delilah," she said.

"You get my vote," I said to Theresa.

"He is a persistent motherfucker, worse than crabgrass. He's going to keep coming back," Delilah said. She pointed at the man in black. "Get in the plane. I need to finish this."

Delilah's goons now stood on either side of me. The one who had his hands in his pocket did have a gun, which he now pressed against my ribs.

"Is someone else coming?" Delilah asked.

"No idea. The guys I came with are dead."

"Is Damien sending more?"

I shrugged. Theresa started to say something but Delilah shushed her.

Delilah nodded to the one carrying the shotgun. He slammed the butt into my jaw. I fell to my knees. Arrows of pain ran through me. As I considered whether my jaw was broken, the other guy smashed the back of my head with his pistol. I face-planted the ground. I swam toward unconsciousness but tried to stayed above water.

I watched Delilah go over to speak with the ones that had put Calvin in the trunk. Her words came to me like I was at the bottom of a swimming pool.

"Soon as I land, I'll send transfers to you. Any bank will be able to make the transaction. It won't be traceable, but you can make up any bullshit you want. Tell them you sold a car or something."

"How about paying us now? What's to say you're going to send us anything?"

"There's nothing to say. I don't have that kind of money on me, jackass," she said.

I was coming out of the pool. The pain in my jaw sharpened my awareness. I pressed a tongue in the corner of my mouth. I found a sharp object that I spit out with a stream of blood. Son of a bitch. I was going to have to ask Benno about a dental bill now—unless they killed me.

I got to my knees.

"You're a tough patch of crabgrass, aren't you? But I'd stay down there if I was you."

I sensed the goon with the shotgun winding up for another blow, but then Delilah shook her head and held up a finger. She turned back to the two by the car, who exchanged glances.

"I think you should give us something. Like half," one of the two by the car said. "You see what they did to my guys out there on the runway?"

Delilah closed her eyes. My busted mouth was bringing me clarity. This was not going to end well.

"I don't have it, you moron," she shouted.

The taller of the two pointed over Delilah to the field north of the airstrip. Theresa cranked her head around, looking in the direction of the finger-pointer.

"Delilah."

"Don't want to hear it, Theresa. I'm tired of this sh—"

"North," Theresa said.

"For fuck's sake. What north?"

Delilah spun around and saw what all of us were seeing. A cloud of dust, flying dirt clods and grass was being created by a white half-ton that hurtled toward the airstrip.

CHAPTER FORTY

I clambered to my feet, grabbed the shotgun right out of the hands of the goon who'd been watching the truck coming across the field. His mouth formed an *oh shit* as I smashed the gun butt into his gut, then pulled back for a swing to his noggin. As he timbered, I took a fast step, moving out of the way of the other goon who rushed toward me. I did my best matador move, letting him flash by, and then I nailed him the back of the head with the shotgun. It was no shovel, but it did the job.

The half-ton was on the airstrip now, peeling out and spinning in a long circle. A door flung open and someone spilled out. I didn't recognize the figure until he was upright, running and shooting. I hit the ground, dropping the shotgun. It skidded a few feet away. Next to the car, one of the goons was planted on the ground face-first. The other had a red bloom on his shoulder.

Everyone ran without knowing where to run.

Except Delilah.

She stood, feet apart, gun aimed at the large man who had just taken out one and a half of her goons.

"Stop right there, Harold."

He kept coming. Why didn't he shoot her? The one he tagged in the shoulder ran past Delilah and toward him. Harold pivoted and fired twice. The goon spun and tumbled like a pair of dice at the craps table.

"Harold!" she shouted.

Harold took a step and then stopped. He peered for a second over at me. I was kneeling between the two I'd knocked out, reaching for the shotgun. He didn't recognize me.

"Leave the shotgun where it is or you're deader than Elvis."

He pointed his gun at me. Then the light went on.

"What the fuck are you doing here, numbnuts?"

While he addressed me he turned his gun toward Delilah. She still had her badass stance and her gun pointed at Harold. The two of them stood off against each other. Theresa had disappeared in the fracas. She must have been in the plane with the pilot.

"I'll put you down," Delilah said.

She didn't seem to know that with Harold less talking, more shooting was better. I figured she was about two seconds from being a corpse on the airstrip.

Harold's shoulders dropped. Even from where I was, I heard the long exhale. I didn't quite believe what I was watching. Harold brought his gun down, and then tucked it into his side holster.

"Listen, I don't—"

He didn't finish his thought, as Delilah fired three bullets into his body. Harold didn't cry out. He went to his knees and then toppled onto his side.

"Shit," she said.

I scrambled for the shotgun. Before I could get to it, Delilah turned and fired. The slug went into my side. Flashes of hot pain coursed through me. I instinctively grabbed for where the bullet went in, like I could somehow stop it from the damage already created. My body bent. I released a groan that came from somewhere deep inside. The shotgun was less than a foot away.

"Forget about it. The next one I'll put in your head." Delilah walked over to me, kicking the gun away.

"Careful. Those things can go off," I said through gritted teeth.

The two goons next to me were up now. Theresa and the pilot were back on the tarmac.

"Jesus, Delilah," Theresa said.

The door of the half-ton opened. Delilah raised her gun, taking a bead on the woman who stepped out.

"Well, well, all the chickens come home to roost. What the hell do you want?" Delilah didn't lower the gun.

"Just give me my share and I'll be gone," the woman said.

The pain might have clouded my vision. It was like I was seeing triple. The three of them could have been sisters.

"I gave you all you're gonna get. You said you wanted out."

"Because of bullshit like this." She pointed at Harold, who had not moved since he went down.

It was hard to think of Harold being dead. The guy was such a force, it didn't seem natural to see his body lying there. It was like killing Paul Bunyan, but not anywhere near as friendly. Harold was a son of a bitch, but I already missed him.

"The money's all tied up in a transfer right now. I'm moving it through a few different systems. When I get settled, I'll route over a final payment. Not that I owe you one," Delilah said.

"You owe me for putting up with you. And I don't believe that you're going to give a shit about me, or any of us, once you're over there. I won't see a dime."

"Believe what you want. Where's Damien?"

"Left him in a barn with Stiltson."

"Left him breathing?"

"Damien is always fine," Reyna said.

Delilah looked over at me. "What am I going to do with you? I know none of these others are going to identify me. Can't be too sure of you."

"Believe what you want," I said.

"Smartass to the end. Hold him up."

The goons beside me, each with their own shiny wound and trickle of blood where I'd nailed them, took my arms.

"Bring him here," she said.

"Delilah, that's enough. Let's get out of here," Theresa said.

"Need to tie up all the loose ends," she said.

"All this gunfire is going to be heard by someone," Theresa said.

"Helluva mess," Reyna said.

"Shut up."

"We need to go, Delilah. Leave him be. He'll probably die anyway," Theresa said.

The pain in my side had made me forget about my sore mouth. I spat a wad of blood on the tarmac.

"What the hell is your name again?"

I rolled my tongue inside my mouth, feeling the spot where my tooth used to be. My jaw wasn't broke, but I was gonna feel this in the morning—if I wasn't dead.

"It's Fischer," Theresa said.

"Right. OK, Fischer. She says you're probably gonna die out here, but I have my doubts. You are a stubborn fucker, otherwise you wouldn't have come out here. Why didn't you leave when I told you?"

"Benno," I said.

The shape of the airplane was starting to get soft. If the goons weren't holding me up I wouldn't be standing.

"Who?"

"You shot his nephew. In the Springs."

"I did what?" Delilah placed the gun on her hip. "Oh wait. That's what this is about? Ha! Harold's boss? Down in Texas."

"Mexico."

"You should have stayed down there. The weather is nicer and the beer is better." She snapped her fingers. "Time is right the fuck up."

As she raised her gun there was a scuffling noise. To my left a large blurry shape stretched out a long arm. Three, no four, five shots. Delilah went down. The goons on the side of me both collapsed. One still held onto my arm as he fell. I went with him.

"You two peckerwoods make one single fucking move and I will take you out."

As I winked out, I was surprised at how much I liked hearing that voice.

CHAPTER FORTY-ONE

When I was a kid I went on roads trips with my parents. One time we drove to the mountains. It was something prairie families did. I sat in the front with mom and my sister got the back seat to herself. I could have sat in the back, but long drives always made me sleepy. I liked falling asleep with my head on my mom's lap. Sound was funny as I car-slept, never quite fully down, only half-aware of the murmurs of voices, along with the hum of the wheels and the drone of our big Pontiac Laurentian's 400 blue-block engine. Dad pointed out the blue-block to those who asked about his car, and many who didn't. Dad called it a Poncho.

The memory of this sensation came back to me as I rode in whatever vehicle I now traveled. It was a big car or a very large truck. In my semi-conscious state, people's voices came out as soft trumpet sounds. What was the name of the horn that Mangione played?

"Flugelhorn," I said aloud.

Some other horn sounds replied, one very deep. It must have been a tuba.

I didn't know who I traveled with. My parents were dead. I hadn't seen my sister in more than a decade. My head was sweaty like it was when I finally lifted it off my mom's lap. Some of the voices, the higher-pitched ones, spoke quicker. There was a deep rumble and then a bang. We were landing somewhere.

Landing.

I was in a plane. My mouth hurt like hell. Who the fuck punched me? But wait, that wasn't the real source of pain. Then that feeling exploded and took over all the other senses. I yelled something, not a word, just a primal sound. Someone, maybe the tuba speaker, lifted me out of the plane and into something else, maybe a real car this time. Air brushed my face. It smelled like pine and pancakes.

My body made a crease, right on the pain line. I screamed and went out.

"Drive faster."

Those were the last words I remembered saying. I urged Dad to bury the needle. Show us what that 400 blue-block was capable of.

I dreamed thick syrupy dreams. Damien was in one of them. He was dancing a funky strut to some of his ska music. He handed me a fat joint, blowing out smoke as he talked to me. Theresa was in the dream too, holding my hand, stroking my hair. Telling me she'd just sold another plot of land to Farmer Joe.

I awoke on a chrome bed with crisp white sheets. It didn't smell like a hospital, but it was clean and bright.

"Thought we lost you," she said.

"Where am I?"

"A friend of mine. Med-school dropout who discovered he'd rather work on animals. Less whining."

Theresa sat across from my chrome bed in a folding chair.

"The Cessna," I said.

"Yeah, that's how we got here. Not sure what you remembered. Harold carried you into the plane, and then out to my friend's car—he lives near an airstrip that crop dusters use. It was only a thirty-minute flight, and another fifteen in the car. Good thing for you."

"Mostly Harold?"

Words came out of me like lava lamp bubbles, floating to the top, but then sinking again without any real purpose.

"Yes, he carried you," she said.

"He's dead. I saw him fall."

A large frame filled the doorway.

"Here's a tip for you, numbnuts. If you're going into a firefight, strap on some protection. Damn, you suck at your job. Why does Benno keep paying you?"

"You were wearing a vest?"

"Those stubble-jumpers must have thought they were heading into something bad. They had a pair of them stuffed in the back of their truck."

Harold walked in and took the chair next to Theresa. He grimaced as he sat.

"Still hurts. Those slugs kick like a mule when they hit you. I guess she didn't want to shoot me in the face. She must have still liked looking at me."

"Thank you," I said.

"Tired of saving your ass."

"What day is it?"

"How the fuck do I know, Fischer. Buy a calendar."

"Benno?"

"Yeah, I called him. It's all good," Harold said.

My vision had cleared up but my brain was still murky. Surfer waves of recognition crashed in, but no one was riding the crest. I let those images swim around for a bit, until they led me back to the scene by the airstrip.

"What happened to everyone? Where's Delilah?"

"She's back with the rest of them. On the tarmac. I doubt she made it." Theresa stared at the floor.

"Those goofs in the red suits will be sorting this one out for a while."

"Red suits?"

"Harold thinks the RCMP go around wearing those uniforms he's seen in old movies."

"In books, too. My man L'Amour wrote about them."

"From a hundred years ago," she said.

"Who was the woman in the truck? She looked like you."

"That was my cousin, Reyna. She was working with Delilah and me. She knew Damien the best, so we were using her to find out some of the banking information we needed," Theresa said.

"If I ever run into that shaggy-haired hippie again I'm—" Harold stopped to cough. "Damn."

"You left her there?" I asked.

"No room in the plane. We needed to get you somewhere quick. She said she was fine. Peeled out of there. Hopefully she was long gone before the cops got there."

"She'll make it," Harold said. "She's got a lot of heart."

"Heart? You get that from another L'Amour book?" Theresa asked.

It hurt a lot, but I laughed.

"Fischer, if you weren't all stitched up and coming back from death's door I'd send you there right now."

"Harold, we all know the tough-guy thing is just for show," I said.

That elicited a laugh from Theresa. We bantered back and forth a bit. My side had a dull ache that told me the painkillers were doing the job. I rubbed my jaw and stuck my tongue in the place my molar used to be.

"What about Damien?" I asked.

"I don't know. Harold said he and Reyna left him and Stiltson in some barn."

"Stiltson's a real guy?"

"Him and Damien were against each other at first, but then joined up when they realized what Delilah was planning."

Harold muttered something I couldn't make out.

"You think everything that went down on the airstrip could be traced back to them?"

"Hard to say. Some people have a way of avoiding the bad stuff,"

Theresa said.

Turned out we were somewhere in northern Ontario. The pilot who dropped us here has already taken off again. Theresa said Delilah hired him from out of Sudbury, and after paying him it was unlikely she'd ever see him again. She wanted me to stay a couple of more days with her friend the veterinarian.

"How do I know he won't put me in a kennel?"

"He's been paid enough to take good care of you."

Harold stayed one more night. He said it wasn't for my sake, as he didn't give a single shit about me. He wanted to rest up before the long trek back to Colorado. I decided to not give him the gears about it. It was decent of him to save my life. Late, the night before he left, he came to my room. He spun the cap off a bottle of top-shelf bourbon and handed it to me.

"Not sure the doc would want me taking that—could thin the blood or something."

"Shut up and drink," he said.

I took a swig. It burned in the best way, and ended with a smoothness that reminded me of late nights spent on the porch with Franko in New Mex.

"That's a helluva lot nicer than Jack Daniel's. You bring that with you?"

Harold took a long pull.

"I found it in a cabinet in the guy's living room. Operating on cats must pay pretty good."

He handed the bottle back to me. A look passed over Harold's face, only a glimmer, and I wonder if I'd imagined it.

"That was a hard thing to do," I said.

"Steal the doc's whiskey?"

"You know what I mean. You put her down."

Harold took the bottle back after I'd drank. He took another swig.

"She was a lying—" He stopped himself and said nothing for a long time.

A machine beeping in the corner was the only sound. It wasn't hooked up to me, so I don't know what it was monitoring.

"Anyway," Harold said.

He took a vial of pills out of his pocket, shook a couple into his hand, and swallowed them. He chased the pills with another pull from the bottle.

"What are those for?"

"Something the animal doctor gave me when I told him what was going on with my stomach."

"You got an ulcer?"

"Who knows. Probably fucking cat medicine. But these damn things work better than anything the guy in Colorado gave me."

I laughed.

"You going right back to the Springs?" I asked.

Harold looked over at the machine with the red light.

"I figure I'll go east for a bit. What was that town I found you in before?"

"Montreal."

"Might spend some time there."

"You speak French?" I asked.

"What does that have to do with anything?"

"Never mind."

Harold held the bottle out to me and I shook my head. If I wanted to be out of here in a couple of days, I didn't want the whiskey to be duking it out with the antibiotics coursing through my system.

Harold took one more drink, then stood to leave.

"Thanks."

"Get yourself a vest, numbnuts."

I watched his large frame fill the doorway, and then I listened to him pad down the hall.

The next morning Theresa came and told me that Harold had left early.

"Thought I'd also say goodbye."

She looked like she just came out of the shower, her dark hair fell down in soft ringlets, and her skin had a dusty glow. Her eyes showed a deep tiredness.

"You're just gonna leave me with Dr. Doolittle?"

"If you're nice he'll give you a cat treat."

The doc was actually a decent guy. He'd checked out his work on me last night, happy with how the wound was starting to heal. My jaw still ached like a bastard, but the pills kept the pain at bay.

"And what now for you?" I asked.

"Time to get out of here. Not sure if the RCMP will make connections between me and Delilah. It will take them a while. She was good at covering her tracks."

"What about Reyna?"

"She'll probably end up with Damien again."

"Really?"

"No, probably not," she said. "She's another one of those who can avoid the bad stuff."

"I always seem to run smack into it," I said.

Theresa kissed me.

"Thanks."

"For what?"

"That asshole in the puffy jacket was going to put me in the ground."

"If I recall, you handled that pretty fine on your own."

She smiled, and kissed me again. This time on the forehead. Her damp hair smelled like the Amazon jungle, or how I guessed something like that smelled. She gave a quick nod, and then was up and heading to the door.

"So you're not going to tell me where you're going?"

"Take care of yourself, Luke."

After she disappeared down the hallway, I called after her.

"Let me know if the tacos are better over there."

***

The guy I named Dr. Doolittle was actually named, Barry Liddle. So I wasn't that far off. I hung out at Liddle's for another week. The doc fed me soup and we played cribbage. Eventually, I moved out of his makeshift hospital room and into a spare bedroom he had in his house attached to his animal clinic. I recalled Franko's nephews Francis and Emil getting patched up by a veterinarian after an extra bad night in New Mex. Maybe I should write a letter to one of those schools that train animal doctors and thank them for their service.

I called Benno and he told me he'd already talked to Harold.

"I look forward to your return, my friend."

"I'll let you know when I leave, Benno."

Surrounded by the turning trees took me back to when I'd almost killed Scarecrow Norman and left Marvelle for what I thought was forever. It was fall then, too. I considered staying with the doc a bit longer—maybe I could sign up as a veterinarian's assistant, tape up some injured paws, or neuter some cats. But when the chill arrived with the yellowing leaves, I knew it was time to head home—or the place I now called home.

The doc gave me a ride in his half-ton to Thunder Bay, where I caught a long bus ride to Toronto. I wasn't in the mood for spending any more time in Canada, I'd had enough. I booked the first flight available to PV. I spent the night in a cheap motel on Lakeshore Boulevard, listening to the traffic and the sound of Lake Ontario lapping at the shore. I called Benno and told him I'd be flying in from Toronto the next day.

The next morning I grabbed a cab to Pearson. I slumped back in the plastic chair in the airport lounge. I surveyed the other passengers waiting for the flight to Mexico. It wasn't cold enough to attract the Bermuda-short-wearing turistas. There were a couple of college kids, both wearing sunglasses, probably fighting the first of many hangovers. Closing my eyes, I picked out the melody of a song playing over some tinny speakers. I couldn't make out the words, but I knew them. *I bought a ticket to the world.* I sure did. I sat up, nodded to the college kids, and walked to the row of payphones.

"Hi. It's me."

"You're alive," she said.

Her voice seeped into me. It was like warm water seeking the center, a low place to rest.

"Yeah."

"Are you OK?" she asked.

"I'm leaving. Going back to Mexico."

"Did you find what you were looking for?"

"You mean who?"

She didn't respond.

"Yeah, I found them," I said.

A long span of silence. I thought I made out a whistling noise, somewhere in her kitchen. I pictured it. The two of us drinking chamomile tea like normal people, considering going for a long walk in the red maples.

"You sound tired, Luke."

"I've had some hard days. But I'll be all right. Need to rest up, swim in the ocean."

The song that was playing in the airport swelled in my ears. It could have been an auditory trick of the mind.

"This is the sound of my soul," I said.

"What?"

"Nothing. I was just thinking of something."

"You're always thinking of something, Luke."

"I just wanted to hear your voice."

"They don't have phones in Mexico?"

I let the warm water of her voice sink into me again. I was the low place.

"It was really good to see you," I said.

She got quiet again. The space stretched out in front of us. The song was over, the whistling sound was gone.

"You need to rest. Go home."

"I'm not sure where that is."

"Sure you do. Goodbye, Luke."

She didn't hang up right away. She gave me a chance to say something but I had no idea what else I wanted to tell her.

I hung up the pay phone and boarded the plane.

CHAPTER FORTY-TWO

Waves of exhaustion swept over me and I conked out somewhere over the Midwest. When I awoke, we were flying over one of Mexico's lush jungles. Passing through customs, I told them I had nothing to check and nowhere to stay, which earned me a meeting in a back room with a few guards. I told them that I'd forgot to book a room at La Esperanza. That's where I usually stayed, or at my friend's place.

"And what is this friend's name?"

"Benno Rodríguez."

The customs guards exchanged glances.

"You are good friends with Señor Benno?"

"We go way back," I said.

"Why are you friends with such an old man?" one of them asked.

"Benno's not old, maybe he's got a few years on me, but he looks great in that fedora he's always wearing."

Their expressions changed. They shook my hand, and one of them patted me on the back. They apologized for the disruption and asked that I not speak poorly of them to Benno. I assured them I wouldn't. Once again I was surprised, but not surprised, at my friend's reach and influence in this part of Mexico—probably other parts, too.

I was set to take the city bus to the Esperanza, when I was met by a man in a tan suit. Of course Benno had sent a car. I didn't even tell him when I'd be there, but his driver had either been waiting for hours, or Benno had gained access to the passenger list coming from Toronto.

I got my usual room and walked the long curved ramp up to the third floor. The hotel Esperanza started out as a hospital back in the day, the ramp being used to wheel patients up and down the floors. The white walls were painted every few years, though the building was feeling its age. I didn't care. This was my place of comfort, where I could soak up the Mexican sun and smell the Pacific air from my small balcony. The Morales family was always glad to see me, welcoming me back with coffee laced with cinnamon and a bowl of fresh papaya.

I sipped the coffee, the voices of dogs and roosters echoing off the white buildings of Puerto Vallarta. On a rooftop across from me, a woman hung laundry. Gulls circled above her, in hopes of procuring a snack, but she ignored them and went on with her morning's work.

The morning stretched out in that languid way it does down here. Flashes of images roamed through my brain. The long straight roads that crisscrossed the landscape I'd left behind, the wheat fields doing their best imitation of a land-ocean, complete with the shush-shush sounds of the wind sweeping through the stalks. I thought of Marvelle, and how it felt driving through that town, and seeing Marguerite again. In my mind's eye, I saw Harold gunned down on the airstrip. But the largest hit man I knew would live to read another L'Amour book. How about me? What had I lived to be able to do?

I went back inside and to the small desk in the corner of the room. I ripped off a page from a pad of paper adorned with the name of the hotel in an elegant script. For the next hour, I wrote Marguerite a long letter. At first the words came out in frozen droplets, but as I wrote both my hand and my heart softened. By the time I came to the last few lines my cheeks were wet. Then I took the letter, ripped it into the quarters, and dumped it in the wastepaper basket. I laid down on the bed, letting all the images and memories drift to the ceiling and to someone else's room above me.

When I awoke, the bright yellow sunlight had turned to a soft purple hue. I padded down the ramp and onto the street, heading for my favorite street-taco stand.

I spent a week following a similar rhythm. Besides exchanging words with the taco vendors, and the woman in the market where I bought chicken mole and fresh tortillas, I spoke to no one. I expected Benno to show up at the Esperanza, or at the El Rayo Verde, where I nightly drained several buckets of Pacificos and crunched on bowls of Cholula-soaked peanuts.

"You seen him, Jimmy?" I asked the bartender and owner of the El Rayo.

"Mr. Benno has been away on business," he said.

"How do you know this?"

"One of his associates told me when they visited to view my monthly books."

Up until that point I didn't know Benno had a share in my favorite spot in PV., but of course he did. Walking up the hill back to the Esperanza, as if reality merged with the thoughts in my head, a familiar figure in a fedora walked toward me. The full moon cast a fat orange light down on him, lighting the soft creamy fabric of his shirt, and making it seem like he glowed with his own light.

I reached out my hand to him and he pulled me into an embrace.

"It is very good to see you again, my friend."

I was surprised by the gesture. I took a step back to study his face.

"Thanks, Benno. You doing OK?"

"Yes, yes. I am only now coming back from my cousin's house—the mother of Benito. She lives in Boca."

It took me a second to place the name. His death, the reason for my journey, seemed so long ago.

"How is she? Did you tell her how her son died?"

"I told her that justice had been served, and I mentioned your name. You would be very welcome to share her table at any time. But for now, come have a drink with me." He gestured down the hill where I'd just come, indicating the direction of his place.

"It's late, Benno. I'm tired."

"I understand, Luke my friend. But come. I have fine shipment of Patron that I would like to share with you… as well as a bit of news."

We walked together down the cobblestones, both of us bathed in that orange moonlight. The dogs and roosters were quiet this time of night. Music drifted out an open doorway, a guitar and a woman's voice intertwined.

"What news, Benno?"

"In time. Enjoy this night."

When we reached Benno's place, a couple sat outside at one of the trio of white cloth-covered tables. They sipped green drinks with salted rims, in front of them were long sticks of camarones. The smell of the garlicky shrimp reminded me that I hadn't eaten anything since that morning.

"You may take those with you. We are closing up now, and I wish you a fine and lovely evening."

Benno tipped his hat to them, and the couple arranged themselves to leave. Inside a man wiped tables.

"Was it a good night, Enricho?"

"A steady flow," he said.

"I will lock up. Feel free to go home."

Benno took a bottle of golden liquid from a cupboard in his office, and two short glasses. He poured for us, then lifted his glass to me.

"I am in your debt, Luke. Once again, you have proven invaluable to me."

I clinked his glass and tipped the drink back into my mouth. As much as I love Pacificos and a good tumbler of bourbon, this tequila fell on my tongue, enveloped my mouth—hell, my whole head—with a fire that didn't burn but rather warmed every inch of my body and radiated out to the air around me. It gave Franko's drink of the angels a run for its money. Being from Benno's private stock, I knew the price tag was high.

"What did you want to tell me?"

"I sense your impatience. Understandable, as your travels have exhausted you."

He reached into a drawer and drew out two envelopes. One had already been opened. He pulled out a letter.

"She is quite resourceful to trace my nephew's background. The letters were first sent to a box office in Boca, but then forwarded to me, as my name was on both envelopes."

He slid the unopened letter to me. It was addressed to Benno, but underneath his name it said C/O LUKE FISCHER.

"Who is this from? There's no return."

Benno read from letter in his hand.

"I don't know you, but I understand that you are family to Benito. I'm not sure of the circumstances, but I do know that my sister Delilah caused his death. For that I apologize to you and the rest of his family. I don't know if you are his father, or are in touch with his parents, but your name was the only one I found. I ask you to send them my condolences. As well, I have forwarded a sum of money that can be released with the information written at the bottom of this letter."

Benno folded the letter and put it back in the envelope.

"I imagine you have met this woman, Theresa?"

"I did. She took me to Delilah."

"It seems that wherever she is now, she is attempting to amend some of her sister's damage. Is that what your letter says as well?"

While Benno read, I had ripped open mine, and scanned it.

"Pretty much. Sounds like she sent me some money, too."

"Hmm. For some, they think money is a solution to all ills. It is not."

"No, it isn't," I said.

"I will make sure Benito's mother receives this."

I didn't tell Benno that Theresa thanked me for saving her life. It wasn't clear whether she meant from puffy-jacketed Larry, or some eventual demise brought on by Delilah. Seeing her sister gunned down must have given her some sober second thoughts. Not to mention, she had access to all of Damien and Stiltson's money. I doubted she would be sending them a package.

"This means I can pay my own hotel bill for a while."

"There is no need,, Luke. I am happy to continue. Feel free to treat yourself to some good meals. If the amount from this woman is enough, plan a trip to the south. Acapulco is a lovely destination. Or perhaps a trip to the northern states might be better."

"Better? Which northern state do you mean? And why better?"

Benno poured us each another shot.

"Do you recall a man named Wilco?"

"What? Of course. He was the guy behind that whole business in Upper Michigan. If it wasn't for Sam, he would have put my lights out for good. But he lived in New Mex. Are you wanting me to go there?"

"I have no business interest in this. But our friend Arkin came across some information. Wilco has disappeared."

"I figured he disappeared right into jail," I said.

Benno sipped the tequila. Out on the street, night birds called to each other with an urgency that I was probably imagining.

"Arkin told me that Wilco served almost no time. Strings were pulled. Then a couple of weeks ago, he was reported missing."

"Maybe someone hit him with a shovel and found a nice place to bury him."

"Perhaps."

"That still doesn't explain you suggesting I go to the northern states. Are you saying Sam has something to do with this?"

"That is the part Arkin said may be of interest to you. Authorities are also searching for her." Benno tipped back the rest of this drink.

"Have you spoken to her recently?"

Most of the exhaustion I'd carried these last two weeks had been released from my body. Sitting in Benno's office on a warm Mexican night, bird songs that sounded like Spanish guitars, and sipping expensive tequila, I was ready to shift down into a nice, easy, and very slow pace. Maybe I'd finally learn how to surf. I could get one of the locals to give me lessons. Ride the corduroy out with the dawn patrol.

"Can you lend me a car, Benno?"

"I have already arranged it, my friend."

ACKNOWLEDGEMENTS

Luke Fischer seems like he enjoys his own company more than anyone else—but he doesn't realize how many people have helped him get on the page. As always, thanks to all my twitter friends, peeps, and writers!

My early readers Theresa Therrien and Martine Proctor gave me excellent notes and gave me a kick in the ass when I needed it (and most writers do). Huge encouragement and eagle-eye catches from readers Kenneth Gray (I owe you a six of Pacifico and a basket of cheese sandwiches), Linda Robinson, Scott Frederick, and Mark Atley mean the world to me. Also Wiley Reiver, just cuz.

Thanks to Jim Thomsen for being an amazing editor with laser-vision, as well being a very fine human. Your work sharpened Luke's world in the best of ways.

For my buddy Phil, you knocked another one outta the park with that cover painting. I couldn't think of a more perfect and beautifully haunting image for this book.

Ongoing support from friends and family members is a vital part of putting a book out there—with special kudos and many hugs to The Lovely who understands what it takes to do this.

Finally, for the readers, new and old, who seemed to like this guy who enjoys a Pacifico or two, and throws more than a decent bunch, you may be surprised how much I think of you all. Your enjoyment of these books exponentially increases my experience writing them.

Cheers, and the next, um, Pilsner is on me.

Find me on twitter, or whatever the hell they are calling it these days: cterlson.

Printed in the USA
CPSIA information can be obtained
at www.ICGtesting.com
LVHW092114021123
762799LV00003B/60